*She pivoted on*
*that would m*

"The animal kingdom must be loose in the city," Nick murmured peering off into the distance. "Those mammoth cats wouldn't be your *man-eaters* by any chance, would they, Miss uh?"

Nick glanced over her head and a worried frown tilted his lips downward. The flesh around his scar puckered slightly. A scattering of fat rain droplets pitter-pattered on the puddles that started to resemble small lakes.

She grimaced. Right now, more rain would be about as welcome as a snake at a garden party. She glanced skyward, seeing a new cloud bank roll in from the east, pushing the blue skies westward over the Everglades. Lightning jumped in the distant sky, but she couldn't hear accompanying thunder, so it must be far away. Dragging her attention back to her uninvited guest, she squared her shoulders, preparing to battle his unwelcome attitude.

Regally, in a how-dare-you-intrude attitude, she answered his not-so-friendly question. "Kerrigan. Kelly Kerrigan. We just came down from the Cincinnati Zoo." She held out her hand coolly.

"Cincinnati?" He chortled dryly, ignoring her hand. "You should have stayed there, safe and sound." He kicked his toe at a large chunk of concrete. "This would be a great time to run back to Mommy...before things *really* get rough." He spread his hand in a sweeping gesture. "You haven't seen anything yet."

"I don't scare easily, Bradley. My daddy didn't raise any cowards." Nor had her brothers cut her any slack for being a girl, especially not Kevin, her twin. She planted her hands on her hips in an indignant stance. The worthless ticket, not much more than mulch in her sweaty pocket, mocked her. "Let me set you straight, Lieutenant—Kenga and Rama are no more *man-eaters* than I am."

Nick's gaze turned insolent, looking her up and down so slowly and thoroughly that she thought her flesh would surely start flaming. He chuckled and she knew he suppressed a grin. The realization irked her but not as much as his next words. "You look like a man killer to me."

Be sure to check out our website for the very best in fiction at fantastic prices!

When you visit our webpage, you can:

* Read excerpts of currently available books
* View cover art of upcoming books and current releases
* Find out more about the talented artists who capture the magic of the writer's imagination on the covers
* Order books from our backlist
* Find out the latest NCP and author news--including any upcoming booksignings by your favorite NCP author
* Read author bios and reviews of our books
* Get NCP submission guidelines
* And so much more!

We also have contests and sales regularly, so be sure to visit our webpage to find the best deals in ebooks and paperbacks!

**Visit our webpage at:**
**www.newconceptspublishing.com**

Tigers Play is an original publication of NCP. This work has never before appeared in book form. This work is a novel. Any similarity to actual persons or events is purely coincidental.

New Concepts Publishing
4729 Humphreys Rd.
Lake Park, GA 31636

ISBN 1-58608-454-2



Cover art by Eliza Black



NCP books are available at special quantity discounts for bulk purchases for sales promotions, premiums, fund raising, or educational use. For details, write, email, or phone New Concepts Publishing, 4729 Humphreys Rd., Lake Park, GA 31636, ncp@newconceptspublishing.com, Ph. 229-257-0367, Fax 229-219-1097

First NCP Electronic Printing: June 1999
First NCP Paperback Printing: November 2001
10 9 8 7 6 5 4 3 2 1

Printed in the United States of America

# *Tigers Play*

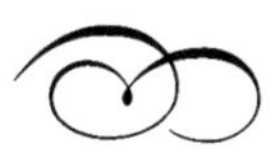

*Elaine Hopper*

Contemporary Romance

New Concepts Georgia

## Dedication

To Dad, Mom, and Aunt Dorothy for instilling in me the will and confidence to make my dreams come true. Aunt Dorothy, take care of Mom. I love you all."

## Acknowledgment

"I'd like to thank the staff of the Miami Metro Zoo and the Florida Fresh Fish and Game Commission for all your wonderful help in researching tigers and the Florida Everglades."

# Prologue

Raging winds whipped wildly around the zoo. Shivers scraped down Kelly Kerrigan's spine. An eerie sound, an even eerier feeling, she expected a fierce gust of wind to sweep her into a different dimension.

She didn't know what to expect not being a native Floridian accustomed to monstrous storms, but an impending sense of doom seeped into her bones like a heavy, cold mist. Everyone from Brian Norcross on Channel 4 Weather, to the sweet old lady who lived down the hall in her apartment building, forecast one earsplitting, fevered August night. If the pictures of Hurricane Andrew's destructive hatred were anything to go by, she'd wish she'd never accepted this assignment.

Derek Karr, her assistant zoo keeper, recanted tales of tidal waves that washed all living creatures into the turbulent seas as if cleansing the wicked society. They were too far inland to worry about tidal waves, weren't they? The eye of the storm loomed nearby, the winds of the most dangerous part of the storm, the eye wall gathering strength, and she wondered if Armageddon lay a lightning bolt away.

Already the winds breezed through the zoo that stood eerily naked. All the animals were secured safely indoors and hurricane shutters had been nailed over windows and doors. The only discernable movement she could see was that of employees double and triple checking safety measures. That and the palm trees bending almost double in the front winds that Chelsea sent.

## *Tigers Play*

She had a sneaking suspicion that it was going to be a night she'd wish to forget, a night to hide for dear life, to pray to the God of mercy like she'd never prayed before. Cautious people had run north, away from the threat of Chelsea's terrifying two hundred mile per hour winds. The airplane ticket her Aunt Meghan had sent her to fly home, mocked her in her pocket, burning her thigh. She should have used it while she'd still had the chance.

She shook the notion away, for it was too late to worry about that now anyway. The window of safety had long passed and the ticket was as useless as an Elvis concert ticket. Besides, her wards needed her. She couldn't afford to let Mother Nature spook her. Still, twinges of apprehension wrapped around her nerves and she prayed that the zoo was as secure as it looked, as her employers claimed.

After all, it had withstood Andrew like a brave warrior. This building had stood tall and proud, refusing to budge an inch even if nearby groves of trees lay broken like matchsticks.

With a fierce flick of her wrist, she rehammered the last hurricane shutter she'd found flapping in the squall. Although the tiger's cage, which resembled an ancient Indian mosque covered by ancient hieroglyphics looked imperturbable, she still lifted a silent prayer for intervention. The tigers were completely isolated on their island, a calculated measure to protect the public safety. Nor could naughty children throw toys or popcorn at them and disturb their peace and solitude. A concrete moat separated them from their visitors by a good fifteen feet. Even a determined cat couldn't jump that. Nor could they shimmy the slick vertical walls. Should their building crumble in the storm, the big cats would be stranded on their island and the populace protected.

She counseled herself to hope for the best and stop thinking maudlin thoughts. Miami, taking no chances after Andrew, boarded up while she prepared the zoo for what was forecast to be the worst hurricane since the dawn of recorded history. This storm, the grandmother of all storms, was predicted to make Hurricane Andrew look like a naughty child. No small feat. She ran her fingertips lightly over the tiger's den, as if to ensure herself it was fortified with steel and iron, up to building code for hurricane specs.

Taking one last look around the deserted tiger's island, she swallowed a lump in her throat and ducked into the tiger's den. She paused several moments while she let her eyes adjust to the dark cave.

"Kenga! Rama!" Her voice sounded scratchy and hoarse. Tears burned behind her eyes but she held them back.

Two adolescent, white Bengal tigers loped to her side in long, graceful strides from the back of the cave, the incandescent lighting making them appear ghostly. Their ears lay flattened against their heads and their fur stood on-end. They didn't need a weatherman to tell them that a dark force threatened to destroy Miami—and perhaps them as an added bonus.

Crouching by the animals in the small space, she scratched behind their ears with her fingertips. Kenga bent her head into the scratching, her honey-golden eyes wide with anticipation, dark with instinctual fear.

"It's time for me to take cover in the office, kiddos," Kelly murmured huskily, still fighting rogue tears. "I brought you steaks," she said, trying to put a note of cheer in her voice. She rubbed her tummy and licked lips that were chapped and cracked from the wheezing winds.

Rolling weary shoulders, she took the steaks out of their container and slid them across the floor. Rama pounced on his, swallowing it whole. He licked his chops, little drops of saliva beading on his muzzle. He sniffed the muggy air permeated by steak and chicken, tilted his head and grunted.

Kelly chortled and flipped him another. "Boys will be boys. Eat up..." *You don't know when you'll get another feast.* She grew morose. *Stop this!* Hurricanes struck every summer. It wasn't as if it was the end of the world. *Was it?* a tiny voice deep in her mind taunted her. She shrugged it away as best she could as she slid a third thick steak to Kenga.

Rama gnawed on his china white T-bone, his paws holding it gingerly as if it were a prized possession. His belly finally full, he hunkered down to ride out the storm, his paw looped over his head as if to drown out the sound of the wind. The golden tip of his tail fluttered up and down as if a marionette had attached a string to make it dance.

Kenga rubbed against her legs, her purr like that of a motor boat. She hugged each cat around their thick necks, in turn. She rubbed her cheek on Kenga's soft head and dropped an angel's kiss on it.

Rama opened a sleepy eye, gazed at her as if she were a silly human, then licked her hand with his sand-papery tongue, tickling her sensitive inner wrist.

She extracted a syringe from her black medical bag, tweaked it with her fingers till the bubbles dissipated and held it in front of her. She glanced at Rama. "This will hurt me worse than it will you." She cringed as she jabbed the long needle full of vitamins into his meaty haunches. He opened his other eye and glared at her as if to say *how dare you!* She rubbed the spot with an antiseptic pad then scratched behind his ears so he would know she meant him no harm. No hard feelings.

She crawled to Kenga and administered the vitamins to her as well. When she repacked her medical bag, she gave each tiger a bear hug and patted them on their rumps.

A lone tear escaped down her cheek and she wiped it away with the back of her hand. "You should be safe here," she mumbled huskily. The cave looked like a fortress. The walls must be a foot thick, maybe more. Still her tongue felt thick and swollen. The beating of her heart pounded out an ominous drum roll. Her gaze roamed the walls of the sanctuary that had stood solid for hundreds of tropical storms and she hoped that at least the eastern most wall was fortified with steel—and prayers.

"Andrew couldn't put a dent in this place," she whispered aloud to assure herself more than the tigers who batted their paws at mosquitos. "Let's pray our luck holds out a second time."

She emptied the container of steaks and chicken giblets into their dishes to ensure they had plenty of food...in case she couldn't return immediately after the storm. With a last fearful glance, she forced a smile to her sad lips and backed out of the cage, slammed the door with all her might and rammed the locks shut with the force of a rifle blast. Her back protesting from being cramped in such small quarters, she stood and stared around her, wondering what sight would greet her after the storm passed.

# Chapter One

When the storm had finally abated, Kelly rammed the entrance door to the tiger's island with might enough to do a Marine justice. Her shoulder screamed from the abuse. To add insult to injury, her forgotten tranquilizer gun slammed against her back like a lead weight. Suppressing a groan, she bit her tongue, then tried again. Although the heavy iron door grumbled and strained a few inches, it still blocked the entrance to the tiger's den as if the Pharaohs commanded mystical guards to seal the entrance for time and eternity.

"What good are big brothers if they aren't around when I need them? Kyle could lift this thing without blinking an eye," she ground through her clenched teeth. She drummed her fingers against the door. "What I need is brute strength—or a little ingenuity," she muttered with a dawning smile, the type that made her older brothers shake their heads and run for cover.

For as long as she could recall, they'd teased her that she was a magnet for trouble. Surveying the holocaust on all sides with troubled eyes, she didn't think she could be held accountable for this, however.

She spied a strong tree branch, about five feet long, no less than 10 inches in diameter, not too splintered or ravaged by last night's raging storm. "Leverage," she mumbled and trudged through thick mud to retrieve it. Her wet leather boots scraped her ankles despite thick tube socks that would never be arctic white again. Blisters already festered in the climbing heat of the day.

Kelly grabbed the sodden branch, and dragged it to the door. She wedged it under the door, angling for the best position and pushed with the determination of ten men, grunting from the extreme effort. Perspiration trickled down her brow and her hair plastered to her head. She stuck her lower lip up and blew at the bangs. They didn't budge.

Ancient-looking hieroglyphics peeked out from beneath layers of slime that looked cursed. A shudder trickled through her blood. Although she'd teethed on her father's safari stories of primitive tribes, sacred animals and native superstitions while her friends drifted to sleep on fairy tale visions of Cinderella and Snow White, doom settled over her. She'd have thought she'd have thicker skin. Some of those shadowy images of old flitted through her mind. With supreme will, she struggled to push them aside to that region of her mind where she relegated unwelcome memories. Otherwise, every creak of the wind or gunshot would have her jumping.

Little by little, the door groaned and shifted, until it slid sideways with the force of a hand grenade. It landed atop several crumbling concrete chunks before falling to the side with a ferocious clatter. She jumped out of the way, seconds before it would have fallen on her foot.

Everything lay in ruins like the aftermath of a vicious battle. Mountains of rubble stood where the mosque should be, testifying to Chelsea's fury. Broken palm trees bent over the tiny tiger's island like scarred soldiers. Shingles and all manner of debris littered the muddy ground. Drowned plants gorged and limp, floated in the new lakes. Lifeless birds, victims of Chelsea's wrath, their wings hopelessly broken, strewn the ground. She stared at them, nameless dread washing over her.

Kelly blinked scalding tears from her eyes, halting dead in her tracks. Scorched air burned her lungs when she inhaled too deeply. "This can't be. It's impossible," she whispered, her words carried away by the wind.

Could she be delusional? She bit down hard on her trembling lower lip. Maybe she dreamed this nightmare. But in living color?

She'd thought people dreamed in shades of gray.

"Ohmigod." She wiped her gritty, sweaty palms down the back

of her khaki shorts then stepped back in total awe, smacking her ankle into a splintered tree that lay ripped from its roots. She ignored the pain that flamed up her leg like serrated hot flashes, her only intent was to find the tigers.

Balancing on chunks of concrete that covered the island, the heels of her boots slipped, making her lose her precarious balance. She doubled over, her arms windmilling to keep her from falling face first in the mud until she found her footing.

"Where could they be?" she mumbled, frantic eyes scouring the tiny island. She swatted another pesky mosquito large enough to saddle and ride in a rodeo.

Taking a breather, she leaned her head back, shaking her heavy hair off her neck. A slight breeze caught at it, blowing it in her face and she tucked it behind her ears. But the laughing wind defied her and blew it across her eyes. She gave up.

Pacing the island, she searched for clues to the tiger's whereabouts. The mosque was gone with the wind. The underground tunnel had been shut tight until she pried it open. Tigers couldn't spread wings and fly. So where were they?

"Where would I be if I were a tiger with nowhere to hide?" she whispered to herself.

She walked a few paces more and stopped short at the root of an ancient palm tree, branches clutching the air like spidery fingers. The amazon lay stretched over the moat, to freedom, to Miami. Her gaze followed its length, and she drew her eyebrows together in a deep frown. "They couldn't have..."

Putting her booted foot on the end of the tree, she used all her might to rock the fallen monster. It didn't budge. It felt solid as the Golden Gate bridge.

"In for a penny, in for a pound," she mumbled and climbed on top of the tree. She stretched her arms out to balance herself, gulping in deep breaths to calm her nerves. She pretended she walked across a balance beam only five feet long and two feet from a padded floor, deliberately blocking out the fact that she crossed a twenty foot concrete moat with no padding. She sucked in a deep breath and fortified her resolve.

Putting one foot in front of the other, she walked the length of the log to the tarmac on the far side of the moat.

"Shoot! If I can walk that monster, Kenga and Rama could run across," she muttered. She teetered back and hopped off the log to solid ground. A large sigh escaped her and she stared at the red-gold sun sitting on the horizon behind the Everglades. Heat shimmered from it as if hell's fires escaped.

She pivoted on her heel and ran smack dab into a chest that would make Conan the Barbarian jealous. Her mouth went suddenly dry.

Strong fingers bit into her upper arms, steadying her when her toe stubbed a large chunk of concrete and she dove headlong toward the ground.

Craning her neck, she lifted her gaze for what seemed miles to the tall stranger who imprisoned her in his vice-like grip.

Her gaze clashed with topaz eyes, not unlike those of the tigers, that probed her very soul. Hers widened in answer. They took in a faded scar that zig-zagged from the far corner of his right eye halfway down his cheek, adding, not detracting from features chiseled out of stone. Without the jagged line, he might have been too pretty.

She studied the man covertly through veiled lashes.

Sun-kissed hair, trimmed short in military regs, complimented bronzed flesh that knew the sun intimately. A green and tan uniform, labeling him one of Florida's elite Highway Patrolmen, stretched over taut muscles. His mouth hovered somewhere between cruelty and tenderness, just like the fingers that bit into her arms. His jaw jutted forward, strongly determined. He wore the wary expression of a man on a dangerous mission, but why did he regard *her* as if she was the enemy?

She arched one finely shaped brow, willing the gerbil somersaulting in her belly to halt.

Not wanting him to sense her fear, she instilled a steely note into her voice when she asked, "Who are you?"

"Lieutenant Nick Bradley of the Florida Fresh Fish and Game Commission," he drawled lazily, releasing one of his arms to dig deep into his pants pocket. He pulled out a black leather wallet. With an adroitness seemingly alien to his size, he flipped it open to flash a tattered ID badge.

She studied the photo ID carefully, examining the picture to make sure he hadn't forged it or stolen it off some unsuspecting mark, sliding discreet sideways glances at him through her thick lashes. The picture looked like a match.

"Trust me. It's authentic," his voice a husky baritone. A ghost of a grin relaxed his stony countenance but his eyes remained narrowed, flinty as steel.

"Okay. What do you and the Florida Fresh Fish and Game Commission want with *me*?" she asked looking at his hand pointedly. She spoke to him in the same tone of voice she reserved for her big brothers when they tried to dominate her. Finally, that training had found a good use.

"Dispatch took a call about white tigers roaming loose a few streets over from here," Nick said. He slipped his wallet into his pocket. His eyes seemed to blaze straight through her as if she were transparent as the wind.

She expelled a pent up breath, wondering if he could hear her nerves jangling. "You think I deliberately set the tigers loose to ravage and pillage Miami?" She chuckled wryly. "Think again." She flipped her heavy hair over her shoulder and smoothed back the damp tendrils that clung to her overly warm neck. Even at sun-up, South Florida in August felt like someone had turned up the broiler full blast.

Distantly, a great ape thumped his chest trying to attract a mate, or maybe he warned off a predator. She couldn't be sure, so she strained to listen for the nuances in the animal's voice, having a pretty good ear for reading animals. Her dad said this talent was her special gift, the one that let her work her singularly peculiar magic with her wards.

"The animal kingdom must be loose in the city," Nick murmured peering off into the distance. "Those mammoth cats wouldn't be your *man-eaters* by any chance, would they, Miss uh?"

Nick glanced over her head and a worried frown tilted his lips downward. The flesh around his scar puckered slightly. A scattering of fat rain droplets pitter-pattered on the puddles that started to resemble small lakes.

She grimaced. Right now, more rain would be about as welcome as a snake at a garden party. She glanced skyward, seeing a new cloud bank roll in from the east, pushing the blue skies westward over the Everglades. Lightning jumped in the distant sky, but she couldn't hear accompanying thunder, so it must be far away. Dragging her attention back to her uninvited guest, she squared her shoulders, preparing to battle his unwelcome attitude.

Regally, in a how-dare-you-intrude attitude, she answered his not-so-friendly question. "Kerrigan. Kelly Kerrigan. We just came down from the Cincinnati Zoo." She held out her hand cooly.

"Cincinnati?" He chortled dryly, ignoring her hand. "You should have stayed there, safe and sound." He kicked his toe at a large chunk of concrete. "This would be a great time to run back to Mommy...before things *really* get rough." He spread his hand in a sweeping gesture. "You haven't seen anything yet."

"I don't scare easily, Bradley. My daddy didn't raise any cowards." Nor had her brothers cut her any slack for being a girl, especially not Kevin, her twin. She planted her hands on her hips in an indignant stance. The worthless ticket, not much more than mulch in her sweaty pocket, mocked her. "Let me set you straight, Lieutenant—Kenga and Rama are no more *man-eaters* than I am."

Nick's gaze turned insolent, looking her up and down so slowly and thoroughly that she thought her flesh would surely start flaming. He chuckled and she knew he suppressed a grin. The realization irked her but not as much as his next words. "You look like a man killer to me."

"How dare you!" Her fingers itched to strike the impertinent smirk off his rugged face. "I don't have time to play games with you."

His eyes narrowed. "I don't play games," he said, a hint of lazy Southern charm lacing his words. Words laced with unmistakable steel. "Wild man-eaters loose in Miami aren't even remotely my idea of fun." He ran his fingers through his hair.

"Maybe somebody's pet tiger escaped?" She flipped her hair behind her, determinedly ignoring the lumbering thump of her heart in her chest. The heavy fall of her hair just grazed her shoulders, flipping slightly up on the ends.

"White tigers?" He shook his head slowly. "None are listed in our data banks. I had Demi double check before driving over."

"Maybe one of your Florida panthers wandered in from the Everglades. Are they tagged with radio transmitters so you can account for all of them?" She slanted him a smug grin.

He regarded her in stony silence, shadows flitting across the flat planes under his cheek bones.

"I thought so," she said. "If you'll excuse me now, I'm busy." She dismissed him regally, twisting out of his grip.

"Looking for escaped tigers?" he mocked with an indolence that pulled her back.

Maybe he sensed she couldn't resist a challenge. Her dad claimed that would be her downfall one day. It came with her fiery red hair and Irish heritage.

Her quick temper snapped. "Look, Lieutenant. I've just had one helluva night. I'm in no mood to deal with your accusations. You have no authority..."

He flashed dazzling white teeth and added, deathly quiet, "But I do."

She let her gaze roam his length, deciding he just might be as dangerous as he looked. Muscle and sinew stretched against his uniform, his long legs strong and daunting. His arms looked as if they could squeeze the breath from her without even trying. But it was the hard glint in his eyes that made her take a step back. Acquiescing, she muttered under her breath, "I hate arrogant men."

"What did you say?" His eyes narrowed to mere slits and he closed the gap between them, backing her against a pile of rubble. Hot breath rasped against her neck and she shivered for a moment before she willed herself to stop.

"I love policemen," she said through clenched teeth, thinking better of provoking this giant. It wouldn't help Kenga or Rama should he arrest her. She might be brave, but she wasn't an idiot.

Strong winds whipped up again, blowing her hair into her eyes. Absently, she pushed it away, tucking it behind her ears, wanting to get away from this man and find her precious charges.

"When's the last time your man-eaters ate?" Nick asked apparently satisfied with her answer. He picked at the rubble, lifting blocks too heavy for her to search beneath. Reluctantly fascinated, she watched furtively as muscles rippled under his shirt when he hoisted the rocks in a pile behind him.

"Don't waste your time looking here," she said matter of factly, her glance skipping to the tree bridge. "I'm pretty sure they escaped."

Nick quirked a querulous brow and sliced her with his icy glare. "What makes you say so?"

Kelly inclined her head to the tree uprooted over the moat. "The storm built a bridge. They walked to freedom." She wished she felt as calm as she sounded. Frankly, the idea of Kenga and Rama loose in Miami scared her. Her fingernails bit into the soft flesh of her palms. Her heartbeat raced as fear gripped her. Otherwise, she didn't think she showed outward signs of fear.

Nick didn't question her assumption. Instead, he asked, "How hungry are they? I need to know exactly what I'm dealing with."

"They ate several steaks and chicken just before the hurricane hit. They shouldn't be hungry for awhile."

"Let's hope not. People aren't expecting to find wild animals under their kids' beds." He chuckled dryly. "If I hadn't witnessed it after Andrew, I wouldn't be prepared either."

"Why are you so obsessed with this hurricane *and* my tigers?" she asked. Her instincts told her this man was extremely worried even if his expression turned stoic.

"Andrew left a bad taste in everyone's mouth. I have no illusions how deadly they are," Nick said. His eyes narrowed. He withdrew his pistol from its holster, flicked the chamber open and peered down it intensely. She stepped sideways, away from the barrel, uneasy when it pointed in her direction.

She couldn't help appreciate that he looked like a pretty handy man to have around in a pinch. He seemed to know his guns. And he could lift pretty hefty weights. She bit back her pride. "Well then, we'll just have to find them."

"What's this *we* business?" Nick snapped the chamber shut, checked the safety and reholstered it at his side. Then his half-laughing gaze glittered over her. "I don't remember inviting you to join me."

"I'm going with you."

"I work alone. You're *not* going out *there*." Nick took the rifle off his shoulder and squinted into the barrel, barely acknowledging her. Finally, he spun it around, an optical illusion making him look like the Rifle Man when he grabbed the butt in his hand. He stood tall and proud. With the wind at his back ruffling his hair, he was silhouetted against the reddish gold South Florida sun.

He wasn't someone she wanted to antagonize. But she had to find Kenga and Rama. What other options did she have but to have him help her search for them?

"Why not? They're my tigers." She faced off in front of him, oblivious to his gun, and lifted her chin defiantly.

"Who'd be responsible for you? Me?" He shook his head, his smile enigmatic. "No can do. I don't have time to babysit."

"I can take care of myself," she replied haughtily, extremely irritated. Trying to appeal to his sense of reason, she reminded him, "They know me. I can bring them in peacefully."

Placing a hand on his forearm, she blocked his way when he turned to leave, she tried one last ploy. "I have a special way with animals."

Nick towered over her, his shadow eclipsing her. Wind whisked palm fronds against his back. Her attention shifted when a bright indigo parrot sailed toward them. It landed atop the fractured palm tree. With its wings fully spread against the purplish and orange dawn sky, she marveled at the beauty of nature in the midst of such hellish destruction.

"Miami's just become the new Mortal Combat zone. Even little old grandmothers are sleeping with loaded guns under their pillows, shooting at anything that moves." He leaned towards her. "How much practice do you have dodging flying bullets?"

"Not much," she admitted grudgingly. She stood taller. "I'll take my chances." She blocked his exit.

"That's zany! Didn't you hear a word I said?" His expression turned to one of disbelief. "Or are you suicidal?"

"You're going," she said as if that explained everything. She lifted her chin defiantly, a hint of a smile tugging at her lips. That almost always worked with her brothers.

He grasped her chin between strong fingers, turning her face first left, then right, and peered at her closely for closer inspection.

His voice became suddenly sultry and gravelly. It poured over her, sugar coating his words. "I don't have ruby red hair and lips, emerald eyes and peaches and cream complexion, and a smattering of freckles."

"What's that got to do with anything, Lieutenant? I was raised with four older brothers and I can out run them, out shoot them *and* out think them! I can do anything as well as you or even better!"

"That red hair of yours will beacon every poacher and criminal within two miles," he said bluntly. "My work requires me to be inconspicuous." His gaze softened. "Besides, you could get hurt."

"I go where my tigers go." She stared him straight in the eye, refusing to back down. "Aren't you being a little melodramatic?" she asked, quirking her eyebrow.

"Just stay put right here where you're safe and get the den ready. I'll do my best to get them back safely."

"How are you going to stop me from leaving five minutes behind you?" she challenged. She calculated plan number two. If he refused to take her with him, she'd take a zoo truck and strike out on her own. Isn't that what she'd planned to do anyway before he showed up?

"Just stay put," he warned. He looked her square in the eye. A lesser soul would have quivered in her boots. But Kelly lifted her chin a notch higher.

"I'll find them alright! With or without you," she promised. Perspiration trickled between her breasts and down her back. The sun floated higher in the morning sky, turning its heat up on a weary, storm-tossed Miami. It must be ninety five degrees in the shade already. She doubted it was nine a.m. yet and dreaded the heat of noon when the sun blazed directly overhead.

"If the National Guard doesn't pick you up first," he drawled. "I can arrest you here and now," he warned, his voice very quiet, very steely. His hand grasped her arm, its grip pure iron again.

"Are you really such a heartless monster?" she spat. He was both handsome as sin and unmerciful as Satan. She looked at his hand disdainfully, shaking it off her arm.

Not backing down from his firm stance, Nick stared her straight in the eye with a trace of contempt. "Are you one of those bleeding heart animal lovers?"

She opened her mouth to speak but he interrupted.

"I have to get the dangerous animals out of Miami before they maul somebody," he said. "I can't take you with me, Cincinnati. I should have hit the road at sun up." Nick muttered. "Let's get out of here before I waste several more hours," he commanded. "Ladies first." He rolled out his arm in a mocking gesture.

She flounced before him, angered she didn't get her way. Her eyes darted back and forth, looking for any hint of movement in the bushes and shadows. Tendrils of smoke sizzled up from the tarmac as if Hell's fires burned close to the surface. Her wet soles squished on the sidewalk.

She strained to hear animal voices and movements. Anything—a growl, rustling in the bushes, the click of toe nails on the concrete sidewalk—to home her in on her tigers. Maybe they'd stayed close to home.

When something thrashed in the bushes, adrenalin shot through her veins. Could Kenga and Rama still be on the zoo property? She peered into the shadows but the thick foliage blocked her vision.

She whistled the tuneless melody that signaled Rama and Kenga to come to her. No response came.

Nick stopped. His brows furrowed questioningly.

"Shh! I thought I heard something rustling in that bush." Kelly whipped the tranquilizer gun off her shoulder. "I want to check it out."

Squatting on her heels, she gingerly prodded at the shrubbery with the tip of the gun, pulling back thick greenery. She tried to lift sections so she could see inside.

"Cincinnati, don't!" Nick warned. "Anything might be in there."

Suddenly, a savage growl bellowed from the bushes. The ground rumbled as if an earthquake trembled. Then a ferocious alligator lunged out. Mighty jaws snapped powerfully just inches from her face. She gasped as her life flashed before her eyes.

## Chapter Two

Startled, Kelly jumped back, away from the horrid monster. The gator vaulted closer, it's snapping mouth showing her a blurry view of its thrashing tongue, a throat cavity that looked large enough to swallow her whole, and rows of sharp, disgustingly filthy teeth.

Fear, unlike any she'd known before, twisted her stomach into a million knots. She waited for the inevitable pain and then darkness when the creature closed his huge mouth over her.

"My trigger's jammed. Shoot it!" Nick yelled.

She grabbed the tranquilizer gun, fumbling with it. She yanked the trigger. Nothing happened. She slammed the useless firearm against the ground, trying to jar it loose. "It's jammed! It must have broken when I fell."

"Shove the gun in it's mouth!" Nick yelled.

She shoved the gun perpendicular in the monster's mouth. Strong jaws snapped it like a twig. So much for those Tarzan movies. Real life never worked like movie magic. Grimacing, she realized that might be her dying thought.

Precious moments had been granted her, even if her attempt to thwart the creature had not halted its ominous advance. She struggled to gain her momentum. Still the monster lunged forward, the clicking of its sharp toe nails against the pavement thundering in her ears. Its beady eyes remained steadfast on her face, their glare mesmerizing. She lunged out of the way.

Hands grabbed her waist from behind, pulling her backward away from the monster's snapping jaws of death. A scream jammed in her throat. She kicked Nick who struggled to drag her further back out of the monster's reach. His huge hand clamped over her mouth. "I've got you. Stop str—ug—gling or we'll fall and both become b-b-breakfast," Nick's commanding baritone dimly penetrated her paralyzed mind. "I have no intention of being gator bait. Work with me here."

Without warning, he dove and rolled, taking her with him. Searing pain slashed her eye as his one-hundred-eighty-pounds slammed her against the asphalt. "Get up and run. Stay away from bushes!" Nick yelled.

She sprinted away then chanced a glance over her shoulder.

Nick rumbled on the ground with the gator, trying to avoid its deadly, thrashing tail. His arms held the gator's mouth shut, but it looked like the gator was inching it's jaws open wider by the second. She knew she had to help him quickly. Even his enormous strength paled in comparison to the gator's.

But her tranquilizer gun had snapped in two. She needed to find a weapon or a diversion.

Feverishly, her eyes scanned the littered ground around her. Broken glass, rocks, shingles and tree branches lay everywhere.

Glancing around, she honed in on a tree she could climb once she launched her deadly missiles. Praying the tree wouldn't topple over, she grabbed a handful of rocks and glass, heedless that it cut her hands to shreds. When she aimed at the gator, Nick kept rolling in her line of vision. She could kill him instead of the gator if she hit him and not the monster.

Worse, she knew if she did nothing, the gator would kill him. She couldn't stand by and let him die. Aiming with the heart of young David when he defeated the giant, she threw several rocks and chunks of glass at the monster. She prayed their leathery friend would forget about Nick. Hopefully, Nick would have the sense to escape, when he had the chance.

One deadly projectile hit the gator in its beady fathomless eye. It screamed and hissed in pain, swinging its huge body agilely toward its new attacker, giving Nick the chance to hurl himself in the opposite direction.

She threw a couple more rocks to ensure Nick's escape then she sprinted for the tree, jumping for the lowest branch. The sapling branch cracked, breaking off under her weight, sending her tumbling on her back, knocking scorched wind from her lungs.

"Get out of there now!" Nick rasped breathlessly, holding his chest.

She ran for the tree and tried to shimmy up the trunk. Rain-slick, the sapling lacked the friction needed to get good hold to pull herself up. Still, she struggled frantically, goaded by the gator's grunting, thrashing jaws. When she peered over her shoulder to gage the gator's location, the outraged monster lunged for her.

"Grab that branch. Pull yourself up. Hurry!"

She slipped. Blood trickled down her cheek where the remaining tree bark scraped her like sharp thorns. She ran the tip of her tongue over her lips and tasted its saltiness.

A loud *crack* like a Roman Candle exploded not less than six inches from her face. She heard blood curdling screams. One was her own voice, she realized detachedly. The other, eerily inhuman, belonged to their leathery friend.

She tumbled atop the monster and recoiled bitterly. Trying to scramble away, all she could feel was it's suffocating, leathery underbelly, it's scaly, rough miniature hands as they hung limply in the air, raking her bare arms, her face.

Eternity seemed to pass and she realized that all she felt was a dull throbbing ache deep in her muscles. Well, she hadn't fallen through Alice's looking glass yet. She still belonged to the real world—even if Chelsea had rewritten the rules.

"The creature's dead. It can't hurt you anymore," he whispered, his voice gentle. He grasped her hand and his strong fingers curled around hers. He hauled her to her feet.

"You're hurt," he murmured, peering at her face. Gentle fingers lifted her chin for a closer inspection.

He whipped a crisp white handkerchief from his pocket and dabbed at the blood that trickled down her left cheek and the nasty gash above her eye, nursing her wounds as if he were a practiced surgeon. His bedside manner was definitely improving. Too much so for her piece of mind.

She stepped back, taking the handkerchief from him and held it over her wound. Too much was happening too fast. She had to regroup, get control of herself.

"You need some antiseptic before you get a nasty infection," he murmured, his breath still warm on her cheek. He didn't seem to notice how she trembled ever so slightly at his touch, but her reaction burned itself into her brain.

"You wrestled an *alligator*. You saved my life," she murmured in awe, then silently cursed herself for sounding like a lovesick teenager.

"All in a day's work," he smiled, a really dazzling smile, making her heart flip-flop in her chest. "Didn't I show you my badge?"

When she nodded her head, he added impishly, "It says, *'To honor, to protect innocent animals, children and fair damsels in distress'*." He chuckled. "Don't tell me you're scared, Cincinnati? You wrestle man-eating tigers for fun everyday."

"I'm cold," she lied, knowing it was unlikely he would believe her in this scorching heat. She wished her traitorous body would obey her commands and not tremble like a leaf caught in an autumn downdraft. "They're not man-eaters!" she protested. "They're big kitty-cats."

"Some kitty cats," he drawled. "I never owned a kitty cat that had mammoth teeth and out-weighed me."

This he-man had a cat? That was difficult to picture and she almost chuckled aloud.

"Thank you for saving my life," she said, bestowing a smile on him. She dabbed at the oozing wound, grimacing when it stung like she'd poured alcohol into the cuts. The sooner she got medical treatment the better. Then she could get back to the business of finding her tigers.

Pivoting on her heel, she intended to walk away gracefully. She could feel his gaze burn into her back and she squared her shoulders.

Miscalculating her steps, she stumbled over the monster instead. She hissed, recoiling inwardly at the sensation of touching that hideous big belly.

"Careful now." Strong hands grabbed her again, saving her from the fall. Nick pulled her back against his hard chest.

Sucking in a deep breath, she gathered her courage. Dang if that leather handbag maker's dream didn't loll over most of the sidewalk, she couldn't help but think. "That thing must be seven feet long," she gasped in awe, mesmerized.

"There's liable to be a whole lot of equally dangerous animals loose in Miami," he mumbled. "I've got to get back to work." He placed his hand on the small of her back and she schooled herself not to react.

She pointed to the office. "The office is just around the corner." She kicked her attacker, recoiling when her toe made contact.

Rustling in the bushes stiffened her spine. Her ears perked. She squinted at the bushes wondering what surprises lurked there. She inched away from it, not about to be caught unaware twice in the space of an hour.

A scrawny, wet monkey, screeching like a hyena, leaped out of the bushes, looking scared to death.

Kelly's heart went out to it and she cracked a grin.

Nick's arms tightened around her.

"Don't be scared baby. Come here," she crooned. She held out her arm, clicking to it.

It cocked its head, studying the humans as if trying to decide if she was truly happy to see them. She was soaked through and through, her fur matted to her body, making her look emaciated. She shivered despite the suffocating heat that rose in layers from the boiling mud baths of the ground.

Chirping, the monkey hopped from branch to branch to Kelly's outstretched arm. She curled her tail around Kelly's arm and dropped a kiss on her cheek. She rubbed her head against Kelly's.

"Looks like you have a friend," Nick said. He lifted a quizzical brow.

She smiled. "I have a way with animals. Warm blooded ones, anyway."

When gunfire clanged in the distance, she jumped.

"Kenga and Rama are no match for bullets," she whispered, her eyes seeking Nick's.

"There's war in Cutler Ridge again," Nick muttered, shaking his head. Shadows clouded his eyes.

"We'd better be going before they shoot Kenga and Rama," Kelly said. The monkey chirped as if to affirm her words.

"You're not going." Nick fixed her with his serious gaze. He narrowed his eyes.

"If it weren't for me, you'd have been gator snack."

"You're not going and that's final," he said quietly, deadly serious. He regarded her like he would the enemy.

Her brow arched delicately and she faced off against him. The monkey leaped to her shoulder. It batted away pesky insects that buzzed around its head. Her tail tickled Kelly's back as it curled and uncurled against her.

"And if I decide to leave five minutes after you? Then what will you do?" She put her hands on her hips defiantly and cocked her chin, remembering she had just about said the same thing to him before.

"Don't do it."

She shook her head slowly. Her hands rested on her hips as they did when her brothers tried to force her to do something against her will.

"You're forcing me to arrest you for your own good then," he stated, his deep tones brisk.

"You can't do that! You..."

"Don't ever challenge me, Cincinnati. I always win."

# Chapter Three

*Right! Bradley always won.* She slowly simmered to a rolling boil, just thinking about the man's condescending attitude. Just because he flashed a shiny tin badge that looked as if it came out of a Cracker Jack box, his word wasn't definitive law. He wasn't even a cop, just a game commissioner. Did he have a God complex, bossing her around the way he had?

She'd find her tigers without him, thank you very much. Since when had she needed a man to bail her out of a jam? Since about never. No reason to start now.

Scathing remarks balanced on the tip of her tongue when he threatened to arrest her. But the cold-blooded-I-dare- you look in his eyes stopped her dead. She knew his type. He didn't play games. She doubted he cracked a smile often or paused to enjoy a sunset.

He wasn't wasting any time. He probably had his rifle cocked, aimed at anything that looked remotely big and feline.

His rear tires spit mud at her in his hurry to find her *man-eaters*. Like a little boy with shiny toy guns, he couldn't wait to play big game hunter.

Her blood pumped double-time through her veins in a rhythm that warned her to hurry. She chewed her bottom lip and stared at the light glaring off his rear bumper as he sped off zoo property. Unfortunately, his guns weren't pretend and his words weren't idle threats.

Standing in the same spot several moments after his sedan disappeared from her view, she mulled over her game plan. The way she saw it, she could sit back on her haunches and hope everything turned out okay, or she could take matters into her own hands.

*No fate,* Linda Hamilton had carved out on the table in the Terminator after she'd finally realized she held the future in her hands. *No fate but what we make.*

The premonition sounded just as prophetic, just as powerful in her own circumstance.

If she cooled her heels here, Nick would hunt the tigers down. His holier than thou I'm-Miami's-savior attitude left no illusions in her mind. He'd shoot the cats on sight, no questions asked.

But if she found them, she'd bring them home safely.

She had to reach Kenga and Rama before he did, or they could put their heads between their legs and kiss their tails goodbye.

Bradley wasn't giving her a choice.

With grit and determination, she marched back to the office, loaded herself down with fresh guns, ammo and a few survival supplies. She felt like Rambo.

Only half an hour behind her blond nemesis at most, she threw her gear into the passenger side of her truck, ordered Derek, her assistant, to stay put and slammed the truck into gear, swerving at the zoo's front gate to miss a flock of flamingoes high-stepping across the street, squawking at her as if she'd brought the hurricane.

She wondered if they were the same birds that had escaped from the women's restrooms where they'd been caged for safe-keeping during the storm. Cracking a half grin, she was glad she'd not been the first unwary soul to open the door to be mowed down by the frantic fowls.

Slowly simmering, she bided her time until the birds cleared her path. She switched the radio on for company and the police scanner for bulletins about the tigers and chuckled when a King Kong-type news flash waxed urgent over crackling air waves.

When she realized it wasn't a movie preview, that Karoake, the zoo's four-hundred-pound ape supposedly terrorized the elderly residents of Golden Cove, she swore softly under her breath. What next? Would the hippos take a plunge in Biscayne Bay? The elephants trumpet down the Dolphin Expressway?

Swerving the truck into a sharp U-turn, impervious to honking horns and irrate expletives, she nearly side-swiped an upside down dump truck in the middle of the road.

She threw all her weight into cutting the steering wheel far left and spun out, nearly missing a roof top sitting dead center in the median.

Driving in a strange city wasn't easy, as she'd found to her chagrin *before* the hurricane. Now it was practically impossible. The map spread out on the passenger seat proved next to worthless. Street signs floated in canals and decorated tree tops like weather vanes. Cars and trees, even roof tops, barricaded most of the roads. Only major roadways had been cleared in the slightest and they were clogged with government vehicles. Vacant-eyed civilians milled about aimlessly like zombies. Bare chested children played in mud puddles oblivious to the danger.

Impatient, she laid on her horn, waving traffic out of her way, flashing her driver's license a few times, pretending she had the authority to pull over traffic.

Miraculously, she found Golden Cove, pulling to the curb with a squeal of her radial tires. In her hurry, she pulled halfway onto the sidewalk, slammed her door and abandoned the truck. Her boss would fix any tickets anyone had the nerve to give her. And if they tried to mess with her personally, with Karaoke as her body guard, she was sure they'd back off in a hurry.

Stuffing her pockets with bananas, she sprinted through what was once the golden gated entrance. One gate hung by a thread. The other lay in the middle of the private park.

Shrill screams pierced her eardrums. Fear sluiced her. A four-hundred-pound gorilla could wreak havoc and destruction. Normally mild-mannered Karaoke might not behave in his typical, lovable manner faced with so many changes and being out of his environment. She couldn't take any chances.

But her gut told her, he wouldn't hurt a fly.

"The ape's going to eat us!" a shrill voice proclaimed in the distance. Kelly couldn't tell if the frantic tones belonged to a woman or to a man. She increased her step from a fast power walk to a jog. Her eyes scanned the compound, looking for the crowd she sensed lay ahead. Rounding a corner, she almost collided with an old woman ambling around with glazed eyes.

"Help us!" A woman's voice screeched in terror.

"Get him before he gets us!" A thin voice wobbled.

She weaved in and out of the commotion, her tranquilizer gun thrust before her—just in case she ran headlong into danger.

Determined, she pushed and shoved her way through a raging sea of stampeding wheelchairs, walkers and adult-sized tricycles manned by hysterical elders into a community known aptly as *Golden Cove*.

"The redhead's going to shoot us!" someone shrieked.

She felt like a salmon pushing upstream. She cradled her tranquilizer rifle to her chest. It gave her a measure of solace.

The sea of wrinkled faces parted like the Red Sea, fearful she was a terrorist commando.

"The Old Man" must be scared witless by these old men. Riled, they jumped around like twenty-year old Olympic champions, intent on getting the *monster* before he got them. She'd be out of sorts if someone treated her that way. Not that she appreciated being thought of as a commando, but with the rifle strapped to her back, she could see where they got that idea.

When she drew near enough to see the source of commotion, she blinked, barely believing her eyes. Radio reports proclaiming a gorilla *terrorized* the residents of Golden Cove were dead wrong.

From her standpoint, things looked exactly the opposite. Far from Karaoke terrorizing helpless residents, little old men and women poked and prodded Karaoke with canes, umbrellas, shuffle board poles and sticks.

Poor Karaoke huddled in a fetal position, arms draped over his head, shrieking like his little cousin the monkey. Like a little boy, he peeked around his gangly hands to see his attackers. Her heart broke.

"Everybody clear out!" she yelled. "Please stop provoking the poor animal!" She slung her tranquilizer gun over her back and held her hands up high in the air before her so no one would perceive her as a threat. She stopped a few feet away from the furious crowd, taking their measure, not liking what she saw. Most everyone waved some form of weapon. They screamed. They yelled.

Their features were contorted with hatred. Heaven knew she didn't want to be beaned by one of those wicked-looking canes and particularly not with the stick that poked trash from the ground. They could crack her cranium with one well-placed swing.

Still, she knew she could fling the gun forward instantly if need be and she felt comforted feeling its weight. She hoped sight of the weapon would protect her. She didn't think she could use it on a person. Still, silently she thanked her father for teaching her to shoot like a pro. King Kerrigan believed in equality and he'd taught his daughter the same lessons he'd taught his sons. He didn't want her to find herself caught in some remote jungle one day, helpless like a prima donna.

He probably hadn't counted on her turning out to be such a tomboy either. A grin played around her lips, despite the dire circumstances.

"He's attacking us!" A normally harmless old lady yelled, twirling her hand bag in the air over her head like a slingshot.

Kelly winced, harboring no doubt the purse would be much more lethal than any ordinary stone. She prepared to duck, tuck and roll. This was one weapon her father and brothers hadn't given thought to.

"Put the purse down please, ma'am," she said as soothingly as she could, feeling like she asked an unruly toddler to put down a hand-grenade. Her voice felt strained and her temples began to throb.

"That ape is going to kill us!" A withered man interjected in her defense. His eyes looked like black marbles bulging from a face that reminded her of a shriveled apple doll.

"We're going to get him before he gets us!" Another yelled, raising cheers from his cronies. Sun, reflecting like a mirror off his shiny head made Kelly squint and turn her head away.

Incited, the crowd pushed in on Karaoke. The ape trembled, his long fingers clenching and unclenching. Fear glimmered in his black eyes. Although glazed, they seemed to recognize Kelly and he made a mieux like a kitten, holding out his hand to her.

"Get back now!" She ordered in her sternest King Kerrigan type voice. If her dad were here, they'd obey him without question. But it didn't have the same effect coming out of a slip of a girl. The crowd ignored her as if she hadn't uttered a word.

"Shoot the ape!" Someone else screeched. He smacked his cane against the wet sidewalk like a child having a temper tantrum.

"Bernie, you got your gun?" A woman shrilled. Kelly's heart galloped in her chest. Her respiration quickened, rasping past her lips in short bursts.

Things were going from bad to worse by the second. The crowd was out of control. She had to act now before someone got hurt.

Hauling her rifle into firing position, she pointed it at the crowd. "I said, get away from the gorilla. Now!"

"She's got a machine gun!" One lady yelled. Another fainted, falling into the arms of three men who lowered her to the ground gently. One fanned her with a palm frond, crooning soothing words to her, smoothing her hair away from her ashen cheeks.

When the crowd gaped at her, and only a few moved away, she yelled again, her voice more quavery than she would have liked. "I mean it! Move away from the animal!"

She lifted the gun butt to her shoulder and pointed the weapon at the man closest to Karaoke. "You first." She waved it until he followed her orders.

Karaoke peeked out, his eyes glazed over in terror. He whimpered like a baby, and her heart went out to him. How could these people not see what a sweetheart he was? How could they be so cruel?

Panic, pure and simple, she presumed. She would probably react the same way if she didn't know what a pussycat this giant ape could be.

Swinging her gun threateningly, she motioned for the fellow to move away. "Now. I'm not messing around. Let me get to the ape."

Reluctantly, the man stepped back. Still, he clutched his cane in a death grip, paranoia gleaming in his eyes.

She approached slowly, more scared of the crowd than the gorilla. Her heart pounded against her ribs. Her knees wobbled. "Step away, please," she said succinctly, wondering why she bothered with platitudes. They inched back like toy robots, their steps stiff and measured. "I'm taking him back to the zoo."

Slowly, she put her hand in her pocket where she had placed Kenga's collar and leash before she left the zoo, keeping a firm grip on the rifle with her other hand. The tiger collar should fit him, too.

She didn't want to upset Karaoke any more than he already was. After all, a four-hundred-pound ape could pulverize her if his adrenaline suddenly pulsed through his veins. Frankly, it was a miracle he hadn't gone berserk before this. No one, human or animal, could take this abuse for long and not defend oneself.

She slid the gun over her back again. Gently, in a gesture of friendship, she held her open hand to the gorilla. "Take my hand, boy. Let's go home."

Slowly, Karaoke lowered his arms. He ambled on his knuckles to her side, his gait lopsided. His soft brown eyes, big and round, sought hers. Tears pooled around the rims. He stopped a foot in front of her regarding her warily, like a soldier offering mercy, not knowing whether she would grant him asylum or death.

"It's okay boy. I'm Kel-ly," she enunciated slowly, pointing to her chest, jabbing it twice for each syllable. "Kel-ly. You know me."

He still looked in askance.

Maybe he'd feel better if she offered food. She'd forgotten she carried incentive and hoped it wasn't squished in her pocket by now.

"Want a banana, boy?" she crooned, sliding a ripe banana out of her other pocket. She peeled it halfway down and held it out to him. The peel draped her hand like an inverted umbrella.

Karaoke sniffed the air as if he suspected a trick, his pug nose wrinkling. These humans were acting crazy today, his gestures seemed to say. She could just read his mind. He thought all the humans had gone over the edge, picking on a defenseless ape.

She sympathized and wished she could soothe his brow.

Carefully, Karaoke took the banana, peeled the rest of the skin off, and tossed it over his shoulder nonchalantly. He stuffed the banana in his mouth, swallowing it in one gulp.

She thrust out her hand determinedly. "Come here, boy.

Apparently appeased by the peace offering, Karaoke hobbled to her on his knuckles. He sat up, stretching his gangly arm to her, placing his hand in hers, his furry, leathery fingers closing over hers in a gesture of goodwill. She smiled gently. "Good boy. Everything will be okay. Let's get home." She squeezed his leathery hand. "Let me put your collar on, okay?"

Karaoke nodded in understanding, giving his consent. Kelly appreciated his keen intellect. If she didn't work with tigers, apes would be her next choice.

She unsnapped the collar and started to put it around Karaoke's neck, when the old man with the cane leapt forward like an ancient Bruce Lee. "Hi yeeah!" he screeched, swinging his cane for all he was worth. Wood splintered over Karaoke's skull.

The big ape stretched to his full height, pummeling his chest with powerful fists, bellowing in rage. He looked and sounded like King Kong. Fear unlike any she'd ever known engulfed her in tidal waves as she watched him grab the cane from the man and snap it over his knee like a matchstick. He hurled the broken pieces toward the horizon and she ducked. It whizzed over her head with inches to spare.

*Oh my God!* Kelly gulped in deep breaths. Her heart thundered in her chest, ready to burst. What had they done! More to the point, what would a four-hundred-pound ape do to these little old people? To herself? She shuddered to think of the possibilities.

She jumped back, fright pushing her with superhuman speed, dropping the leash like she would the metal part of a scalding curling iron, and grabbed for her tranquilizer gun with shaking hands. Her fingers trembled when she tried to pull the trigger.

Where was her cool when she needed it? King would not be impressed at this instant.

But Karaoke moved faster. With one swift jerk, he pulled Kelly to him, swinging her in his arms as lithely as if she were a rag doll.

Kelly's breath came in short gasps. Perspiration rolled off her brow and ran down her back in rivulets. She took a deep cleansing breath, trying to soothe her nerves.

"I'm not Faye Raye!" she muttered brokenly under her breath, pushing against his hairy chest. She squeezed her eyes shut tightly, wondering what her father would do in such a situation.

Simple. He was too smart to get into a situation like this. He wouldn't have stepped within ten feet of the animal.

"The ape's got the girl!"

*Duh! Tell me something we don't all know.*

"Serves her right for playing with prehistoric monsters!" Somebody else shouted.

Had they never heard of empathy? Or sympathy?

"We've got to save her." Another screamed.

"Call the Miami PD!" A second voice of reason shouted.

*Finally, voices of reason.*

"Run before he gets us too!" Still another screeched.

*So much for that reprieve.* She struggled to free herself, but Karaoke grasped her tighter, hauling her closer to his chest. She turned her nose away, vowing to buy him a vat of underarm deodorant when she got him home. *If* she got him home.

"Put me down, boy. I'm not going to hurt you. I won't let them hurt you again." Kelly crooned, trying to eradicate all traces of fear from her voice. Still, she detected faint quivering. Her pulse fluttered like a candle in the wind. Her heart couldn't take much more before it surely would burst.

The gorilla's nostrils flared in and out. His eyes narrowed, panicked. Blood trickled down his left cheek. His grip tightened and he bellowed a warning roar she felt sure all of Miami *and* Ft. Lauderdale could hear. She wondered why no policemen had come to her rescue yet. Surely, someone else would have heard the news reports. It felt as if she'd been here for a century. Didn't anyone else care that a gorilla roamed loose through Golden Cove?

"Get back!" An authoritative voice commanded.

Kelly's neck snapped to her right. Nick. Thank God he'd found her. Exquisite relief flooded her and she went limp in Karoake's arms. She let out a long, scorched breath. Her pulse started to slow. Her heart sang in recognition.

Her sunny-haired savior had arrived—tall, strong and laughing in the face of danger. She smiled tremulously at him, forgetting how mad she'd been at him only an hour before.

"Stay absolutely still, Cincinnati," he gritted between clenched teeth. He held a sister gun to her tranquilizer rifle butted against his shoulder, peering down the sites.

"He's injured, Nick," she said, her compassion for the ape suddenly flaring in her bosom. Something tender deep inside swelled up. "Don't hurt him," she whispered, her breath ragged.

"I'm trying not to. If you'll stop jabbering and let me concentrate." The sun glinted off his hair like spun gold. His lips thinned in concentration. His scar stood out on his cheek, almost silvery in the harsh light of noonday.

No man had ever looked so dashing or so handsome.

Her hero.

"Shoot him in his rear where there's more meat. You don't want to hurt him," she pleaded.

"I'm a little more concerned with your safety and the safety of all these people right now, Cincinnati," he muttered, his voice deep and gravelly. He squeezed the trigger gently. A dart flew swift and true, landing in Karaoke's shoulder.

The gorilla swatted at it like he would at a pesky fly, mieuxing again in consternation. Then he slumped, the arm that held her prisoner falling limply to his side. The huge body fell over in slow motion.

Her gluteus maximus hit the muddy concrete sidewalk with a thump. He curled up in fetal position, sucking his thumb like an infant.

In two bounds, Nick knelt and gathered her in his warm arms, pulling her tightly against him. "Are you okay?" His voice was husky with concern. His free hand smoothed her hair away from her face.

She nodded, melting against him.

He lifted her high in the air. She snuggled her head against his chest, her ear listening to the strong, rugged beat of his heart, and her own thumped in unison. Two hearts. Two bodies. One spirit. She smiled dreamily against his lithe chest.

Carrying her to a picnic table where he deposited her gently, he ordered, "Stay put!" His voice came out nowhere near as gentle as his arms. His eyes narrowed, threatening her to disobey.

Instantly, her mood changed to one of wariness. She was on alert. Had she misread him so badly? She frowned in consternation, her eyes narrowed, seeking his.

"Don't hurt Karaoke!" She jumped to her feet following him, all gratitude, all warm, cuddly feelings forgotten in light of the new threat to one of her animals and his sudden bruskness.

Nick rounded on her, his hands on his hips, his eyes shooting daggers. He towered over her menacingly. "If you interfere in my job one more time, I'm arresting you. Now, stay put!" Nick pivoted on his heel and strode to where the ape lay semi-conscious on the ground.

She ran after him, grasping his forearm, swinging him around to look at her. "He's zoo property. It's my job to apprehend him!"

"You don't know when to quit, do you Cincinnati?" His words were very quiet. Deathly quiet. She barely caught them. But she well understood the menace in them.

"I've got an animal on the loose in Golden Cove and you want to play games. I don't have time!" He whipped a pair of handcuffs from his back pocket and snapped one side on her arm.

"You can't do this!" she gasped, twisting in vain, not knowing whether to be appalled or stunned. The cold steel bit into her soft flesh.

"Watch me." He chuckled mirthlessly. Glancing around, he crooked his forefinger at the woman with the lethal purse. She ambled over, her purse swinging deceptively harmless from her wrist. She smiled at Nick. Sunlight winked off her silvery curls.

"Will you watch my prisoner while I move the ape to safety?" He worked his charm on the woman and Kelly grimaced, wondering how anyone could buy his obviously false charisma, deliberately forgetting she'd succumbed only moments before.

"Certainly, Sonny. Should I whack her if she tries to get away?" She held up the purse menacingly. Glee effused her face with warmth.

"What have I done?" Kelly asked, her eyes wide, hurt. The indignity humiliated her and she stiffened. Her uniform felt wet and sticky and she chafed. She still smelled like Karaoke and she tried not to breathe too deeply.

"What did you say, dearie?" The silver bandit asked holding her purse up again. She smiled sweetly, her chin dimpling.

"Nothing," Kelly said with a wry twist of her lips. Zookeeper's school hadn't taught her how to deal with this species.

Snapping the other half of the cuffs to the old woman, he said, "I'll be back as soon as I get the gorilla loaded in my trailer. If she gives you any trouble, just yell."

"She won't." The woman smiled beguilingly.

Flashing a mischievous smile to Kelly, he swatted her rear playfully.

Kelly jumped, stunned. His fingers scorched her even through the thick khaki pants. Impossible waves of awareness shot through her and she cursed herself for her weakness.

"I'll get you for that," she vowed through clenched teeth. "Don't turn your back on me," she added under her breath.

"We'll help you move King Kong," the karate man chimed in. "If you get his shoulders, Bernie and I will each take a leg. Simon will help you if your end's too heavy."

"I'd appreciate it," Nick grinned.

Kelly fumed, tapping her foot, watching out of narrowed eyes.

The silvery bandit added her two cents worth. "It'll be easier if you use that wagon over there we use for groceries. The hurricane didn't touch it."

"Where's it at, Lil?" the karate man asked.

She lifted her unencumbered arm and pointed. Her forefinger jutted out. "Just inside the clubhouse door. I put it in there so no one would trip over it."

"Good thinking." Nick applauded.

"I'll get it," Bernie said as he hobbled to the club house. Momentarily, he hauled a Red Flyer wagon behind him like a little boy in a Norman Rockwell painting. He had to zig-zag around cups, fallen branches and pieces of roof.

Kelly watched closely as the men hoisted Karaoke's limp body onto the wagon. The ape's huge frame spilled over it, his knuckles and toes grazing the steaming concrete. Kelly bit her lower lip to keep from crying out.

"Put his head in the wagon and you two hold his legs, and you hold his arms on his chest," Nick directed. He crossed Karaoke's hands over his chest as if he were praying. He tucked his feet into the end of the wagon.

With a grunt, Nick tugged the wagon behind him. Bernie and Si ended up pushing from the rear. The crowd limped behind them, ogling the strange sight, not realizing nor caring they made even a stranger sight.

Kelly shook her head, impatient to get the cuffs off. Did Bradley even plan to release her upon his return? Would he return, she wondered, or leave the silver bandit in charge of her indefinitely? She chafed, sitting on the picnic table, her elbow on her raised knee, her chin on the palm of her hand. She watched the procession as she would a circus parade.

Finally, Nick returned, sauntering toward her leisurely as if he hadn't a care in the world.

With a sigh, Kelly asked, forced sugar sweetness in her voice. "Are you planning to release me *this* century?"

Nick regarded her leisurely, his gaze slowly taking in her measure. "I don't know. I told you to stay put, twice. And you didn't listen. I'm beginning to think you're a troublemaker with a capital T, Cincinnati. Why would I complicate my life by letting you get underfoot again?"

"Who says I'd be underfoot? I was doing quite nicely until you showed up." She wouldn't let him get her goat again. At least she wouldn't show it. He-men like Bradley loved to lord it over women. She refused to give him the pleasure. At least, not more than she had to. Hand-cuffed, he had her at a large disadvantage. But that wouldn't last forever.

"You were about to become Mrs. King Kong before I showed up!" Nick howled, laughing at her.

Turning to his accomplices, Nick bowed, a twinkle in his eyes. "I appreciate your help. She'd have fled the scene for sure if not for you."

Kelly shot a quelling stare at Nick. How dare he!

"My pleasure, young man. The bridge club in Newark will never believe this. I can't wait to call them!" She held her arm out for Nick to unlock the cuffs that bound her to Kelly.

The woman's jerking motion yanked Kelly's arm out of it's socket. She almost stumbled off her picnic table perch.

Pay back would be sweet, she promised herself. She favored the lieutenant with her sweetest smile, imagining all sorts of delicious retribution.

"Be careful of this one," she whispered to Nick.

"Why?" he whispered conspiratorially, leaning his head toward her, the gleam in his eye downright merry.

"She's a sly one. Like a fox. Don't take your eyes off her."

"I won't," he promised, snapping the cuffs to himself. Then he slid his silvery sunglasses over his eyes, making his expression inscrutable.

"Time's wasting. Let's go," he said, striding forward, catching Kelly off guard.

Her shoulder screamed from the abuse when he tugged unmercifully. "Remember me? Quasimoto?"

"Keep up. You've already made me waste another hour finding those tigers."

"*I* delayed you? I didn't ask you to play Lone Ranger. You did that on your own, cowboy."

"What'd you expect me to do when I heard some crazy red head had a gun in Golden Cove trying to commandeer a two-ton gorilla? How many crazy redheads are chasing after escaped zoo animals?" Nick turned those insidious glasses toward her. His lips quirked. "It had to be you."

Kelly fumed. She bided her time, quelling her anger as best she could. "No one asked you to play hero. I distinctly remember telling you I can take care of myself."

"Sure. You were doing a dandy job when I showed up. You were about to go shopping for wedding dresses and tree houses." He laughed outright. "Tell me. What was your plan of action?"

Kelly remained silent. He knew darned well she hadn't one. Karaoke had caught her completely off guard. She hadn't counted on the silver brigade inciting Karaoke to King Kong type antics. *Wedding dress, my foot!*

Nick opened the passenger door of his sedan and stood aside like the gentleman she knew he wasn't. "Slide in."

Kelly cleared her throat. "What about these?" She held up their cuffed hands.

Nick unlocked his side of the cuffs, regarding her soberly. He held it tightly.

"Well? Are you going to unlock *me*?"

"I think we'll wait for the authorities. When they get the ape they can take you back to the zoo, too."

Kelly stared in disbelief. Her temper snapped, despite her resolve to the contrary. "You're joking. You'll be sorry if my big brothers ever get their hands on you!"

Nick's eyebrows furrowed skeptically. "Nope. You almost got yourself killed back there. You're a danger to yourself. You..."

Static crackled on the radio. "...tigers sighted in Cutler Ridge..."

"Damn! I can't wait around." He sprinted to the driver's side of the sedan and hopped inside. He revved the engine and glared at her.

"You're going to leave us here?" She bent, staring inside the dark car, wishing she could read the expression in his eyes. Whoever'd created those silver tinted sunglasses should be hung.

"I'll let the oldsters watch the gorilla. He's caged and can't cause further harm." His lips pursed. "You however, would escape and bring Miami to her knees."

Kelly lifted a quizzical brow. "How drole. Everyone's a comedian. So what do you propose?"

"I'll have to take you with me. Get in and fasten your seat belt. Next stop: Cutler Ridge!"

## Chapter Four

"You can't go in there Sir," a National guardsman informed Nick, his rifle ready to remove Nick's head from his shoulders. He looked ready for combat, barricading the road leading into Cutler Ridge. He could be a poster boy for the Armed Services.

"We're on official business, Lieutenant." Bradley flashed his badge through the window. "Please let us pass."

"What is the nature of your business, Sir?" The man did not budge an inch or bat an eye. He stood tall, straight and proud.

"Bradley of the Florida Fresh Water Fish and Game Commission. Tigers were sighted in this area less than half hour ago. I'm here to take them in."

"I'll have to get clearance from my Captain, Sir."

Kelly leaned forward in her seat, flashing her sweetest smile. "Sir." When he didn't respond, she repeated louder, "Sir."

This time, the man leaned in her window. "I'm the zoo keeper in charge of the tigers. They haven't been fed in well over twelve hours—which means they're starved."

"Yes, Ma'am." The lights of understanding hadn't lit his eyes yet.

"Tigers are carnivorous creatures...they consume a diet of red meat. I imagine they're getting pretty desperate by now."

"In other words, man, don't be daft! You'd make a mighty tasty tiger morsel." Nick chortled. "Can we pass now to capture those man eaters before you start looking like supper?"

"Yes, Sir!" The lieutenant stood back, putting his rifle at parade rest. "Be careful, Sir!" The man snapped smartly to military attention.

"So this is beautiful Cutler Ridge?" She looked this way and that, examining Chelsea's horrible destructive powers. Her heart ached for the poor people who lived here. It looked like they'd lost everything. "Chelsea must've been throwing hail and brimstone when she ripped through here last night," she whispered in awe, unshed tears stinging the backs of her eyes.

"They should know better than to name storms after women," Nick murmured keeping his eyes glued on the road. "They got what they deserved."

"You mean because we're wildly temperamental or some such malarkey?" She wrinkled her nose, snorting at his totally chauvinistic views and turned in her seat to glare at him.

"You said it, Cincinnati." The gold flecks in Nick's eyes twinkled merrily at her, taking some of the bite out of his words. His lips tilted upward and her heart melted.

Would she ever learn? She'd had plenty of experience with four older brothers teasing her constantly. Yet, gullible as she tended to be, she fell for their tricks every time. Well, almost.

"Magnetic center must lead through Cutler Ridge and Country Walk - just like the Bermuda Triangle. Damn if this storm didn't take the same path as Andrew. It's downright eerie. Buying property here would be like building on the San Andreas Fault." Nick ran unsteady fingers through his blonde hair.

"It really did that?" Kelly asked in astonishment, unable to tear her eyes from crumbling houses, if they could still be called houses. They were roofless, windowless and in many cases, missing walls and even second stories.

"This looks like pictures of Mexico City after the earthquake. Look over there, people are digging through the houses."

"What for?"

"Survivors," he said, ominously. Their gazes locked for a second. "Maybe looting." He shrugged his shoulders, frowning. "Disasters like this bring out the best and the worst in people."

"Are we close to the sight where Kenga and Rama were sighted?" Kelly wanted to know. Her pulse quickened and her breath grew

"What for?" His attention was focused on the opposite side of the road.

"I think that child needs help." Before Nick had brought the sedan to a complete stop, Kelly jumped out, running to the boy, adrenaline pumping through her veins pushing her forward.

Cursing under his breath, Nick pulled to the side of the road, grinding his brakes, then hopped down from the sedan to follow Kelly. He swore under his breath softly.

"Hi. I'm Kelly. This is Officer Bradley." Kelly motioned behind her at the tall blonde man who gazed down at them. His shadow loomed over them, stretching across the lawn.

"Offither?" The boy seemed to focus on the word, his voice hesitant. Perhaps because it was a word denoting authority and during crisis situations, many people sought authority. Even normally independent Kelly.

"Yes, son." Nick stooped to the boy's level, putting a huge hand on the boy's shoulder. "Is something wrong? Are you lost?"

"Where do you live?" Kelly asked, her nerves shouting, tingling all the way down to her toes. Nick put his other hand on Kelly's arm, restraining her and she looked down to catch the worried lines drawn around his mouth. His message communicated itself - be silent. She took a deep breath, willing herself to calm down.

The boy pointed to a destroyed house behind him. The roof was gone, probably decorating Cuba now, the side wall had imploded and the second floor hung precariously, groaning and moaning, threatening to buckle any moment. "My mommy's trapthed in there. She says Katy's hurt real bad."

Alarmed, Kelly sought Nick's gaze over the boy's head. "I want my mommy." The child cried, sobbing gently, tears racking his tiny frame. Plump tears trickled down his cheek. His lips quivered.

Kelly hugged the little boy close, rubbing his back, shooshing him softly, giving him her strength. "Shhh! We'll help you find your mommy."

"And get my sisther?"

He could be no more than six years old. If he weren't ragged and dirty, he'd be quite adorable. But Chelsea had left her mark on him. It looked like she'd dumped a ton of mud on everyone in Cutler

Ridge.

"Help me, please! Somebody help me." A distant voice sobbed brokenly, over and over. "My baby's hurt. My beautiful baby..." The voice faded into hiccoughing sobs.

"Oh my God, Nick." She grabbed his sleeve, digging her fingers into his arm, not realizing she'd used his Christian name for the first time. "I hear them. I think I hear them!"

"I heard something too." He lifted his chin regally, listening intently, like a tiger in the wild. His muscles contracted beneath her fingers.

"Offither. Mommy's crying *real* bad. Can you help her?" He stared at Nick and Kelly with puppy dog eyes. Tears ran down his cheek, leaving twin trails where they washed away the dirt. "The theiling hit Katy on top of her head. Mommy was trying to get her out and the second floor started to fall." He touched his cheek where angry red abrasions swelled under the dirt. "It hit me too, but I ran. Mommy said to get help...will you help my mommy? Please!" The child rambled as fast as he could, about ready to hyperventilate.

"He needs medical attention and it's a safe bet there aren't any doctors around. Get your bag out of the truck then follow me. I'll have to go in," Nick said with steely resolve.

"You can't go in there!" Alarm clutched her heart. He might get hurt—or worse!

"How else do I get them out?" He turned those curiously golden eyes on Kelly, making her feel twelve-years old again.

"Not alone. You need help!"

"Who do you suggest? "

"Radio for the National Guard, find some neighbors..." she said breathlessly.

"Cincinnati," his voice ragged with raw emotion. "There isn't time to wait. The house is about ready to come down. It's now or never."

"But..." He left without listening to her objections "...you could be killed." She squeezed her eyes tightly, clenched her fists and balled up her innermost courage. "I'm going with you."

"Like hell you are!" Nick rounded on her. Steely hands grabbed her shoulders, clamping down hard. The pads of his thumbs rubbed the hollows of her neck, almost making her forget the urgency of the moment. "Stay here with the child. Keep him safe. And find me some help."

"Who, Nick?" She felt at a loss. She knew no one here, didn't know who to trust, who might help. Spreading out her hands before her in helpless array, she repeated, "Who Nick?"

"Try the Guard? Maybe the neighbors."

"The house could fall any moment..."

"Precisely. That's why you can NOT go. That's final!"

"There's no time to argue. You need someone and face it Bradley...I'm the only one you've got." She sucked in a deep breath, ignoring how it scorched her lungs, ignoring the little voice of reason in her head that told her to run for the hills.

Nick heaved a giant sigh. He looked over his shoulder, studying the house. Then he took two giant steps to the boy and knelt down to be on eye level with the tyke. "What's your name, Slugger?"

"Mattie Wilson." His little face crumpled when his mother screamed again, this time more agonized. "Mommy! Katy!"

"Miss Kelly and I are going to get them out. But I need you to stay right here and guard my car."

His voice was too deep, too husky. She suspected he struggled to hide his own fear. Yet, her heart lurched. He remembered her name. It rolled on his tongue like ancient Irish brogue, the way her father liked to say it.

"But Mommy! Katy!"

"It's a real important job. Think you can handle it for me? Tell, you what champ. I'm going to deputize you."

Kelly lifted one finely arched brow. The man exercised a wonderful rapport with kids. She wondered how he got it. This enigma of a man would prove worth further exploration. Much more exploration.

"Let me doctor you up real quick. Okay Mattie?" Kelly opened her bag and rifled through it quickly. "Gotcha!" She picked out a tube of antiseptic gel that should work just as well on humans as on animals, twisted off the cap and squeezed the tube from the middle.

Quickly but gingerly, Kelly swabbed Mattie's face with antiseptic. He screamed and jumped back but she soothed him best she could. Then she bandaged him up. "There now. You're all fixed up, young man." She hugged him, smoothing his hair from his face with slightly shaking fingers. "Don't you worry about a thing. Officer Bradley and I are going to get your mommy and Katy out of that house right now. They're going to be all right." Kelly crossed her legs at her ankles, hoping she spoke the whole truth.

Faint sobs assailed Nick and Kelly as they entered the crumbling structure. Carefully, they picked their way through debris, stepping over pictures, dishes, clothes, toys...

He stumbled over a little girl's baby doll. Immediately, it cried, "Mama, mama," while it's china eyes fluttered open, staring vacantly, accusingly at him. Nick stared back, his mind accessing memories he'd thought safely, permanently tucked away, relegated to another life, to his other self.

His little girl, Ashlea, had owned a doll just like that, a doll she had loved dearly. It was that damned doll that she'd left outside in his mother's yard prompting her to venture outside alone after dark to rescue it... or so his mother had told him tearfully. Nick felt as paralyzed as if the roof had caved in on him. Painful memories, overwhelming guilt, unbearable grief consumed him as he locked gazes with that damned doll. It seemed to mock him, to curse him, to tell him he was too late...

Nick cursed loudly, he kicked the doll with a fury that scared even him. Kelly looked askance at him, her wide mouth drawn in concern. Shock mirrored in her expressive eyes.

That doll encased a demon, one that tortured and tormented him. It mocked him, blamed him. Unable to withstand the accusing glare one minute longer, Nick stomped over to the doll, closed its eyes and put a couch cushion over it, smothering the demon inside. It was easier to blame the doll than to blame himself. When he turned around, Kelly frowned silently. Her brows drawn, her mouth puckered in a silent mieux, she looked like she wanted to ask him what was wrong, but had thought better of it.

"Help us. Someone please help my baby." A voice moaned, snapping him out of his self-absorption, reminding him why he was in the crumbling house. Sobbing followed the impassioned plea.

He followed the sound, stepping on top of the debris everywhere. Kelly followed close behind, leaning on him when she lost her balance. They ducked beneath the doorway into the living room.

The moaning and pleas for help came from this room, he was certain. Chelsea had vented her fury in here, ripping and shredding with no feeling, no thought, just blind senseless rage. Blind anger threatened to rip through Nick, but closing his eyes briefly and clenching his hands into fists, he quelled it. This wasn't the time or place to lose his cool.

Sharp eyes scanned the room. Chunks of roof, wall, beds, couches and even broken trees lay in rubble. In the end, he had to search with his ears. He found the woman sobbing, cuddling a blonde-haired girl, who lay unconscious in her arms, blood trickling from a nasty gash in her forehead.

A chunk of concrete block wall pinned the woman's legs, rendering her incapable of moving her lower body. Anticipating how heavy the blocks were, most likely both legs were fractured in several places. When their gazes clashed, he read terror, pure and undiluted in her eyes. He wondered if his shone with dual emotions.

Kelly knelt beside the woman, compassion oozing from her. "Your little boy sent us. He told us we'd find you here," she spoke softly, assuringly. She laid a soothing hand on the woman's shoulder.

"Thank God." The woman sobbed. "Thank God. Mattie found you. I knew he would. He's a good boy, my Mattie. He's a good boy..."

Nick feared the woman was in shock. Her skin looked deathly pale beneath her Florida tan. The pupil's of her eyes dilated. Her lips blued around the edges. However, his main concern lay with the girl.

He sucked in a deep breath, nonplussed for a moment when he saw the child's face; so angelic, like a little pixie, framed by baby fine blonde hair that cascaded to her shoulders. She sported a pert little nose and lips that bowed as if Cupid had blessed her with a double dose of love. He bet her laughter tinkled and that her eyes glowed when she played with her baby doll. He felt a twinge of guilt for trying to smother it. He would get it for her if, no he corrected himself fiercely, when she awoke.

It was difficult to tell just by looking at her if she was breathing, and for a moment, he couldn't breathe himself. The air rushed in, but it wouldn't expel. Gently, he leaned over and spread his hand over her chest, like one would an infant, to feel if it rose and fell.

"Is she breathing?" Kelly whispered.

Nick nodded his affirmation, expelling a sigh of monumental relief.

Still, there was no cause to celebrate yet. An untidy crimson puddle coagulated alarmingly on the floor by the child's side. The child's flesh burned his. Fever raged within the tiny body. Dehydration proved a real threat, and like her mother, so did shock. There was no telling how much blood she'd lost or if she were concussed.

The girl gasped for air, although he refrained from adding that to the answer he gave Kelly. They had to get her to safety and medical attention quickly—or else.

He didn't want to think about *or else. Or else* brought back too many painful, paralyzing memories.

He needed Kelly's help to get the mother free and hoped she proved stronger than she looked. There was nothing preventing him from lifting the child except her mother's arms. He wanted desperately to cradle the little angel, to let his strength flow into her fragile, battered body. Then he thought better - what if her back was injured? He could cause her more harm. He straightened, looking down contemplating his best move.

"What are we going to do Nick?" Kelly's words spilled from her tremulously. Tears welled in her luminous emerald eyes.

"Is my baby okay?" the woman cried. "Is she going to be alright?"

Her eyes pleaded with Nick to tell her everything would be fine, but he couldn't. He didn't know. He averted his eyes, thinking again of his own tragedy...

The woman started sobbing, her body shaking uncontrollably. "I'm going to lose my baby, aren't I? She's going to die."

" I don't know." Nick turned back, mumbling. "Not if I can help it. Not if I can help it," he repeated under his breath.

They had to decide quickly. If they moved the girl, they could seriously injure her. If they left the girl and her mother where they were for much longer, the house could collapse, completely burying them, or the girl could die from any number of assailants: shock, loss of blood, or internal injuries.

None of the choices to him were good. But they were his and he was stuck making them, and he had to do so fast. Waiting too long, was in reality making a decision to do nothing, and that he couldn't live with. Better to take action and be wrong, than to take no action at all.

Pushing his own demons to the back of his mind where they belonged, he told the hysterical woman, "I'm going for help. I'll be right back. I promise."

"Don't leave us. Don't leave my baby!" she implored.

"I'll be right here," Kelly said. "I'm not going anywhere."

"But..."

"I'll be back." He threw over his shoulder. He ran to his sedan, keeping his eyes peeled for anyone who could lend a hand.

They had to have help. There was no way around it. He yanked open the door to his Sedan where Mattie lay sleeping on the front seat. Nick snatched the radio and called to find assistance. It seemed like a year before anyone answered his SOS, but finally, a voice crackled at the other end of the line. Then, he had to guess at his location. Everything looked so different, so eerie...like the eve of destruction, the end of the world, a little voice taunted him.

The approaching night was downright spooky. He wasn't the type to scare easily, otherwise he couldn't track poachers alone in the Everglades, or stare down packs of wild dogs and come out the victor. Yet, shivers crept down his spine standing out in the middle of this disaster zone.

As soon as he'd given his whereabouts, Nick grabbed the animal stretcher and dashed for the house. He swore under his breath when he stumbled over broken, rain-sodden lumber ripped from someone's roof. All he needed was to break his leg and become part of the walking wounded.

Saving the girl had become an obsession. He had to help that child. He had to get her to safety and medical care. Nothing else mattered.

As Nick entered the house, he heard the woman's sobs again.

Her pleading rang in his ears, taunting, tormenting till he wanted to shut out her cries, shut out the world. He could identify with her, understand her, and yet, maybe because of that, he wanted to shut out her pain. He'd locked away his own pain for so long, so well, that he hadn't let anyone near him since...

He shook his head to clear his mind of the disturbing images that had haunted him day and night for more years than he liked to recall. He didn't think he possessed the capability to love anyone again.

But this little girl was getting to him. And if he were completely honest with himself, Kelly had gotten under his skin too. It must be the stress from the hurricane causing him to feel so out of character. Perhaps it was the atmospheric conditions, and not just plain stress. Either way, these feelings were unwelcome. He didn't want them. He didn't want the pain they elicited. It hurt too much to love someone...

Without realizing it, Nick had come full circle. He stood inches from the mother and daughter to whom he was their last hope, their only hope. He had to act quickly, for night would be falling soon, and with it, the last rays of the sun's warmth and guiding light. Predators would crawl out from their holes, both human and animal.

"Thank God you're back," Kelly whispered, her voice raspy, almost breathless. Stars twinkled in her eyes when she lifted her gaze to meet his. Twin circles pinked her high cheek bones. He caught his breath. He hadn't seen anything so beautiful since his Melissa. He cut his thoughts short and broke the gaze, rebuking himself for such thoughts at a time like this. Forcefully, he turned his attention back to the injured people relying on him.

Bending on one knee, heedless of the sodden debris soaking through his jeans, Nick spoke gently. I'm going to put your daughter on this stretcher I have with me, here, see?"

The woman nodded in comprehension.

"I'm going to take her to safety. And then, I'm going to come back and get you out." His sharp eyes examined the woman's pallor, her shallow breathing, noting how white and drawn the knuckles were that clutched her baby to her. He didn't want to leave her here, but he could only carry one of them at a time. Nor did he think it would be an easy task to lift the debris from her legs. He only hoped they weren't crushed, mangled or possibly in need of amputation. Hurriedly, he pushed the last thought away lest he became overwhelmed with the magnitude of the task before him and he became useless. If he cleared his mind, kept his heart out of this, he could do it. He'd will himself to be an automaton, a robot with a back of steel and the arms of an angel.

The girl's pallor alarmed him. Again he wondered if she were still breathing. He took a deep breath, preparing himself mentally. Gently, Nick cradled her head in the crook of his right arm and gathered her against him. Vaguely, he noticed that Kelly watched closely.

"Kelly, hold the stretcher still while I put Katy on it."

Kelly hurried to do his bidding. "Hurry Nick. We don't have much time..."

He took care to lift the child very, very carefully, all the while, praying he did nothing to bring further harm to her. Damn, but he wished he had a proper stretcher and backboard, a neck brace, and help so that he didn't screw this up. He took off his belt and tied the girl to the makeshift stretcher as best he could and he prayed she wouldn't slide off. Her legs hung off the bottom, dragging the floor. Kelly held the board tightly, preventing it from shifting.

"I can't lift her by myself. The board's too heavy." This was no time for stupid heroics. "I need you to lift the other end. Can you do it?"

"I don't know." Kelly sounded worried. She eyed the child dubiously. "I'll have to try."

"Try your damndest. Now's the time to prove to your brothers that you're as strong as they are."

"It's now or never, right?" Kelly screwed up her face and squared her shoulders. Wisps of her red hair clung to her forehead and her cheeks where perspiration trickled over her flushed face. "I'm ready."

Nick picked up his end of the stretcher, the end where the child's head rested. "Go ahead and lift. You'll have to be navigator."

"I finally get to tell you where to go?" Kelly's face split in a tight grin.

Nick smiled back, even if it was strained. How did she do that? Make him laugh in the face of such adversity? The woman constantly amazed him. "Yeah. You get to tell me where to go and you can even tell me I told you so."

Kelly lifted, grunting through clenched teeth. Stress lines etched her normally smooth skin. Her knuckles turned white on the makeshift stretcher.

They struggled, panting to carry the stretcher outside. The house grunted and groaned, pieces of plaster falling intermittently, warning that more was to come. They had to duck out of the way of a particularly large chunk that probably would have knocked one of them out cold. He deflected it with his elbow which now ached like the devil. Fortunately, he could move it around thus he didn't think it was broken.

"Are you alright?" Kelly asked, her voice warm, sultry.

"I've been better," Nick said, grimacing, trying to ignore the instant warmth coursing through his veins. "I'll survive."

Finally, they reached the front door. It had never taken him so long to cover 100 yards before in his life. He swore he'd never become a paramedic.

With the last of their strength, they hauled the stretcher outside the door, then slumped to the ground together.

"Hey! Are you alright over there?" A male voice hailed from across the street.

Nick turned, summoning his strength from his very loins. His shoulder brushed Kelly's breast. "I need help over here. I've got two injured people. One's still trapped inside." His chest rose and fell heavily.

Kelly was panting heavily, holding her hand to her throat.

"Are you alright?"

She nodded that she would be. "I'm just a little winded."

Turning his attention to the child, Nick laid his hand on the child's chest again and leaned his ear near her nose. She breathed, but very shallowly. It bothered him how still she lay, how completely unconscious she appeared.

"Hang on, over there. Help's on the way!" The fellow called.

"Thank God!" Nick mumbled. He leaned his forehead on the

child's soft hair. Relief flooded over him. He knew they weren't out of danger yet, but now there was a prayer. With other strong backs, they'd lift the heavy mortar that trapped the girl's mother and get her out of the house - hopefully before it crushed everyone inside.

He felt a comforting hand smoothing his hair from his brow. Gentle fingers ran through it, then settled on his neck where they rubbed lightly. Kelly seemed to sense his inner turmoil. Was she in tune with his moods? Or maybe his face was an open book?

"Move over guy." A serious voice spoke gently beside him. Nick hadn't heard his approach, and he jumped, startled. "Felix and Luis are going to take the girl to the hospital. Do you know her name?"

"Katy Wilson, I think," Kelly said. "Her little brother's in our car over there." She stood, pointing to the sedan.

Nick mourned the loss of those gentle hands massaging his neck. Her soft skin, her gentle touch, had felt better than anything he'd known in years.

"This isn't your house?"

"No. The little boy who lives here asked us to help. I couldn't find anyone else, so we went in."

The man clapped Nick's shoulder. "That was mighty good of you. You both look all tuckered out. By the way, name's Hunter Hughes."

"Nice to meet you, Hunter." Nick shook the man's outstretched hand. "Bradley. Nick Bradley of the Florida Fresh Water Fish and Game Commission. And this pretty lady is Kelly Kerrigan from Cincinnati. I don't know about you, but, I'm pretty spent." Nick ran his hand through his hair, absently. "The girl's mother's still inside. She's trapped under a chunk of the wall. It's gonna take some doing to get her loose...and I don't know how long the house'll stand." Nick straightened, stretching his aching muscles. His eyes narrowed as he viewed the destroyed neighborhood again.

"I've got two more guys coming in a jiffy. We'll get the lady out. Let's get a head start. Maybe we can do it before they get here."

Nick put a restraining hand on the man's arm. "It's dangerous in there. I can't make you go in."

Hunter shook his head, pursed his lips. "We've been digging an old man out of the house across the street for the past couple of hours. I couldn't live with myself if I knowingly left someone to die."

Two burly men loped across the street. Hunter consulted with them briefly, turning to point at the girl. Within mere moments, they had the girl in the air as easily as they would have lifted a single three pound weight.

Nick watched as Felix and Luis carried the girl to a beat up Chevy van across the street and loaded her in the back. The one called Felix crawled in the back with her while Luis got behind the steering wheel. Slowly, he pulled the van away from the curb, dodging crashed cars and fallen trees.

The house creaked eerily, warning the men to hurry. Nick exchanged glances with Hunter and Kelly. They pursed their lips, no words necessary, and trudged into the house. Nick led the way. It looked like the ceiling was sagging. Time slipped away. The sands in the top half of the hour glass were almost gone...

"Where's my baby? Where is she? Is my little boy alright? Thank God you came back," she cried. "You came back..."

Hunter took off his shirt and laid it over the woman. He put the back of his hand to her forehead. "I think she's in shock. She's freezing."

"He was sleeping in my car a moment ago, peaceful as a cat in a windowsill." He wiped gritty hands down his pants legs. "Let's lift this wall off her and get her out of here...before..." He'd been about to say, before we all become pancakes, then remembered the woman's hysteria. That would have been a tactless remark. Where was his mind? Far in the past. Or with Kelly?

Man, but he was a jumbled up mess today. Category five hurricanes had a way of messing with his mind. He thought he'd gained control over his life, but the past 24 hours had turned it upside down again. He pushed his hand through his hair, brushing it out of his eyes.

Hunter gave him a knowing look. Nick watched him test the big chunk of wall on the woman. It didn't budge. That meant they'd have to find a lever of some sort to hoist it off her legs. Kelly started moving smaller chunks out of the way. Hunter and Nick followed suit. When they had cleared the area as best they could, they looked at each other. No help had arrived. The house was creaking louder now, grunting as if the second story would cave in any minute. They couldn't wait any longer.

"Get out now, Cincinnati. We'll finish this."

"I'm not leaving you..."

"Get out while you can. Don't argue with me woman!"

"I'm not leaving until we get her out," she said with finality. She jutted her chin and her breasts out defiantly.

"Then make yourself useful. Find something we can use as a lever. It has to be strong, metal preferably, something that won't break while were lifting this wall. If that wall falls on her again..." Nick ministered to the distraught woman, her flesh burning his where his fingertips touched her cheek.

Kelly looked around, prodding here, poking there, looking for anything that fit the bill. Anything at all.

Then she spotted something. She tugged an old fashioned lamp post, the type that reached from floor to ceiling, from where it was trapped under rubble. She grabbed it, tested it for strength. Once she was satisfied it wouldn't bend easily under pressure, she took it to Nick.

He examined the post, grunted in consent. "This'll do. Help me lift that wall off her, would you? Help me wedge it under here." He speared the pole under the debris, then leaned on it with his shoulder. It groaned but started to move. "Like this..."

Hunter crawled under the piece of wall hanging over the woman. Mercifully, the woman had passed out a moment before.

"It's not hurting her is it?" Nick enquired. He breathed in deeply, gathering his strength.

"No, it looks clear." Hunter took the proffered post from Kelly. "On three, we'll lift," he told Nick.

"Okay." Nick got a better grip on the end of the lamp post.

"One. Two. Three!" Hunter yelled. The men heaved with all their might. Nick groaned, gritting his teeth, straining his muscles, trying to lift with his legs. Beside him, Hunter ground his teeth, a guttural sound rising from his throat. Kelly stood back, mesmerized, holding her breath.

Through clenched teeth, Nick moaned, "I think it's moving.

We're getting it."

"Keep pushing, it's going, going..." Hunter cheered them on.

A piece of roof crashed behind them. Plaster sprayed them. "For heaven's sake, Cincinnati, get the hell outta here now!"

"I'm not leaving you. You might need help."

"Let's give it one last college try. Push really hard."

Nick pushed with all his might, exasperated that Kelly wouldn't listen to him. He could feel it moving, lifting. Then, suddenly, it flipped, and crashed. The men had to jump out of the way, for it didn't go in the direction they were pushing, but at least it was off the woman.

Nick, Kelly and Hunter knelt by the woman carefully examining her.

"Her legs look real bad, Nick," Kelly told him in awe, her hands trembling.

"I've seen mountain lions caught in bear traps that looked better than she does," Nick agreed. "She really needs a stretcher, or we'll hurt her..."

The house shrieked it's final warning groan. There was no doubt it was going to come down. Plaster showered them, a fine particle dust storm that looked like nuclear fall out made him cough and splutter, forcing him to cover his mouth with his hand so he could breath. He had to duck the big chunks of plaster that hurled from above with the force of comets. He held no false illusions. They may be miniature, but painful as grenades.

"No time!" Kelly yelled. "It's now or never!"

Hunter hoisted Sheryl over his shoulder, crab-running as if he were maneuvering through tires in an obstacle course. Nick pivoted on the ball of his foot, adrenalin pumping through his veins at quadruple rate, pushing him to get the hell out of there. Just as he was about to leave the house, Kelly stumbled, falling on her knees.

"Help me, Nick!" she cried, frantic. She scrambled to stand, pushing off the floor with scraped hands and elbows. The soles of her shoes skid out from under her when she couldn't find a good foothold on the piles of debris. Fear darkened her eyes to the shade of an evergreen forest and she thrust her hand out to him, imploring him to help her.

*Oh Lord.* She was going to die. The roof was starting to fall. Walls were caving in.

He thought his heart would burst.

He dove for her, cradling her beneath himself, tucking his head over hers in a fetal position. If the house fell on them, he'd bear the brunt of the avalanche.

Just as the house groaned its final death throes and the ceiling started to collapse, he snatched Kelly tightly around her mid-section.

Oblivious to the pain jabbing just about every muscle of his body, to the awkwardness of holding Kelly, he dove, rolled and tucked under a large oak table he espied a few feet from him. The bulk of her body, slender as it was, made his task near impossible, but what choice did he have?

Not even milliseconds later, the house fell sideways, no sturdier than a stack of cards, but a heck of a lot heavier.

# Chapter Five

Nick didn't know if the slate table would hold the weight of the roof, or crack in two like a fault line. But no other sanctuary presented itself. It represented their only chance and he gambled that it would hold.

In reality, the house crumpled in less than the time it would take to unlock the front door, but to Nick, it dragged on about as long and tortuous as sitting through *Gone With The Wind* without an intermission.

The nuclear fallout distended like a mushroom cloud. He coughed so hard he nearly choked. Tenaciously, he shielded Kelly with his body, holding her tightly as if that would stop his world from caving in.

He felt rather than heard her gasp against his chest when the house settled, but she was a trooper and didn't scream like most women would have.

He murmured soothingly as he smoothed her hair away from her face. "We'll be okay. Don't worry." He didn't know if he spoke the truth, but he said it as much for his own peace of mind as to comfort the woman in his arms. Somehow, the sound of his voice, even thick from a combination of raw fear and the gritty dust lodging itself in his throat, seemed to slow her respiration, still her trembling against him. Or maybe it was the reassurance of his words, simple as they were.

He dropped kisses on her silky hair, not sure why, but somehow the small action comforted him as it seemed to comfort her.

When he inched his way to the side of the table after several silent seconds to see if they could safely escape their self-imposed prison, roof tresses hurled from the vicinity of the one-time roof as if Zeus hurled lightning bolts from Mt. Olympus. He dragged her back to the center of the table to wait longer, lest the sky split wide open, seeking sacrificial lambs as it had the night before.

Deafening silence fell. Several moments dragged by before Nick realized that the house had settled, that there would be no further flying projectiles, and that by the grace of God, the table had held. Carefully, he opened one eye, then the other to survey the destruction.

He whistled long and low under his breath. Half the roof had missed crushing them by less than an arm's length.

Plaster dust hung in the air like volcanic ash. He could taste it on his lips and licked his tongue over them to remove the grittiness, spitting out the little chunks of plaster before they lodged in his throat. Everything was coated, including his weary body, making him feel like Casper the ghost.

"Come on, Cincinnati. Let's get out of here."

She quivered in his arms as if she were a small, trapped animal. "Is it safe?"

Nick twisted a hunk of skin to make sure he numbered among the living and that he wasn't having another vivid nightmare. It stung alright. This wasn't one of his many nightmares. He wasn't six feet under.

So many nights, he awoke in a cold sweat, beads of moisture soaking his body, screams curdling deep in his throat. Sometimes, he remembered these nightmares. Always, there was a child in peril, a child mangled, mutilated reaching out for him with bloodied, soiled hands through silvery, whirling mist. The hands turned into huge furry paws...paws with claws unsheathed, raking his naked body, spewing his life's blood, seeking his soul.

Just the thought sent shivers through Nick. Apprehensively, he looked at Kelly, half-expecting her to turn into the dreaded predator of his nightmares. Other than the heavy plaster coating Kelly like clown make-up, she looked human enough. Priority one was to get her out of the disaster zone before further catastrophe struck.

Still, he lay atop Kelly for what seemed an eternity until her squirming prompted him to lift his weight from her.

"That was close," she said in short punctuated bursts as if struggling to breathe.

Reluctantly, he loosened his grip on her although he didn't release her completely. He ran his hands up and down her arms to see if she were whole. "Too close."

"We'd better see how the boy's doing. He's been alone for a long time." She looked askance at him, her eyes wide and luminous as a wild animal's.

Finally, he released her. "Stay right here. I'll be right back. I want to see something." He crept gingerly from under his makeshift cave. Sharp tingles shot up his toes, into his feet, his ankles and along his leg. Asleep, the left leg dragged like dead weight until he stopped to massage the worst of the kinks out of his calf. He didn't need a charlie horse when his mission had barely begun.

The rest of his muscles screamed in protest when he stretched like a grizzly, rolling first one shoulder to get out the kinks then reaching as high as he could, clenching his fingers into a tight fist, then uncurling them slowly. He followed suit with his other hand.

Squinting, he craned his neck to search the heavens, noting how fountains of pinkish-lilac light pierced the clouds, streaking the sky with pastel watercolors. Silver rims fluctuated around fluffy clouds as they floated past the setting orange-yellow sun. A rainbow formed a wide arch over the Everglades.

Someone barbecued sirloin strips and hot dogs in their backyard. His empty stomach grumbled, chastising him for neglecting it. He couldn't help but salivate, wishing he had the luxury of throwing a tenderloin or two on his grill then kicking back on his lounge chair with the Stephen King novel he was reading. When he thought of everything spoiling in his fridge at home, he grimaced. Half the city must be barbecuing on their butane grills while he and Kelly munched on stale candy bars, canned Spam and drank boiling soda.

After Andrew, he should have learned his lesson and installed a back-up generator. Electricity could be down for weeks, even months in some parts of the city and generators would be more costly than all the gold of Avarice. At least he had put one in at his mother's house. Twisters had touched down indiscriminately throughout Dade county, with Cutler Ridge acting as magnetic center, drawing the brunt of destruction.

"Nick..." Hesitantly, Kelly peeked out from her hiding place. "Is it safe? Can I come out?"

"Come here." Nick beckoned to Kelly, holding out his arms. She ran into them, hugging him fiercely. She melted against him and he noted how well they fit together. "Are you okay, Cincinnati?" Her bright copper head bobbed up and down.

Nick hoisted Kelly high in his arms. Determinedly, he shut out the past...at least for tonight. Now wasn't the time or place for self-pity. His sworn mission had yet to be completed.

"Let's get out of here." He strode purposefully, carrying Kelly with the ease of a man in top form.

He set her down gently when they cleared the debris. Elation filled him when she reached out and squeezed his hand. He squeezed hers back, refusing to release it when she tugged gently. His fingers intertwined with hers and she gave him a gentle smile. They walked hand in hand to Nick's sedan, their arms swinging in silent camaraderie.

Peeking in the window, he saw that Mattie slept peacefully, curled up in a fetal position, sucking his thumb.

Leaned over his shoulder, she whispered into his ear, her breath warm on his neck. "Isn't he adorable?"

Nick agreed, but for the lump in his throat, he couldn't voice an answer. He opened the door gently, awaking the boy.

"Where's my mommy? Where's Katie? Are they okay?" A tear trickled down Mattie's cheek. He rubbed his sleep-filled eyes with balled up fists. He stretched his shoulders and yawned widely, rolling his shoulders back. "I want my daddy."

"In a little bit, slugger," Nick said.

"You promised me I could see Mommy." Tears welled in the boys eyes.

"And you will, Mattie. Very soon," Nick said.

Kelly pulled her hand away and knelt by the boy, hugging him close to her chest. "Where's your daddy?" She shot alarmed looks at Nick then at the house.

He read her unspoken question as easily as if he read close-captioned TV. Was Mattie's father trapped in that mountain of rubble that was their house? Had they left someone in there?

"At the hospital. He's a doctor. His boss made him work last night." His red head strained off her shoulder. "I was supposed to protect Mommy and Katie." *And he'd failed.* The unspoken sentiment tore at the suddenly still air.

Nick heard Kelly's sigh of relief while his gut clenched. The guy's duty had nearly cost him his family, just as his own had cost him his. Knots tied up his stomach so tightly, he felt nauseous. This hit too close to home.

"He promised we'd be all right. He said the storm wouldn't come in this far." Tears swam in his eyes. "He promised."

Taking the boy from Kelly's arms, he swung him into his own. Man to man, he said in as steady a voice as he could muster, "Your daddy couldn't have done any better. He'll be proud of you. As I am."

Mattie sniffed back tears on a hiccough and wiped his runny nose on his grimy shirt sleeve. "Really? But they're hurt..."

"That's not your fault. You got help for them. You saved them." *He hoped.* He hugged him close. "You're a bonafide hero. You'll probably get a medal for this."

Mattie stopped crying on a jag, a sunny smile lighting his face. "You really think so?" Then he looked at Nick skeptically. "Will I get my picture in the paper?"

"You bet. And I'll get you and your family free passes to the zoo." Kelly smiled at him over the boy's shoulder, her heart-shaped face glowing, her eyes softer than he'd seen them, crinkle lines at the almond shaped ends attesting to the fact that she could laugh and lighten up.

Maybe there was more to her than bleeding heart animal activist or hard-hearted zookeeper. In different circumstances, he might want to explore those suspected facets of her personality.

But he had a mission to do. All in all, he calculated that he'd been delayed about a day total now and he grimaced. He didn't like interruptions. He didn't like added baggage. It slowed him down, made him sloppy. And that was unacceptable.

He put the boy on his feet gently then reached for his cellular phone. Nick punched his office number onto the key pad, the strangely musical tones sounding like a staccato *"Mama told me not to come"*. Somehow, that thought rang in his ears as if an omen, but he refused to dwell on that thought.

Demi answered, her soft voice weary and frazzled as if she hadn't slept in days and torn out half her hair.

Headquarters was probably about as quiet and calm as a riled up hornet's nest. Garcia would have at least a dozen government types breathing down his neck to round up the dangerous animals. Maybe now they'd give them the staffing they needed. Maybe but doubtful, he grimaced. Game commissioners were expected to be super men.

"Let me speak to the Chief." It wasn't a request. He tapped his foot impatiently during the exaggerated wait. Reaching out, he pulled Kelly to him. She felt good against him, leaning into him, seeming to enjoy their togetherness. He refused to dwell on the implication of his action.

"Bradley? Where in holy carnation are you?"

Nick held the phone away from his head, his ear ringing with Garcia's growl.

Kelly must have heard him for she arched her head back and tilted one coppery brow at him. From this angle, her lashes looked impossibly long and lush, creating black fans on her ghostly white cheeks. Minute plaster particles dusted them.

The chief's voice rose several decibels as he invented several new words unfit for Mattie's ears. Kelly and his own for that matter.

He covered the receiver with his hand to mute the sound.

"Don't you ever answer your phone or your pager?" the chief barked, his tone belligerent, his patience obviously stretched way past its limits.

"I've been busy. Listen Chief, I need..." He leaned against his sedan, one foot curled behind him. Kelly snuggled into him making it hard for him to concentrate on his conversation. It hadn't been such a good idea to hold her. He rubbed his chin against her satiny hair, his beard catching in the silky soft tresses. It had been a lifetime since he'd let a woman get this close. Maybe two lifetimes.

It sent thrills through him that he couldn't do anything about. Not here. Not now. Not that he was sure he even wanted to.

With supreme effort he dragged his attention back to his boss not quite blocking out the fact that Kelly rubbed against him in impossible places, probably without even realizing it. Just the steady rhythm of her heart beating against his made his breathing shallow.

"No. You listen, Bradley. Get back here pronto!" Static crackled over the line. Distant sirens whirred.

"The tigers..." he began patiently as he could. Garcia tended to get hyper when pushed. And he'd never been more pushed than now.

"Forget the blasted tigers! I've got a situation here..."

Mattie tugged on Nick's arm, his topaz eyes imploring.

Nick shook his head, frowning. He covered the phone transmitter with his hand. "Not now, Mattie. I have to talk to this man for a moment..."

"But, Mr. Nick!" Mattie yanked with more rigor.

"Shhh!" Nick held up his index finger commanding silence. The breeze ruffled his hair.

Across the road, a short, balding man spray-painted three foot high red letters on his splintered garage door. Before his eyes, 'All-State' appeared in spiderery scrawl, the red-spray paint dripping like blood. Even the houses bled here. Again he had the feeling of being swept into a Stephen King thriller.

Then the man stepped back, stared at his handiwork and shook his head. Weary shoulders slumped and he threw the can onto the ground in disgust and stalked away. Nick didn't blame the guy one bit. His house was totaled, more holes than walls and he had one giant sky light. Namely, no roof.

Next to him, Mattie pouted, but kept quiet.

"I've got a situation here, too, Chief. I can't leave..." He couldn't exactly say he had man-hungry tigers roaming in downtown Miami with Mattie a foot away, all ears. The child was scared enough.

"I don't care a rat's ass if your head's stuck half way down an alligator's throat! I'm calling you in. Report now!"

There was no way he would call off his search. Kelly would just go without him and land herself in trouble again, deep trouble. He could sense it. The hairs on the back of his neck stood on end. And innocent children like Mattie ran about without a clue to the danger lurking nearby, maybe as close as that deserted house across the street.

He wouldn't leave them alone and that was final. "Can't hear you, Chief..." Nick tapped his finger nail on the receiver. "Hey, Chief! Where'd you go?"

Kelly twisted in his arms. His lips tilted slightly and he winked at her.

Her wide mouth grinned mischievously. Stars twinkled in her eyes. The laugh lines deepened. Her hand cupped her mouth to mute the sound of her laughter.

"I know you can hear me, Bradley. Don't go playing lone wolf again. I'll have your badge!"

"Are you there, Chief?" Nick covered the transmitter again to muffle his voice. "Stupid phone must've gone dead." He flicked it off, completely disconnecting it with deep satisfaction. He tossed the nuisance through the window. It bounced on the seat and thudded to the floor.

"That was very naughty." Kelly's laughter tinkled as her eyes danced with devilment. Her pert nose tilted up at him, the late afternoon sunlight catching the faint dusting of freckles bridging it. They faded into the complexion of her cheeks. Her sassy grin elicited an answering spark in him.

He had trouble keeping his mind on the business at hand. He shrugged nonchalantly, trying not to take the situation too seriously. "Don't worry. He needs me too badly to fire me. More likely, he's scared shitless I'll walk out on him in the middle of this." He'd been fired before. Garcia always hired him back. Pleaded with him to return. It was getting to be ritual.

"Mr. Nick. Miss Kelly!" Mattie pleaded, desperation lacing his voice. "I have to go pee-pee!" The boy held his crotch, hopping from one leg to another. "Real bad!"

Nick frowned. He looked around. No restrooms in sight. Oh well, "Desperate situations..." Nick muttered.

Releasing Kelly gently, he took the boy's arm. He escorted him to the partial cover of his open sedan door. "Turn around. Right here." Putting his hands on the boy's shoulder, he turned him around. "Kelly, close your eyes," he said with a wink in her direction. He stood between the boy and prying eyes. "Go pee pee right there." Pointing to the grass, he commanded, "Don't wet on the car. Got that, slugger?"

Mattie shook his head, tossing his coppery curls. He did as told.

"Can I open my eyes yet?" she asked.

"I'm done!" Mattie ran around Nick's legs.

Nick grabbed the radio, bringing it to his mouth. He'd try to reach the Guard. Like traffic cops, they were never around when you needed them and putting a microscope up your rear when you didn't.

Static crackled loudly in his ears. He broadcast an SOS. After his third call, the Guard finally responded.

Nick was filling a captain in on his situation, asking for help, when he heard the boy screech, "Groucho!" The boy's voice lowered a decibel. "Come here, kitty. Here kitty, kitty, kitty." Mattie hunched down on his heels, holding out his hand as if he held a tasty morsel. The cat wasn't fooled. Slowly, he spider walked toward the cat, the soaked grass squishing beneath his feet.

Turning, Nick watched, unconcerned, as Mattie played blood hound.

When the child was within a foot of the big tom cat who regarded him as if he were a peasant, it licked first one paw, then the other meticulously. After his bath was finished, he loped off without warning, his haunches catching an easy stride.

In a flash, the boy sprinted after his pet.

"What the hell!" Nick growled, rumbling erupting from deep in his chest. This didn't bode well. He had a bad feeling about this... "Mattie! Get back here. Forget the cat!"

Kelly echoed him, her voice an octave higher than his. "Come back, Mattie!"

When the child didn't respond, Kelly gave chase. Her hair bounced on her shoulders. Her gait rolled unsteadily as she zig-zagged around shingles, branches, even couches and chairs hurled across the destroyed lawns.

Nick hesitated a second, murmuring into the radio, "Hold on a sec..." He dropped the handset, letting it dangle, then sprinted after the boy. Muck grabbed at his feet. Threads of lives lay unraveled everywhere, like mixed up jigsaw puzzles. It was a lousy obstacle course, one he'd hoped never to see again after Andrew's wrath was cleaned up.

The boy ran amazingly fast, but the darn tiger tabby streaked away like the Midnight Special.

Kelly almost caught the boy several times just to have him slip out of her grasp, her fingers clawing thin air. Stumbling, she almost dove flat on her face, but she caught her balance at the last second.

"Stop, Mattie!" Wind whisked her warnings away, or they fell on deaf ears. Mattie continued the chase, his face flushed, the bounce in his step exhilarating.

"Mattie, stop!" Nick had no clue where they were. The cat dodging hither and yon, cutting through yards and crossing streets with no particular logic. No human logic at any rate.

Finally, the big tom tired of the chase and let the boy scoop him up. Mattie cuddled his pet like a fluffy teddy bear, squeezing him tightly. The cat meowed a warning, but the boy ignored it, playing with the long tail. No wonder the poor animal had run!

Nick wasn't taking any more chances. He grabbed the boy's collar, holding on. "Didn't your mother ever teach you not to run away like that?" Nick reached over to scratch the cat's head.

Groucho purred loudly as if he hadn't just caused a passel of trouble.

"You're on my black list." The cat just smiled and leaned further into Nick's fingers, his whiskers flicking, his eyes closed in ecstacy.

Kelly joined them, reaching out to pet the feline's head. Her breath was accentuated with sharp, short bursts of air. "Pretty kitty," she crooned.

When he lifted a quizzical eyebrow in disbelief that she didn't want to strangle the mangy feline, she merely shrugged her shoulders. "I love cats."

"Of course," Nick said dryly, shaking his head. To Mattie he said, "Where are we, slugger?" Nick looked for street signs, landmarks and any clue of where they were. It was hopeless. One building looked like the next — ripped to shreds, tumbling down, roofs torn from their supports. Faded water-logged furniture, was tossed both inside and outside the destroyed structures as if a giant child had thrown a temper tantrum in the midst of playing with her dollhouse.

Chelsea had wiped all trace of personality from this neighborhood, like military housing where all houses looked alike, only worse.

Dusk was setting which didn't help the tone of foreboding. The August sun was dipping below the horizon, shimmering hazily as if it didn't have a care in the world. Very soon, predators of night would scavenge the streets, delighted to find all manner of debris, thrilled to find a young boy like Mattie.

"I dunno." Mattie shrugged his shoulders. "Nothing's the same." His eyes took on a haunted quality as he turned on his heel, his gaze scanning the war zone.

"Can you get us back home?" Nick asked, haunched on his heels to be eye level with the boy.

"Yeah."

"Lead the way, Mattie. Don't run off again."

"Miss Fugazzi says I'm the very bestest line leader!" He puffed his chest out with pride, bouncing his cat up and down.

Nick fell slightly behind, seeking tiger tracks as unobtrusively as he could. As twilight settled, gunfire rolled like an incessant drum beat.

Someone yelled nearby in Spanish. Nick knew a few words, but he couldn't follow the rapid-fire litany even though he strained his ears.

Suddenly, several youths jumped out of the shadows of one of the few houses that still stood. Menacingly, they surrounded the trio. Mattie cowered, clutching his cat so tightly it growled.

The tallest member of the group, a swarthy kid no more than twenty, planted himself in front of Kelly. Black leather, criss-crossed by zippers hugged powerful muscles. When a wicked grin split the kid's tawny face, Nick caught the glint of a diamond chip in his gold capped front tooth.

He kept his face expressionless as Kelly smiled, putting her hand on Mattie's shoulder to guide him around the gang. He took their measure, debating whether or not he could take on four, maybe more young men in their prime, suddenly feeling old even though he was only thirty-three.

The tall juvenile sidestepped, blocking Kelly's path. With a mere snap of his fingers, he motioned his friends to circle.

Kelly pulled Mattie back against her and her arm crept around him protectively. Mattie stood stock still, squeezing the growling tom cat.

A nefarious smile curved the leader's lips. His eyes danced with rabid glee. He only had eyes for Kelly and he didn't care if they roamed her length. A twinge of jealousy fired Nick's veins.

"What are you doing out here, pretty lady? Did you come to visit?" the leader asked, his voice dangerously quiet, slightly accented. Pitch black eyes scanned her slowly, lasciviously, making Nick want to deck him for his impertinence.

"We're just taking the boy and his cat home," she stuttered. So much for showing no fear. People like this thrived on fear. Now, she was feeding it, the last thing she should do. Nick closed his eyes, gathering his strength. No fear, Kelly girl, he wished he could tell her. Don't panic. Stay calm.

A tattoo peeked out from his rolled up shirt sleeve. And did he detect the glint of cold steel peering out his pocket? A switchblade? Or a Saturday Night Special?

As if she had received Nick's telepathic command, she pretended that everything was normal. Quietly she asked, "Did you see any white tigers?"

"Just Tony." The youth on her left snorted. "On my cereal box this morning." The teens snickered, their teeth arctic white against their olive skin.

"Thanks, anyway," Kelly smiled falsely. "I think I'll ask that lady over there." She tried to push Mattie through the circle, following. No fear, Kelly, Nick thought. They can smell it.

The circle tightened forcing her to stop dead in her tracks, pulling Mattie up short against her. Nick remained silent, watching for any sign of weakness, biding his time. When Mattie squeezed the cat too tightly, he groused, his haunches working against the boy.

The tall youth pulled a pearl-handled switchblade, twirling it in Nick's face. Kelly's eyes widened fearfully. Her knees trembled.

"Leave us, pretty lady? You just arrived," he spoke deceptively softly to Kelly only, as if Nick didn't exist. Yet, he didn't lower the knife.

"Yeah, and the party's just starting."

"We have to get the boy home. His mother is worried." Kelly pleaded. "You're scaring him," she whispered, her voice raspy. Her chest heaved.

"If I were you, I'd worry about myself," the tall one said, rotating his knife mere inches from Nick's face.

Kelly's eyes were glued to the knife, mesmerized in fact. She couldn't tear her gaze from it.

Nick knew they couldn't accompany them. And they definitely couldn't let the boy go with them. That was the first rule of survival - never go anywhere with would-be abductors. You were as good as dead if they got you alone.

With his index finger, the other man traced the outline of Kelly's jaw, then tilted it towards his lips while Nick bristled. The boy stepped impossibly close to the woman, so close his breath mingled with hers. The tip of the knife pointed at the soft underbelly of her throat. "Do you have something to trade? Something I might want, chica?" He released her chin and let his finger trail lower. "Maybe we can work a deal."

Kelly's eyes narrowed but she didn't move away. Then he caught the flash of fire and indignation in her eyes.

His muscles coiled, tensed. She wasn't going to back down, just as she hadn't with him. He felt her heat rise.

Sugar so sweet it would throw him into a coma passed her lips. "I have something for you."

He lowered the knife, closed it and slipped it into his pocket. Then he put his lips on hers, let his hands crawl over her. For the brief moment before Kelly lifted her foot and stomped his toes with the full force of her body and shoved him away so hard he stumbled, dazed.

Suddenly, Groucho leapt from Mattie's arms attacking the youth's face. Twin guttural screams rose from the youth's throat and Groucho's. The cat flew up in the air, his claws bared. His back arched, his fur stood out, he screamed like a demon just released from the depths of hell.

"Run, Mattie. Run!" She pushed the boy, stumbling, falling flat on her face when a foot came up tripping her, throwing her headlong to the ground, knocking the breath from her lungs, silencing her screams.

The cat twisted like a Doberman pinscher were after him, arcing his powerful hind legs, razor-sharp talons thirsty for blood. He swiped the kid's face, digging deeply. The kid threw the cat as he screamed in agony. He clutched his face, jumping up and down. The cat shot away like a bullet.

Chalk one up for the fur ball.

"Get that mutha!"

"Run!" Nick commanded, shoving Kelly ahead of him.

They didn't need further prompting. The boy ducked between the kids, avoiding their clutches as they grabbed for him. Their attention refocused on Nick and Kelly. They sensed his threat, and they seemed intent on capturing Kelly.

Another knife waved in his face and he stopped dead. The last glimmers of the sun honed in on it.

"Is that your cat, hombre? Are you responsible for that demon from hell?"

He just stared at the knife, assessing the situation, looking for weakness in the enemy. His ears strained for any sounds of help. Nothing sounded close.

"Get him! Forget the cat!" the injured kid commanded, clearly the leader.

Kelly clutched the boy's arm, hanging on it. "He didn't do anything to you. Can't you just let us go? We'll forget we saw you."

Now! When the kid was distracted. Nick pivoted, battle ready, swinging his leg in a wide powerful arc. He connected with the first attacker's groin. Then he lowered a karate chop on the back of a neck, felling another. Then two more youth jumped him from behind, knocking him to the ground, pushing his face in the mud.

Nick arced his back with all his might and threw his attackers off. Lunging at them, he threw himself on top of the heap. They struggled, rolling in the mud, fighting to the death.

Meanwhile, the tall youth grabbed Kelly, twisting her arms behind her back, yanking her sharply when she tried to stomp his feet and bite his hand.

"That was one giant mistake, chica," the youth spit in her face. He extracted a razor sharp knife and held it to Kelly's throat. "You're going to pay for that little stunt." The knife pressed further into her throat and she held her breath.

"Gringo! I've got your lady." White teeth flashed in the midst of the teen's snarl. The diamond glittered. "Give it up *now*, or I'll slice her throat!"

The fight drained out of Nick instantly. Lying still on the ground, he thought furiously for a way out of this mess.

The youth he had pummeled hauled him rudely to his feet, then shoved him forward. Nick stumbled almost knocking into Kelly.

"One more sound, one more stupid move like that," the youth promised, his nostrils flaring, his lips thinned in a steely grin, " and I'll slice her neck and throw her in the canal."

"You'll both be gator bait," promised the adolescent he'd kicked.

"Then what are you going to do to me? Kill me?" Nick laughed, sarcastically. "Why don't you let her go? Then you and I will fight. Right here. Right now. Like real men."

The kid thought about it. Then he bared his uneven teeth again. The gold cap gleamed in the soft moonlight. A cricket chirped nearby. Rustling stirred in a vacant house. Rats, Nick presumed. Or hungry cats. Perhaps, a tiger tracking its prey, tracking them, ready to pounce.

"You won't get away with this. He called the guard. They're on their way."

"She's bluffin, Raf. They didn't call nobody," said a teen that sported three gold hoops in his right ear, one in his left ear. Nick presumed the rips in the elbows and knees of his denim was a fashion statement.

"Yeah! They was just chasin' that mangy flea bag," a tattoo-covered adolescent said.

"If you believe that, I have beautiful ocean front property to sell you in the Everglades." Rafael's lips turned up in a smirk verging on a snarl. "Not!" He scratched his chin, absently rubbing the day's growth of stubble making it itch. "They didn't call the Guard but they're *Feds*!" Rafael circled Nick. "Look at his uniform. He's a cop."

"What are we gonna do with them, man?" a youth asked apprehensively, shuffling his feet, kicking dirt in their faces with the toe of his boot.

Kelly looked around the group, noting how very young they were but how very dangerous they looked. Especially the one with the diamond chip in his tooth. The one called Rafael. The gleam in his eyes was definitely feral bordering on lunatic. He was wired and ready to blow.

"What do we always do with The Man when he invades our turf? We ice him. Feed him to the fish."

"What about la chica?" a still pimply faced youth asked, licking his lips. Saliva beaded on them as if he were rabid.

"She'll join him...after I have a little fun with her." Rafael trailed a long, lean finger down Kelly's cheek, tracing the curve of her jaw, following it down her slender throat and stopped where the swell of her breast pushed out the stretched neck of her T-shirt. He leaned forward, strong tobacco on his breath searing her cheek, making her cough and feel as if she had just swallowed a dirty ashtray.

Kelly tried to step back away from the youth's unwanted touch that slithered along her flesh.

"Hold her tighter," he told the youth that had her arms pinned behind her. He got up in her face. "You owe me." He leaned forward and kissed her violently, stealing her breath and her dignity.

She twisted, struggling with all her might to escape, but she was held fast, their fingers biting into her arms so hard there was no doubt she'd be bruised. Karaoke had been far gentler.

The youth's lips became more demanding and his tongue demanded entry.

"Let the girl go," Nick commanded. "You go through with this and it's rape."

"Get rid of the gringo," Rafael murmured against her lips. Determined to escape, unable to think of anything else, Kelly opened her mouth wide then brought even teeth down as hard as she could on the boy's bottom lip. Simultaneously, she stomped his foot with all her might. Distantly, she heard howling, as it clamored with the ringing in her ears.

The hands that had held her like a vice only seconds before slackened. With one violent wrench of her body, Kelly was free and fleeing as sure as if she were the fleet footed Mercury of ancient legend.

"Run, Cincinnati!" Nick yelled encouragement in a panting voice that assured Kelly he was nipping at her heels, pushing her forward. That, and the infuriated yells of the dreadful gang as they yelled obscenities at their back.

She felt the wind at her back, felt her heart pounding like a jackhammer against her ribs and her breathing came in short, raspy bursts. Wet grass made her feet slip and slide. Several times, she almost fell headlong, but Nick caught her, steadied her.

It felt good to be free, to have the wind whipping at her hair, to put as much distance as she could between herself and her wanna be captors. It felt good...

Kelly's thoughts stopped abruptly, turning to panic. Dead ahead, almost invisible in the black night, was a concrete wall that must be at least fifty feet high. Cars whizzed by on the highway overhead, unfeeling, uncaring mechanical monsters that seemed to laugh at their desperate plight.

Insects buzzed as if nothing extraordinary had happened or was happening. Cicadas sang their nightly song, only now it mocked her, taunted her. She pushed through a swarm of gnats, her arms crossed before her face. Gnats were the least of her concern. She spit one away that landed on her lips.

Swift on her feet, Kelly turned right and almost ran headlong onto the sharp slope of a steep canal. Skidding to an abrupt halt, her arms automatically went out like a windmill to steady herself while she balanced precariously on the edge of the miniature cliff that looked over swirling, murky waters barely discernible under the heavy cloud covered night.

The water gurgled below. Cicadas chirped louder. Heavy vehicles droned overhead. Yet, she was all alone save for Nick.

"Don't stop now," Rafael's voice mocked. "Finish the job for us."

Fiendish laughter rang out in mocking chorus.

Desperate, Kelly backed herself against the wall. Nick positioned himself in front of her in a battle ready stance while she searched the wall for cracks and any sort of footholds that they could climb to the safety of the highway above.

When she glanced over her shoulder, her heart dropped to her knees when a fearsome sight met her eyes.

Rafael faced Nick twirling a gold plated dagger two inches from his face.

## Chapter Six

Put your weapons on the ground slowly. Get your hands in the air," a gravelly baritone voice with the slightest trace of a well-educated Southern drawl, boomed through a fog horn.

"Thank God!" Kelly whispered. Her jagged fingernails stopped clawing the concrete in an effort to find handholds up the crumbling wall. It was the only thing that protected the highway from Cutler Ridge residents. All the horrible tension that knotted her shoulders and clenched her gut ebbed from her exhausted body.

The youths brandishing sharp knives not more than two feet from Kelly and Nick froze. Their black eyes widened fearfully.

"Shit, man!" Rafael exclaimed, grasping his knife as if his life's blood depended on it. He had a debt to repay and he looked as if he'd carry it through to the end regardless of the damning consequences he'd have to pay. He advanced a menacing step. His hideous scratches gleamed sickly purple in the dim starlight.

"Get behind me!" he hissed. He didn't await her response, but shielded her with his body.

She grabbed his shoulder, peering into the demonic eyes of the enraged gang leader. She didn't spy a single trace of mercy in those black beady eyes, not one ounce of fear or regret.

Nick's muscles bunched, as if he were ready to combat the youth bare handed if necessary. He lifted his hands in a defensive karate position. His muscles tensed.

"Stay back, Cincinnati." He whispered through the corner of his mouth. "This may not be over yet."

The two men started circling each other again, slowly, taking each other's measure. Kelly held her breath. She'd seen fighting roosters look friendlier.

Rafael twirled his knife menacingly in Nick's face. Starlight glinted off the serrated blade. Their feet shuffled in the dance of death. Rafael jabbed without warning.

Nick jumped back, forcing Kelly to jump too.

"This is the United States Guard and you're under arrest. Don't move. Repeat do *not* move or we'll shoot." Approximately twenty to thirty guards jumped out of the back of an army truck and secured the dead end street, barricading entrance and escape. They carried semi-automatic repeating rifles and wore their crowd-control gear. Their boots pounded the pavement heavily, making them sound like an entire brigade.

She could barely see them as they blended so thoroughly into the velvet backdrop of night.

"It's the blessed Guard!" another youth said in a stage whisper. His hand opened and his knife clattered benignly to the pavement. Moonlight bounced off it mesmerizing her. Her gaze was glued to that knife.

She thought just how close that bloodied dagger had come to spilling their blood tonight and chills racked her body. She twined her arms around her mid-section, reminding herself they were safe now, that the gang members couldn't touch them.

Several guardsmen jogged to them, apprehending Rafael and the other gang members. It took four burly men to drag Rafael from the scene, kicking and cursing demonically. Two held his wrist, pressing forefingers against the small bones of his wrist until he dropped the blade.

"Don't think this is over, gringo. I'm going to get you for this! I'm going to slice your throat and rape your woman, and then I'm going to feed you to the gators...." He writhed in his captors grasp and she wondered if four men had enough strength to hold him. Curses trailed behind him as the wind whisked away his threats. She watched in fascinated dread until he evaporated into the dark blanket of night.

"We're safe now, Cincinnati. The calvary arrived."

"Thank God!" she said barely loud enough to hear over the droning traffic above.

Nick pivoted on his heel, hauling her to his chest before she had an inkling of his intentions. His lips descended on hers in a searing kiss that made her sizzle from the inside out.

Stunned, she didn't respond, but she didn't struggle against him either. His lips were hard and demanding and she wasn't sure if his kiss was one of punishment or extraordinary relief.

Slowly, her arms twined about his neck.

His embrace tightened around her waist and he lifted her so that her feet dangled midair.

She only knew he sparked sensations in her she'd never felt before, that none of the men she'd dated had begun to touch.

Someone cleared their throat for attention nearby.

Nick released her lips reluctantly. When he looked down at her, his eyes were dark with passion.

She shuddered in his arms, loathe to leave his warmth.

Nick set her on her feet gently, curling his arm around her waist, his fingers caressing her waist. His touch felt possessive and although she never thought she'd want someone to own her, the idea of having this man possess her, intrigued her. She hooked her arm around his waist, reveling in the feel of his steely strength. She leaned against him, drinking in his strength until they were interrupted by a voice in the dark.

"Uh-hmm. I'm going to need both of you to accompany us to the post. My colonel's going to have some questions for you." With the moonlight at his back, the man's expression was difficult to read, almost impossible. But his voice sounded impersonal and professional. Tall and rigid in stiff green and black camouflage fatigues and black laced boots, he looked more like a robot than a man.

A very welcome robot.

"Pardon me for asking, but how in the world did you get so filthy? You must have gone for a swim in the swamp." The captain turned away and acute embarrassment flooded her. "I think I can talk the colonel into letting the both of you use some of the emergency water to clean yourselves up."

Nick and Kelly looked at each other without a word. They *were* certainly a mess, especially Nick. Not only was he flour coated with plaster dust, but that was cemented by the mud Rafael had smeared his face in. "You look like the creature from the Black Lagoon." She told him with as straight a face as she could, but it was a losing battle.

"You look like a geisha doll." He grinned good-naturedly, mischief flickering in his eyes.

If one her brothers' had said that, she'd have punched them in the gullet. But under the circumstances, she veiled her eyes with her lashes and elected not to retort to his jibe. There were worse things an attractive man could call her.

"The truck's waiting for us. Y'all hop in the back with the men." The captain strode to his truck. "Gireaux, up front with me!"

But she had a burning question that couldn't wait. "We had a little boy with us," she said breathlessly as she trotted to the Captain's side. She lifted her right hand to about waist level, parallel to the ground and smoothed thin air. "He's about this high, with red curly hair and freckles."

"He answers to the name of Mattie Wilson." Nick's shadow meshed with hers.

"He's about five years old. And he might have a big tom cat with him." Her gaze scanned the crowd that looked more like faceless shadows than people. None of them looked child-size. However, it was hard to tell with the moon hiding behind clouds, and Miami as black as a desert night except for the truck's high beams.

Soldiers secured the site efficiently as automatons. Superior officers issued commands to their troops above the distant and not so distant sounds of gunfire, sirens and night insects singing their nightly symphony.

She felt as if she were standing on the shore of the River Styx, watching souls pass from the land of the living to the land of the dead. Still, she clung to the first ray of hope she'd had in hours, since that dreadful storm.

The captain's lips twitched into what might suffice for a smile. "We picked him up on the edge of Cutler Ridge. He told us where to find you." Reaching in his pocket, he withdrew a red and white box of cigarettes. Tilting it, he tapped the bottom with his forefinger, rustling the cellophane wrap. A filter tip poked out the top about a quarter inch. "Smoke?" He held the package out to first Nick, then her.

She shook her head. "No, thanks."

Nick passed also. "Where's the boy now?" His head turned in a slow swivel. "I haven't seen him."

"One of my lieutenants took him to his father at Jackson Memorial. He'll be fine." After withdrawing the cigarette, he slipped the cigarette pack inside his shirt pocket. He stuck the cigarette between his lips and struck a match. Once it was lit, he inhaled deeply, narrowed his eyes and looked at them through the haze. He extinguished the flame and the match tip glowed red. The acrid smoke burned her nostrils.

"Any news on the kid's family? The little girl?" Nick said, his voice thick and husky. He batted away a mosquito which decided to try its luck with her. She smacked it, grimacing when her neck stung from the impact.

"Did she make it?" she asked, her heart turning over. She watched for any change of expression in the man's face to gauge if he told them the truth.

"I don't have any knowledge about that. We only found the boy. Sorry." Someone called him away and they were left standing alone staring at his retreating back.

"Do you think they're all right?" she asked. "Katy looked so pale. She'd lost so much blood." Her fingers combed her hair back from her face. "She couldn't be more than four years old...just a baby."

The clouds drifted away and the moon shone full on Nick's face. Normally golden brown, dark pools rimmed his irises and they looked almost black. Their expression pushed her back a step. They looked more than haunted, tortured.

Empathetic, her heart heavy with fear, she put her hand on his forearm. In a shaky voice, she asked, "You don't think she made it?"

He stared into the distance so long, she asked hesitantly, "Nick? Is everything all right?"

As if coming out of a stupor, his muscles jerked beneath her fingers. "I don't know. I told you these storms were killers, nothing to take lightly." He sounded as gruff as he had when he'd first announced he thought of Kenga and Rama as man-eaters.

Although at least ten degrees cooler than the day, the evening still must have been ninety-something. But she felt icy cold inside. She didn't know why, but Nick had changed. It was if he'd shut down, or shut out the world. She withdrew her hand from him.

Between Nick's strange behavior and learning absolutely nothing about Katy Wilson and her mother, frustration coiled in the pit of her stomach. She was anxious to get out of here and back to their mission. They were still no closer to finding the tigers than when they'd left the zoo. They were wasting time. Why did they have to talk to a military colonel? She and Nick were civilians. What could a colonel possibly want with them?

A megaphone boomed. "We're rolling out. Everybody in the trucks."

"That's our cue," Nick said. He grasped Kelly by the waist and boosted her into the back of the truck. Several hands gripped her arms and hoisted her up.

One of the men who must be Gireaux, broke off from the contingent and jogged to the front of the truck. He tossed his fatigue cap in the cab before him, then hauled himself into the passenger seat.

The revving engine sounded like the drone of a giant mosquito and the back of the truck vibrated even though the tires hadn't moved a centimeter.

"I'm going to get you, gringo!" Rafael yelled from the back of the truck. He snarled, bristling. She had no doubt he itched to get revenge, and fear licked up her spine. Instinctively, she recoiled as if she'd come face to face with a rattlesnake.

Nick's head jerked up, and his gaze dueled with the embittered black scowl of the gang leader.

Rafael struggled to be free of his bonds, but he was securely manacled, not to mention the contingent of guards surrounding him, holding him back. The teen was no longer a threat, just an obnoxious nuisance.

"What's wrong, gringo? Cat got your tongue? Chicken?" He snickered, enjoying his joke. His friends cackled beside him.

"Stuff it, bad boy!" One of the guards shoved him back against his seat.

"Make me!" Rafael spat at him, then flashed his smile. Somehow the diamond chip seemed sinister. Evil.

Nick watched in silence, but she felt his muscles coil beside her, felt his tension as if he were ready to spring into action.

She snuggled up against Nick. When his arm dropped around her shoulders, she dared a glance at the gang leader from under cover of her lashes.

His eyes never left them, his lips curled in a sinister twist. Even handcuffed, he looked menacing. The hateful threats, the scowls, scraped her nerves raw with anxiety.

"I'm about ready to gag you, Son," the guard next to him said. "I've had more than enough of your mouth."

"If you lay one finger on me, Gramps, my brothers will get you."

Someone yelled from Kelly's end of the truck. "We're here. Lock those delinquents in the brig, Gates. Take Sheridan, Nelson and Rodriguez with you." The men started to shuffle out of the truck.

Nick extricated himself from Kelly and jumped to the ground lithely. He held out his hands for her. Grabbing her by her waist, he swung her to the ground as easily as he would a small child.

"If I were you, gringo," Rafael said as the guards shoved him off the back of the truck. "I wouldn't go to sleep."

Kelly's eyes widened, her fear heightening to super sensitive levels. Her head told her that the youth's threats were idle but her gut told her otherwise. She couldn't prove it. In fact it seemed ludicrous, tied up and guarded the way he was. But deep intuition warned her to be careful. She held Nick's arm, standing tall at his side. She did her best to mask her expression.

"Don't worry about him, Cincinnati." Nick reached over and squeezed her hand. "He won't see the light of day till we're long gone." Nick looked the young man up and down, taking his measure. "Besides, he's nothing to be scared of without his *toys.*"

"I can break your neck with my bare hands," Rafael said, sneering.

"Move it out, punk!" The guard behind Rafael prodded him, none too gently, to move forward. "Shut your mouth."

"Make me!" Rafael rounded on the man with violence in his

eyes, a sneer on his lips. The deep scratches on his face were dried with blood and looked exaggeratedly wicked.

The guard shoved him into the mud then smiled. "Get up, boy!"

The youth glowered at the burly man as he struggled to get up. He looked like a flailing flounder on dry land with his hands cuffed behind his back. Fresh mud glopped on his face and he struggled to wipe it from his eyes. Curses spewed from his lips.

Finally, the guard yanked him up by the cuffs then pushed him forward. Rafael stumbled a few steps.

Kelly hadn't noticed that the captain stood at her side. She jumped, clutching her throat when he spoke. "My colonel wants to speak with the two of you."

Kelly looked down at herself then at Nick. She'd seen sorrier sights in her life, but rarely.

"The colonel wants to see us *this way*?"

The captain barely spared them a patronizing glance that he would bestow on a buck private. "Let's get you two to the showers first. Follow me."

Without waiting for acquiescence, the captain strode purposefully down a row of tents. Several men and women milled about in army fatigues. It would have looked like The Swamp on the old MASH reruns except for the multitude of children running to and fro, and the men and women stumbling about as if shell-shocked. Infants screamed, miserable in the heat, demanding formula that was in short supply. Dogs bayed at the moon. Kerosene lanterns, flashlights and even a campfire, lit circles of light throughout the darkness. Shadows flickered eerily. Mosquitos lined up as if to make withdrawals from the blood bank.

Kelly stayed close to Nick, awestruck by the sight of so many homeless, battered people. Children ran by in make-shift slings, sweaty, caked in layers of mud in varying degrees of dryness. Young men limped, sporting bandages as if they'd come off a battle field. Women wondered about aimlessly with vacant expressions as if the full impact of this tragedy hadn't quite sunk in. All manner of trash littered the ground and she picked her way carefully lest she stepped on a roofing nail or shards of glass.

She couldn't prevent her mouth from watering when she smelled hot dogs grilling. It had been hours since she'd eaten so much as a Milky Way. She tried not to breathe too deeply and ignored her grumbling stomach as best she could. First things first.

The captain stopped abruptly. She walked into Nick's back. "Sorry," she mumbled, backing up two steps.

"Men's latrines to the right. Women's to the left. You can have five minutes of water each." He turned and looked at Nick again. "Maybe I can get you ten."

"Very funny," Nick muttered.

"Okay, swamp boy," Kelly laughed. "But I'm going before he changes his mind." She headed for the showers, feeling better already. Then a thought struck her. What about her clothes? What good would it do them if they put these smelly rags back on? "Captain?" She waited till the captain turned to her. "Can we get a clean change of clothes?"

The captain looked at her with narrowed eyes.

"Ma'am," the captain said, a twinkle lighting his eyes. "I'll have someone bring you a pair of fatigues. Afraid that's the best I can do."

"I imagine you'll throw our duds on the fire?" Nick asked dryly, stripping out of his torn shirt.

"No, sir," the captain said, shaking his head. I could get arrested for burning hazardous waste. I'll have them buried. Deep."

"Everyone's a joker," Nick said, heading for the showers.

"Who's joking?" the captain said, grinning from ear to ear.

Her gaze riveted on Nick. Despite the absence of electricity which had initially made tent city appear dark and gothic, her eyes had grown accustomed to the dark. But it wasn't really dark. Moonlight and starlight cast their silvery sheen on them. Soldiers walked by with flashlights that beamed rays of light along the alleyways between tents. Kerosene lanterns lit tent walls, silhouetting often embarrassing images that made heat burn in her cheeks. Or maybe she was as nocturnal as her tigers.

Enough light shone on his bared shoulders to illuminate fiery red scrapes and scratches where nails and broken boards ripped his skin.

"You need medical care," she said soothingly, her bleeding heart overflowing. Tentatively, she touched one of the scrapes with gentle fingertips. Embers ignited deep within her, fanning higher when she felt the burning heat of his bare flesh.

"Yeeow! That stings." He flinched, moving away as if stabbed, glowering at her. "I'll wait for a nurse."

"Ungrateful bastard," she mumbled under her breath. She rubbed fingerpads together that still tingled.

But she had the devil of a time keeping the appreciation out of her gaze that fell on his bronzed chest matted by softly curling golden blond hair, hair her fingers itched to tousle. He didn't just have a health-club physique. His muscles were genuine, labor-authentic. His flesh was bronzed by spending hours in the sun, not some tanning booth. Of course, he could have spent hours sunning on Miami Beach, but he was too vital to lie still for so long.

As her gaze traveled lower, she registered how a soft line of golden blond hair disappeared tantalizingly under the waistband of his slacks, how his washboard flat stomach slimmed to narrow, whipcord thighs. She saw bare-chested men all the time and never gave them a second thought. Why this one should make her cheeks burn and make her loins ache, she didn't know. She didn't even like the sensations spiraling inside her, but she could no more deny her attraction for Nick than she could stop searching for her tigers.

Perhaps the reason was that he was sexier than any man had a right to be.

When she raised her eyes to his, she caught a flicker of mirth mocking her. With supreme effort, she fought down the heat flooding her cheeks and she pretended to study a military vehicle.

He sidled up to her, raising her temperature a minimum of ten degrees. His breath rasping on her neck, he asked, his voice so low only she could hear it. "Would you like to be my private nurse?"

She fought to retain some semblance of control, but he made it almost impossible. She knew he knew darned well the effect he had on her. No less than solar flares. Some perverseness inside wouldn't allow her to admit the spark of attraction she felt for him. Not as long as he wanted to put a bullet into Kenga and Rama.

She couldn't understand how she could find him the least bit attractive under the circumstances, but she did. Saving children and damsels in distress gave him points. Slaying dragons, even alligators, was a bonus, too.

Still, she knew nothing about him. Not really. Not to get close enough to nurse his wounds.

"Do I look like Florence Nightingale?" She favored him with her most regal glare.

He moved closer and murmured in her ear. His breath was warm and moist on the sensitive flesh of her neck. "You don't fool me, Cincinnati. You're a sucker for hard luck cases or you wouldn't be so concerned about those man-eaters."

She bristled, forgetting how alluring he was half-naked. Between clenched teeth, she sneered, "Stop calling Kenga and Rama *man-eaters.*"

He had the gall to laugh. To outright laugh at her.

She could slug him. Then, she thought better of it. He could arrest her for attacking an officer of the law. So she simmered quietly, biding her time. She'd wait until the chance presented itself to slip away from him in the dead of night. Then she'd find her tigers, leaving him in her dust.

She'd show him what a bleeding heart, tiger-loving female could do.

But, she grimaced, it was hard to prove to anyone, even herself, how strong-willed and determined she was in ripped, filthy clothing, caked with grime, looking no more dignified than a birthday party clown. She barely took herself seriously this way.

When a young private laid a set of freshly laundered fatigues and army-issue towels over the shower stall for them, she slipped under tepid water, away from those unmercifully teasing eyes.

It felt so wonderful to sluice off the muck that clung to her. It felt like it had invaded every body cavity. Heedful that she only had five minutes, she rushed that which she wished she could savor.

Neither the towel nor the fatigues were soft on her skin. Rather, the towel was so stiff it bristled against her like a brillo pad. The starched slacks practically stood up by themselves and felt like iron when she first slipped her legs into them. Only the green t-shirt felt soft against her flesh and it molded to her like a second skin.

She'd never worn fatigues before, hadn't even been sure what they were. Oddly, she felt combat ready. All she needed now were combat boots and an automatic pistol, maybe a few hand grenades to complete the outfit. After today's events, she craved fire-power. Miami was a combat zone and she wouldn't make the mistake of underestimating it again.

She chafed waiting for Nick to join her.

When Nick joined her a few moments later, a wicked gleam blazed in his eyes. She was glad she'd taken the time to wash her hair so that it hung silkily to her shoulders. Her coppery tresses had always been one of her best features, at least one that men could decently admit to admiring.

However, his gaze glided a half a foot below her face and she knew he was admiring something else. Drat this clinging t-shirt. It was supposed to be uni-sex, but it was anything but. She crossed her arms over her chest to hide her budding nipples, cursing herself for her weakness. She turned her back on the tune of his laughter, her spine so rigid it would shatter with a good wind.

"The colonel's waiting for you." A fresh-faced lieutenant stood at attention, his gaze riveted to Kelly also.

She bridged the men and felt negative energy pass through her as if she were a conduit between two live wires.

"Lead on, Lieutenant," Nick ordered gruffly, an edge to his voice. He put his hand in the small of Kelly's back and she was miffed to find it was a perfect fit. He brought up the rear in their formation as the lieutenant escorted them to the colonel's tent.

The officer stopped in front of a tent that was flanked by two military policeman with the initials MP cuffed on their upper arms. The taller one sported five stripes. The other only had four stripes on each arm. They held rifles across their chest, and stared straight ahead. When they saw the lieutenant, they tapped their heels and saluted him.

The young man saluted back smartly, a jaunty snap in his wrist. Behind her, she felt Nick twitch.

"We're here to see the colonel."

The taller one spoke, no more emotion in his voice than a computer would have. "Is the colonel expecting you, sir?"

"These are the two he wants to see, sergeant."

"I'l l announce you, sir." The taller one who wore a name tag over his pocket that told her his name was Gutman, ducked inside the tent. The flap lowered and they waited. Muted voices drifted to her but not loud enough to make out the words.

Again, she wondered what business a military colonel had with her. What interest could he possibly have with a zookeeper and a game warden? Did he want them to testify against the street gang that had tried to give them tonsillectomies sans anesthesia?

She'd return for that trial without hesitation – *after* she found her tigers and took them home.

A swarm of gnats descended on them as they chafed and she batted them away.

After what seemed an eon, the sergeant returned and held open the tent flap. "The colonel will see you now."

Kelly walked under the flap with only a slight downward tilt of her head.

Nick bent at his waist to clear the tent doorway. Then he stood stiffly beside her, his demeanor 180 degrees changed from that of a few moments before.

The lieutenant ducked inside, swept off his cap, came to attention and saluted the colonel.

The colonel saluted back. "At ease, lieutenant." An intelligent gaze took her measure, then Nick's.

Chancing a glance at him, she noted that his features were expressionless, his eyes devoid of emotion.

She turned her attention to the colonel, taking his measure.

He looked distinguished. Silver dominated short, cropped hair with a few strands of mahogany peppered in. Piercing, brown eyes bore into her. A square mouth set above a strong jaw gave him an indomitable air that verged on intimidating. His shoulders were broad and straight and although he wasn't standing, she presumed he was a tall man for he sat high and straight in his chair. At a guess, she'd say he was fifty-something, her father's age.

Styrofoam cups littered the colonel's desk, drips of coffee lingering in the bottom. He shuffled stacks of files, straightening them into semi-neat piles. Straightening to his full height, he leaned forward holding out his hand. She'd been right. He was tall. Probably six foot two or three. About as tall as Nick. "Welcome to tent city."

He spoke softly, exuding a thick Southern drawl.

Nick, then Kelly, shook the proffered hand. The grip was firm, authoritative, the grip of someone who meant business.

Holding her breath, she felt tension in the air so thick it was like swimming through fog. What was wrong? She stood tall keeping her eyes trained on the colonel, for she had no idea what constituted military protocol.

The colonel folded himself into his chair again, stretching back, his inscrutable gaze still boring into them.

Nick sat. She followed his lead, not sure how she was supposed to behave in this strange military world. Growing up with her eccentric, widowed father was the exact opposite of this setting.

"Captain Carey tells me that the two of you looked sorrier than a fox dragged in by the hounds when he saved your necks from the Knights." He cracked his knuckles loudly, one at a time, making her wince. "Would you mind telling me *why* in the name of Dixie they were after you? Drug deal gone wrong? Gun running?" He paused for a pregnant second.

She couldn't believe her ears. They thought she and Nick were the bad guys? *Unbelievable.* It sounded like time for her to make a thirty-five cent phone call to her father's attorney.

She sat very still, listening, watching every nuance of the colonel's face. But it was like trying to read a foreign language she'd never studied.

This was one cool character.

When he got no response, he continued, leaning forward. "Just *why* were they trying to carve you up?"

"Do gangs need a good reason?" Nick asked, coolly. Sitting tall, he hardly flexed a muscle.

"Maybe. Maybe not. You tell me." He motioned for his aide. "Do you want coffee or soda?"

"Cola?" She suspected that coffee brewed on a Bunson Burner would taste more like motor oil.

"I'll have the same," Nick said. He reached over and squeezed Kelly's hand.

The colonel nodded his head and the soldier slipped silently out of the tent. Shadows flickered on the tent walls, dimming every time a gust of wind blew the kerosene lamp or the colonel touched his desk.

"Let's start from the top. Mind if I smoke?"

Nick and Kelly shook their heads. The colonel extracted a fat Cuban cigar from his pocket, struck a match and took a deep puff. Exhaling, he stared at them through the haze of smoke. Nick lifted a quizzical brow.

One of the perks in this Godforsaken hell hole. Want one? He held one out to Nick. His shadow took on monstrous proportions on the tent wall.

Nick shook his head. "No thank you, sir."

The colonel leaned back in his chair and propped his feet on his desk, crossing one leg over the other.

"Well?"

"I guess they were mad when we threw the cat in the gang leader's face." Nick's voice remained steady as if he read a news cast rather than relived an emotional ordeal. But then, maybe he did these sorts of things routinely in his line of work.

"You did what?" He half snorted. His cigar paused mid-air.

"She threw the fur ball from hell in the kid's face," Nick reiterated matter of factly as if it were an everyday occurrence. A grin split his placid face. "You should have seen the fur fly."

"And then, he pulled a knife on you?" Leaning forward in his chair, he jotted a few notes on his blotter, punctuating his thoughts with the occasional, "Uh huh."

"Then, his friends jumped us. We fought them off..."

"Nick fought. I ran," Kelly said.

"Then they cornered us and next thing I knew, the calvary arrived." He raked his fingers through his still damp hair.

"Uh huh," the Colonel said. "Why'd you throw a cat in the kid's face." He took a deep puff of his cigar then regarded her critically through rings of smoke. "A cat isn't necessarily a weapon of choice."

"He pulled a knife on us. We didn't have a choice. It was self-defense." A defensive edge laced his deep tones.

"*Why* did he pull a knife?" Inhaling deeply, the colonel blew out more rings of smoke, squinting his eyes.

"I guess we invaded his turf," Nick said, shrugging as if it didn't matter why the youths took offense to them.

"And?" The colonel clearly held reservations.

"That's it." Nick was a man of few words.

"You have anything to add, Miss Kerrigan?"

She shook her head slowly and tucked her hair behind her ears. "We didn't do anything to them."

"Why were you there then?" His imperious gaze told her that any idiot should know better than to wander about in a war zone after dark.

"Mattie ran after his cat. I had to find him." Well, any idiot would realize she couldn't leave a little boy to fend for himself in such surroundings.

"Mattie's a little boy," Nick said. Although he sat, he was stiff as if at attention. She didn't have to touch him to know his muscles were hard as boards. The tension was almost suffocating.

"We saved his mother and sister from a falling house."

"Whoa! I lost you. Cats. Collapsing houses. Runaway kids..." He dropped his feet to the floor with a loud thud then leaned forward on his elbows. "I've had better luck questioning Ruskies! Maybe if you tell me *why* you were in Cutler Ridge in the first place, we'd get somewhere!"

"Excuse me, sir."

The colonel nodded. "Come in, Lieutenant. Freshen my coffee, please."

The aide backed into the tent balancing a stained cafeteria tray holding an array of cheap canned sodas and hot coffee. She marveled that his fatigues looked crisp and fresh even in such sweltering heat.

Nick pushed his chair back, standing to help the lieutenant. The officer poured syrupy liquid into the Colonel's cup while Nick poured soda into Styrofoam cups for himself and Kelly.

The colonel tapped his ashes into an empty soda can. The smell gagged her and she coughed.

Nick handed a cup to Kelly who gratefully accepted. Cupping both hands around it, she tilted the cup to her lips and took a sip. The effervescent liquid slid down her dry throat smoothly, despite it's warmth. It seemed even the military couldn't commandeer such a precious commodity as ice this close to ground zero, so soon after the storm. At least, they weren't giving it to their guests.

"We're trying to find my tigers..."

The colonel bolted out of his chair, knocking it over. He strode around his desk in three long strides to tower over her. "Did you say *tigers*?"

"She means her *man-eaters*," Nick said dryly.

Kelly rounded on Nick, spitting dry ice. "They're *not* man-eaters. They're in far more danger from you than you are from them," she said quietly, trying to keep her emotions in check. In the back of her mind, it registered that the colonel's actions weren't those of a man on her side. Her spine stiffened as if a thousand needles stabbed her.

"Why pray tell do you have tigers, young woman?" With the disdain with which he snarled the word *tigers* he might as well have said *fire-breathing dragons* or *Godzilla*. Adrenalin spewed into her veins. Her nerve endings stood at attention.

Nick turned to the colonel. "They're not precisely her tigers. She's a zookeeper from Metro Zoo. I'm from the Florida Fresh Water Fish and Game Commission. We're tracking her tigers for obvious reasons."

"Obvious reasons?" Kelly said, deathly quiet, clenching her hands in her lap.

"Before they maul somebody."

"They're as gentle as lambs..." She sent him a look to kill. At the very least it should have given him pause before making another crack about her *man-eaters*. He knew those were fighting words.

"Young lady..." The colonel said, raising his eye brows in disbelief. "I have a whole stack of reports on my desk over there about some wild animal whose been marauding and *eating* livestock and domestic pets. There's reports of livestock carcasses throughout Dade County. Family pets missing. Some found mangled, half..."

Kelly held up her hand, not needing to hear the rest of the gory details. "But Kenga and Ram..."

The colonel faced off against Kelly as if he was going to let all hell loose. Instead, he spoke so low she had to strain to hear him. "Tigers aren't kitty cats, Miss Kerrigan. I'm going to order that my men shoot to kill on sight."

She grasped the colonel's arm, pleading. "You're wrong. Kenga and Rama wouldn't do that. I bottle fed Rama myself. They don't have a vicious bone in their..."

The colonel shook her hands from his arm as if she carried the Black Plague, his expression twisted in disgust. He stared at her long and hard before continuing.

"You're letting emotions cloud your judgment, young lady. I can't afford to do that. Right now, their menu consists of Tabby, Fido and Elsie. Next, it'll be someone's kid. Do you want that on your conscience?"

"Then, colonel," Nick said quietly, the voice of reason. "You'll let us be going on our way to find those man-eaters before that can happen..."

The colonel glanced at his wristwatch. "No can do."

"Are we under arrest?" Nick took a big gulp of his soda.

"It'd be easy enough to check out your stories - though I tend to believe you..." He wiped perspiration beading on his brow with his arm. He took another puff from his cigarette and stared into the smoke as if it would foretell the future.

"Is there a problem then?" Kelly asked, uneasy to voice her suspicions.

"Curfew started at 2000 hours." He consulted his watch again. Kelly saw the fluorescent glow of its digital face. "It's almost 2100 hours now."

"What's that mean?" Kelly whispered. If ever a family had been the opposite of military-minded, it was her eccentric family. These military terms might as well be Chinese as far as she was concerned. She looked at Nick and lifted her brow.

He whispered, "2100 hours equals nine p.m."

"But that's early. We're adults." She bristled at being treated like a child.

Nick murmured in her ear, his warm breath doing strange things to her insides. "This is martial law, sweetheart. It's a whole new world. Get used to it."

"Who died and made you G.I. Joe?" Although she supposed being a game warden wasn't that dissimilar to being a soldier.

"We'll give you a tent for the night to bed down. In the morning, you can grab some grub and be on your way by 0800."

"But surely, Colonel," she reasoned. "You can't expect me to share a tent with him?"

"Tents are in short supply. You're lucky I don't just give you a knapsack and tell you to camp under the stars."

"But I hardly know him..." Righteous indignation welled in her voice. She tossed her head and stared at the men, each in turn.

"I didn't tell you to sleep with the man. Just go to sleep in the same tent." Amusement gleamed in the colonel's eyes. He looked at her as if to ask if she were for real.

She flamed with indignation. It wouldn't surprise her if her cheeks glowed as bright as her hair. The idea of sleeping with Nick was preposterous. Absolutely ludicrous. She'd sooner sleep with a hyena. But her fingers still tingled where she'd touched him.

From beneath veiled lashes, she studied him covertly to see if he'd taken offense to the colonel's words.

"Thank you, sir." Nick stood, grasping her by the elbow, his hand cool and firm on her. If he felt answering sparks, he didn't show a sign of it. His glare told her she had better behave.

Defiantly, she jutted her chin in the air. No man told her what to do, not even her father. She was tired of this one lording it over her, badge or no badge.

"The lieutenant will show you to your tent." He dismissed them without another glance.

But she wasn't ready to retire for the night yet. Especially not with this man.

"Do you think we can get something to eat?" The smell of hotdogs grilling tantalized her. Her stomach grumbled. Her salivary glands worked overtime.

The colonel flicked her an unconcerned glance. "See our guests get some chow, lieutenant." He folded himself into his chair and dug into his stack of paperwork as if they weren't there.

"Follow me," the lieutenant said. He lifted the tent flap and held it.

As she walked under the flap of the tent, the colonel said dryly, "Happy hunting. I hope you have permits for all that artillery."

Her fists clenched and unclenched, but wisely, she didn't utter another sound. Inside, she seethed.

"All that I need, sir," Nick said.

She kept quiet. Did she need permits? She was on official zoo business. It hadn't occurred to her to ask for something as insipid as a permit when Chelsea had practically obliterated Miami from the map. Or when her tigers were loose and at the mercy of kooks with guns that just might think they'd make dandy trophies.

Away from the colonel's suffocating presence, she inhaled deeply. The man's insufferable attitude scraped her nerves raw.

They twisted and turned through tent city as if they traversed a rat's maze. For all she knew, they could have been traveling in circles. One tent looked about as inviting as the next.

The smell of hot dogs and hamburgers grew more ardent. Picnic food had never smelled so heavenly. Her mouth watered. Her stomach contracted.

They turned a corner to the sight of firelight dancing on an open campfire. Bedraggled people around the fire looked like war refugees. Several pairs of vacant eyes turned on them and she shuddered as if looking into the soulless faces of ghouls.

# Chapter Seven

She stopped dead, staring at the bedraggled people, wondering if she stared into the eyes of the last living souls on earth.

But that was crazy, especially when she knew that her father and brothers slept safely in their home in Cincinnati. They were probably worried to death about her, but they worried in comfort, abject luxury compared to this, with precious air conditioning to cool them and decent food to eat. Again, she wondered what had ever possessed her to leave such civilization.

Just a week ago, the answer had been clear. Freedom. Independence. A chance to prove herself as the youngest of the Kerrigan brood, not to mention the sole female in an otherwise all male clan. She wanted to make a mark in the world without help from her powerful father.

Hurricanes. War zones. Military rule. None of these things had never occurred to her. Not even remotely.

This didn't seem like a different country. It felt like an alien world.

Squaring her shoulders, she buoyed her courage. What better place to prove herself than in a wild, brave new world?

She studied the people with new eyes. They'd stared into the face of death and come out victorious. They were survivors, heroes and heroines.

"Hot dog or hamburger?" Nick broke into her thoughts, his words seeming absurdly frivolous in comparison to her brooding.

She shook off the feeling of doom and forced a light note into her voice. "Hot dog." She followed him to the dancing fire, feeling its warmth on her face, the smell of burning logs and cooking weiners seemed too good to be true. "Smother it with mustard."

"You might as well order gourmet food." He snorted, grabbing a slightly crispy dog from a paper plate near the camp fire and plopping it into a bun. When he handed it to her, their fingers touched.

She jerked away, anticipating miniature lightning bolts. To cover her heightened attraction to him, she moved away, taking a seat on a downed tree trunk.

He joined her, sitting so close his thigh burned into hers as he took a big bite of his burger. Juice dribbled down his chin and he wiped it away with the back of his hand, grinning at her.

Cognizant of the intense feelings he ignited in her, she scooted about half a foot down the water-logged tree. Half turning, she studied the shadows flickering across his features, piqued when he laughed at her.

"Haven't I proved myself to you, yet? I don't bite."

"So you've not bitten me." She held up her fingers, ticking off his list of offenses smugly. "You've done plenty else. Let's see...you arrested me. Handcuffed me. Nearly got me killed. Not much difference," she retorted, glaring at him. She forgot she held the hot dog and spoke with her other hand, the hot dog shaking in the air. "I wonder why I don't trust you?" she said with heavy molasses in her voice.

He sidled closer, his voice low and husky. "You should be grateful I saved your pretty neck."

"And I saved yours. We're even. I don't owe you a thing." Even though she knew the score wasn't even. He'd saved her a few more times, at great peril to himself for which she was grateful. But she wasn't ready to let him know how grateful.

He stuck out his hand with the hamburger still in it, then grimaced, pulling it back. Switching it to his other hand, he stuck the right one out again. "Maybe it's time we made a truce. Friends?"

"Partners." She put her hand in his a shade reluctantly. *Friends* might be too strong a word. He might apply the wrong connotation.

He studied her, his expression inscrutable as he held onto her hand. He held the strategic advantage, his back to the light. Every nuance of her expression lay open to him while his lay hidden in shadow.

She knew she should pull her hand away, that she should sever contact, but she didn't want to. His touch made her warm and tingly all over. It made her feel somehow safe in this alien world.

"I'm curious what made a petite woman like you become a zookeeper? Why do you work with *man-eaters?*" His thumb rubbed the back of her hand hypnotically.

Casting him an almost reprimanding smile, trying her best not to melt at his touch even as she melted from the muggy heat, she chuckled. "That's a pick-up line if I ever heard one. *What's a nice girl like me doing in a job like that?* Can't you think of something more *original?*"

"Maybe. But I want to know anyway. It's not exactly in the main stream."

She slanted a side-ways glance at him from beneath her lashes. Was he for real? Even her macho brothers accepted women working side-by-side with them in non-traditional roles. "It is in my family." Visions of her home, a miniature zoo in its own right, curved her lips in a smile. On any given day, they shared their domain with at least a dozen animals, mostly exotic.

"Tell me about them," he prompted, smiling into her eyes, coaxing her. He bent his leg at the knee, rested his elbow on it and made himself cozy.

Frowning, she shook her head. "I don't want to bore you..."

"You just told me they're interesting."

"I did?" She didn't recall that. Her older brothers interesting? They were just typical men.

"I have the time if you do." He exuded charm. Good thing he wasn't trying to sell her a used car.

Why not talk to him? They had time to kill. And she wanted to stall returning to the tent alone with him. This was as good an excuse as any.

"My father, King Kerrigan, is the head zookeeper at the Cincinnati Zoo. He's had a love affair with animals since way before meeting my mother. They met on safari in Africa..."

"Trapping tigers?"

"Tracking an elephant herd," she corrected. She paused to take a bite of her now cold hot dog that settled in her stomach like a chunk of quartz. "Mom retired when she found out she was expecting Kyle, my oldest brother. Kane and Kenneth followed quickly and she never regretted her choice. At least that's what King says."

"You don't know? She's never told you?"

She stared at him, not sure she wanted to answer that question. Not that it pained her exactly as her mother had died before she could recall, but she still felt a niggling sense of loss that visited her in dreams sometimes. She wondered just how much she should tell him.

"Penny for them," he said, nudging her gently.

Heaving a deep sigh, she stared at the twinkling stars that didn't seem to know or care that Miami lay in ruins, that haggard, homeless people gaze upon them hoping for miracles, for absolution.

When she was little, her father had taken her and Kevin on his knees, held them tight and told them that their mother lived in those stars. That when they saw one twinkling, it meant she smiled down upon them. Ever since, she and her twin had taken to waving at twinkling stars and they symbolized her mother's love.

A lopsided grin tugged at the corner of her lips and she moved her hand ever so slightly in a wave that the lieutenant would never notice but that she hoped her mother would see and answer.

One nebula outshone all its sister constellations, almost like the night long ago in Bethlehem which had changed the world. Maybe this one would change hers. She took it as a sign to proceed with her story.

In a slightly husky voice, she continued. "She died in a car accident when Kevin and I were babies." She favored him with a sad smile. "Kevin's my twin and he's a zookeeper, too."

"Where's he?"

"Still in Cincinnati, with King, Kyle and Kane. Kenny and I are the only ones who spread our wings. Kenny's a missionary in Port-au-Prince, Haiti. He always said that his calling was to serve God, not coddle wild animals..."

"Sounds like my kind of man." Although the words could be

construed as fighting words, they were said without menace so she couldn't take offense. Not much anyway.

"You'd probably like Kane even better. He's a cop."

"And Kyle?"

"Another zookeeper. He and Kevin are in India procuring more animals for Cincinnati. They probably don't have a clue that Hurricane Chelsea ripped through Miami."

Nick held up his hand and counted off brothers. "Kyle, Kevin, Kane and Kenny." He shot her a quizzical, teasing glance. "Did I miss any?"

"Nope. There's only the five of us. We were enough to keep King busy."

"No wonder you're a tomboy."

It was her turn to lift her brow and tilt her head. "If I am, it's because I grew up in a houseful of men. I didn't learn how to cook till I was in my teens and my Aunt Meghan took pity on me. But I knew how to bandage an injured dog or cat."

"Do you think you could put a few bandages on my back if we could talk our hosts into giving up a few first aid supplies?" He shifted awkwardly as if it pained him and she remembered the fiery red scrapes.

"Let me see," she said, turning him around so that his back faced her. She pulled his shirt from his slacks and lifted it over his shoulders, telling herself the whole time that she was his nurse.

But she doubted nurses felt this way about their patients and she chided herself, vowing anew to remain cool and composed around him, afraid she'd set herself an impossible task.

"What's your professional opinion, doc? Will I live?"

"You'll live, but antiseptic and a few band-aids might help. You don't want to get an infection." She motioned to a passing soldier to come to her aid. He listened attentively and a few minutes later, he returned with the required medical supplies.

She murmured a *thank you* and favored him with a wide grin when he deposited them next to her.

Nick looked over his shoulder, shooting a wicked grin at her. "Are you ready to play doctor, Cincinnati?"

She glanced around her. Only embers remained in the fire. Her light was dying out. Nor was the ground sterile, not that she expected that here, but reasonably clean would be nice.

"Not here. In the tent." At least she could lay out the supplies on canvas, instead of mud, soot and debris. She tugged his shirt down and ordered her heart to stop drumming wildly. Gathering the supplies, she stood and waited for him.

He stood and motioned for their lieutenant who'd been keeping a discreet distance but who hadn't taken his eyes off them. "We're ready to turn in for the night. Will you take us to the hotel room?"

Embarrassment blazed from her toes to the tip of her head. "One more remark like that, and you're on your own, Bradley," she hissed behind him, scandalized. If only Kyle or Kevin were here...

"I'll be good," he said. But she could hear the smile in his voice even though his back was to her as he followed the soldier, his gait as lithe and easy as a lion's.

"Here's your tent," the lieutenant said after taking them through the maze again. "You'll find two cots, bedrolls, and a kerosene lamp inside. Latrines are two aisles over, three tents to the right. If you need anything, there'll be patrols up and down the aisles all night long. Let them know. Reveille will be at 0400. Ignore it if you can. Night folks."

"Night," they answered in unison.

Nick motioned for Kelly to go first, then he followed her. He lit the kerosene lamp wick with a lighter he dragged out of his pocket and turned the blaze up inside the hurricane glass so that light flooded the Spartan tent. Moths performed their nightly ballet on the outside wall of the tent, silhouetted by the light. An occasional soldier passing by casting shadows through the thin walls. Nick strung mosquito netting over the tent door to keep out unwelcome nightly visitors.

She knelt on the hard ground, spread out her medical supplies on the canvas floor next to the cot on the left and sifted through them to find what she needed. "Come over here. "You'll be my first human guinea pig."

He sauntered over and sat heavily, eyeing her speculatively. "I thought you had tons of experience."

"On animals. Just about every kind you can imagine. I even

doctored an armadillo once that'd been struck by a car."

"In case you hadn't noticed, I'm not an armadillo." His laughter mocked her.

"I hadn't noticed," she lied, dryly.

When he sat there staring at her, making her as uncomfortable as a cat in a dog pound, she took the offensive. "I'm only going to put some gel on your back and bandage it up. It's not major surgery. Stop being a baby." Her gaze dueled with his. "Now are you going to take that shirt off, or shall I?"

"I'll let you." He held out his arms to her.

"Take it off," she commanded, no nonsense in her voice. Honestly! Men were more trying than wounded tigers.

"When you sweet talk me like that, how can I resist?" he mocked. But he pulled off the shirt and she was less than half a foot from that strong chest that radiated enough heat to keep the Ohio Valley warm all winter.

She poured witch hazel onto a cotton ball, patting his wounds as gently as she could.

"Did your dad remarry?" He flinched the first time she touched the alcohol to his scrapes and she waited for a moment before continuing. This time, she warned him first.

"He dated, but no woman was brave enough to put up with the Kerrigan clan."

"That bad, huh?" His teeth gnashed when she dabbed more alcohol on him.

"Between five rowdy kids and the animal kingdom?" She chuckled at the memories. "One poor woman wasn't watching where she walked, and she stepped on our pet tortoise. Shelly had crawled out from under the couch unnoticed — until then." She cracked a devilish grin. "To hear her scream, you'd think someone shot her."

"I once put a baby alligator in my step dad's jeep."

Her smile broadened. "What'd he do?"

She squirted the medicinal cream from the tube and rubbed it into his wounds. He flexed his shoulders and his muscles rippled beneath her fingers. Did he know that he set off bottle rockets in her stomach when he did that? The sensations they sparked warred with her common sense, but they were proving stronger.

"Grounded me for a month."

Trying to keep her voice steady, she said, "Kevin and I put a garden snake into King's car before he went to see the Wicked Witch." Memories of the tongue lashing and spanking didn't dim the mirth bubbling inside her. "We had to clean animal cages at the zoo every Saturday for the whole summer but at least he didn't marry her." She chuckled. "Ever clean a rhinoceros cage? I think you got the better deal."

She rubbed the residue from the cream down the legs of her fatigues and then cut a long strip of gauze. "Hold this," she ordered, dangling it over his shoulder like a snake.

Their fingertips touched and a shudder coursed through her. What was happening to her? Had Chelsea wrecked her magnetic center? Were the high and low pressure fronts affecting her equilibrium? She shirked away from his hand as if burned.

She guessed at the length of paper tape and snipped it off the roll then hung it from the edge of the cot. "Let me have it."

He handed the gauze back to her and she bandaged the worst of his wounds with the mummy gauze and put a few band-aid type strips on his smaller wounds.

"You're a much better patient than that armadillo," she said on a self-conscious laugh, gathering up the medical supplies and moving away.

He turned and regarded her oddly.

"Cincinnati?"

She didn't lift her eyes and busied herself with the task at hand. "Yeah?"

Still not looking at him, she crossed to her side of the tent and started to turn down the bed role. She did her best to fluff the army-issue pillow that felt as if it could be filled with concrete. No one would bother stealing the towels or pillows from this bourgeois motel, at least.

"Thanks. You make a darned good Florence Nightingale."

Their eyes met across the tent and held for several seconds. His were darkly unfathomable and heaven only knew what he could read in hers. She hoped he couldn't see in them how much his bared chest and sultry voice affected her. Hopefully he couldn't see her well in the flickering light.

He stretched out on his cot, leaning up on his elbow.

"Good night, Cincinnati."

"Good night, Lieutenant." She turned her back on him and punched her pillow. Then she burrowed around her covers as if she was a cat getting comfortable. It was too hot to consider crawling under the covers. Even at three in the morning, she suspected the temperature had topped eighty. But at least it wasn't as stifling hot now as it was mid day when she could have flipped pancakes on the road.

"I figure if we sleep till 0600 and grab some breakfast, we can roll out of here by 0700, tomorrow. That'll give us about six hours sleep and we can get an early start." Nick outlined his plans.

If she got up with reveille, Kelly thought, she could elude Nick and find her tigers without him. Then he wouldn't have a chance to shoot Kenga and Rama. But how would she get around? Her jeep was back in Coral Gables. He had the only keys to the his sedan. She fumed silently. It looked like she was stuck with him. Unless she got a ride back to the zoo and started all over...

"Hey, Cincinnati? You didn't hear a word I said, did you?"

"You said we'd get up at 0600 and leave at 0700, right?" Under her breath, she murmured, "whatever that means." She rolled over, trying to find at least a semi-comfortable position and her eyes met his.

"I said we'd better get some rest. 0600 comes mighty early and these cots," he eyed his distastefully, "are hard as rocks."

"At least they're dry." She tucked her hands under her chin, curling her knees to her abdomen.

"Sweet dreams, Kelly. You did well today. Your dad would be proud of you." He leaned over the side of the cot and doused the kerosene light.

Darkness shrouded them and she felt cocooned in the heat.

"Thanks," she mumbled, rolling to her side so that her back was to him. He was making it too hard to dislike him, to stay mad at him. Yet, how could she harbor tender feelings for a man who professed to think of her precious tigers as man-eaters? A man who believed they were responsible for the vicious carnage that littered the city. How could she be falling in love with him?

Her thoughts brought her up short. *Falling in love with him?* She couldn't, she told herself. Impossible. She wouldn't allow it. She'd let her guard down after she saw how tender he was with Mattie and his sister, but that was before he reminded her how much he hated her babies. How hard-hearted he was to the gentle creatures.

Suddenly, gunfire rang in the distance. Angry shouts neared. Visions whirled in Kelly's sleep-drenched mind - the house collapsing, the little girl, unconscious, bleeding, the switchblade drawing nearer and nearer to her face, mesmerizing her. With a jolt, she bolted upright in the dark, a scream rising in her throat.

It wasn't merely dark. It was pitch black. There were no lights, not even stars. She must have tumbled into a black hole.

Hands reached out for her, grasping her shoulders, seeking her face. A voice, distant, indiscernible said something, but she didn't understand, didn't want to understand. She screamed again, struggling to get away, to free herself from the terror it reeked.

Groggily, she began to realize where she was - inside a tent, on a cot that was hard as a concrete slab. The voice, warm and deep, began to make sense, to wrap itself around her as a cocoon, safe, desirable and wholly enveloping. The voice belonged to Nick who was crooning softly in her ear. His lips brushed her earlobe, lightly but provocatively. His warm tongue flicked inside, lathing her with warmth, igniting desires she didn't know existed.

She arched into his caress, her arms snaking around his neck drawing him to her. He slid his body alongside hers on the cot forcing her to turn sideways to accommodate his length, bringing her breasts into contact with his warm chest. Tingles shivered all over her and she laughed deliciously, letting her hands explore the wonder that was him.

Nick's hands roamed her body too. One hand trailed lightly up her side until it lingered at her breast. His lips plundered hers seductively, demanding surrender, seeking union, giving passion.

He moaned into her mouth. His hand cupped her breast, squeezing it gently, seeking out the nipple, rubbing it. His hips ground into hers in an age old rhythm, pressing, straining, seeking the warmth for which he longed.

Lost in passion, Kelly pulled him closer, opening her mouth wider, losing herself in his need, her own quickly building.

When he broke his mouth free from her lips and sat up, she protested. "Sit up, Kelly."

When she sat up, he lifted her shirt over her head and threw it behind him. Her breath lodged in her throat, her heartbeats pounded rapidly. Then his hands encircled her waist, his touch scorching her. Slowly, his hands trailed up her back till they reached her bra, fiddling with the snaps. It seemed an eternity, then the offending garment was loosened, strewn behind her and her breasts swung free. But only momentarily.

Nick cupped each breast in his hands, testing their weight, learning their shape. Then he leaned forward, capturing her lips, plundering them until they were swollen. His fingers rubbed her straining nipples, softly at first, then grew more demanding, working her into a frenzy until her breath was torn from her lungs in ragged gulps.

He tore his lips from hers and trailed hot kisses down her throat, lingering in the hollow as she arched her head back, letting her hair swing freely behind her. It tickled her back. Then, as if lured, Nick's tongue flicked and darted its way down her chest until it found one creamy mound. His lips kissed, then his tongue lathed in concentric circles until it claimed one rosy peak, kneading and suckling, taking its whole into his mouth. They groaned together in ecstasy.

When he tore himself away to give attention to its twin, Kelly whispered breathlessly, "Let me undress you." She took off his shirt and flung it behind her. She longed to feel his bare chest against hers and she pressed into him, lifting her lips to his kisses. His skin against hers burned, lifting her to heights she'd never dreamed. She rubbed herself against him, not caring that she was building in him a fire that could only be quenched in the time honored way of men and women. She longed for a union she'd never before experienced, yet knew instinctively would lift her to the realms of Heaven and beyond...

After an eternity, or was it mere seconds, Nick lifted himself off her. She heard the loud crackle of a snap being unpopped and she knew he was taking off his pants. Her chest weighed heavy. She couldn't breath. She couldn't move. She could only long to feel him deep inside her.

# Chapter Eight

"What the he..." Nick lifted his head from Kelly's soft as satiny flesh and swore softly. Sirens wailed. Horns tried to rupture his eardrums. People shouted frantically. Man made lightning bolts flashed through thin tent walls illuminating the small space eerily. The sounds grew ominously closer dimly alerting Nick to a sinister change in the air.

Nick lowered his head tasting Kelly's sweet lips one last time before meeting their destiny. His fingers stroked her sleek hair, so silky soft, smelling like gardenias in full bloom. He knew it would sparkle like rubies in the brilliant Florida sunlight and it mesmerized him. She had the most glorious halo of hair he'd ever laid eyes on. He just wanted to bury himself in it and forget the rest of the world.

Greater sensations assailed him. His groin nestled against her ached excruciatingly eliciting moans from his very soul. When he slipped his tongue inside her mouth she shivered beneath him exquisitely. He knew he only stalled the inevitable moment when he had to pull away from her womanly warmth, a warmth he had been denied too long.

Reluctantly, he pulled away feeling suddenly cold, lonely. "We can't get a break, can we Sweetheart? We'll finish this later," he drawled languidly. He lowered his head, kissing a pert nipple.

When he tightened his embrace, she arched impossibly close, her nipples hard and erect, her slender throat beckoning his kisses, her womanly core rubbing against him making an answering explosion in him eminent. He cursed the circumstances in which he found this exquisite creature in his arms for he didn't want to let her go but he must. His higher mission called.

Dark, emerald eyes brimmed over with passion when she lifted her guileless gaze to his. She shivered erotically in his arms and he almost hauled her back into bed, damn the consequences.

He hated to, but he pushed himself up and off, careful not to hurt her.

With a shuddering breath, he knelt, groping in the dark to find their clothes. He hadn't felt so effected by a woman since...

No he wouldn't go there. Not here. Not now.

Kelly sat up, swinging those exquisite legs a model would die for to the floor, the legs he wanted wrapped tightly around his waist. She murmured in an intoxicatingly husky voice with a slight tremor of fear, "What do you think is happening outside? Do you think they found Kenga and Rama?"

Nick wanted to take her in his arms, tell her everything would be okay, but knew he could not make such promises. Instead, he tossed Kelly her T-shirt. Then he turned his shirt, right side out and tried to slide his arm into the sleeve.

There was no way.

"Wrong shirt. Switch," he chuckled softly at the joke on him.

He tossed her the T-shirt. When his shirt hit him in the face, he stumbled backward. He caught himself with his hand. Kelly's warm laughter trickled over him like a hot mountain spring.

"Imp," he grumbled, slightly irritated. He wondered when his flesh would cool down, when he would start breathing normally and if she knew just how agitated he felt.

"Do you think they're okay?"

"You know that if they were found in city limits or if they attacked someone..." If the guard had found them, they were wounded or dead. The colonel had ordered shoot to kill. However, Nick did not want to worry Kelly unduly. They would find out soon enough what had the compound in such an uproarious state of chaos.

He doubted that the tigers could cause such a ruckus - unless they roamed loose. Then they would hear gunshots, wouldn't they?

"I'm ready," Kelly mumbled.

Nick seriously doubted that, but the darkness prevented him

from seeing her face, from probing her eyes. But the twinge of anxiety in her tone clued worried him.

Her mind dwelled on those damned man-eaters! How unflattering!

"Let's find out then," Nick murmured. He grabbed her hand to pull her behind him. Unable to resist her satiny softness, however, he pulled her to him. Soft lips trailed tender kisses along his scar. When she cupped his cheek with her soft, gentle hand, he closed his eyes in exquisite torture. No one had ever touched him so.

He lifted his head reluctantly, the static of her hair making it cling to his cheek.

"Let's find destiny," she drawled.

He wondered if truer words had ever been spoken. "You may not like destiny once you find it," he warned. He brushed her hair away with the back of his finger.

"It can't be ignored," she said breathlessly.

The double meaning struck him between the solar plexus.

When he saw the nod of her head silhouetted in a flash of light, Nick took Kelly's hand in his. He squeezed it supportively, then pulled her behind him. Her hand felt very small, very fragile in his and he wondered anew why a slip of a woman like her devoted her life to such dangerous, sinister man-eaters as her tigers.

A young soldier in a hurry, bumped into Nick, nearly knocking him down.

"Sorry, Sir." The boy stumbled away at a trot.

"Are you okay?" A worried frown marring her perfect forehead.

Soldiers rushed about the command post. Medics bustled importantly, setting up a mobile triage unit. A private wheeled a stretcher in front of them.

Imminent danger permeated the air.

Nick squeezed her hand. "I'm fine. Stick close to me. Something's going down."

She looked up at Nick, her eyes wide, inimitably curious. Amber flecks pooled around the iris making her eyes curiously gold. Her exquisite profile lay in shadow.

He felt an overwhelming urge to sweep her back into his arms. Sucking in a deep breath, he lifted his face to the sky, letting the cool morning breeze cool his heated flesh.

Dawn loomed an hour away. A blanket of twinkling stars slowly faded away and a falling star bolted through the Heavens like a chariot. All except the tail disappeared leaving a smattering of angel dust glimmering in the Milky Way.

Nick and Kelly paused, admiring its brilliance, forgetting the bustle about them.

"Wish upon a star?" Kelly whispered to him, her breath warm on his neck.

"What do you wish for?" Nick wanted to know, envisioning her supple body beneath his under the moonlight in a place far, far away from all this commotion and chaos, in a place where lovers could take their time and enjoy one another for eternity...

"I wish for..." Kelly's voice trailed off. Her eyes gleamed with mischief and crimson stained her cheeks. She bit her lower lip with small pearly teeth. "You know if I tell you, it won't come true!" She wailed. Lowering her voice, she added, "I imagine you already know."

"I can make a wild guess. One out of two..." Tigers, or him. Which was it? He wasn't sure he wanted to know. He might lose the bet.

A Humvee multi-purpose truck rumbling to a halt next to the stretcher broke the magical spell. Instinctively, Nick pulled Kelly away, shielding her body with his.

Several medics rushed to the truck. More horns blared. Further commotion erupted. Soldiers jostled Kelly pushing her into Nick.

"Let's get a closer look," Nick yelled above the noise. He pushed and shoved his way through the crowd, keeping a tight hold on Kelly's hand, pulling her behind him.

"Can you see anything yet?" Kelly asked. She stood on tiptoe, straining to see over the crowd. "What's in the truck?"

Nick strained his neck but the crowd pressed against him too tightly.

Damn! He couldn't see a thing in this human sea of turbulence.

"Let's get closer."

"I'm trying Cincinnati. Stay close," Nick said, tightening his hold on her small hand, feeling very protective of her.

When they reached the truck, MP's holding rifles barred their way. Kelly looked at Nick, a frown creasing her pretty face. She bit her lower lip beguilingly.

"What's happening here, soldier?" Nick asked the closest MP.

The young man looked down his nose imperiously at Nick making Nick quirk an eyebrow. Who did this upstart think he was anyway?

"That's classified information." The soldier lifted his rifle higher, pushed it out a hair's breath in silent, but unmistakable warning.

Nick ran his hand through his hair, frustrated. He sighed deeply. He peered over the soldier's shoulder trying to catch a glimpse of the figure they were placing on the stretcher. They wouldn't go to this amount of trouble for a tiger, especially not a presumably dangerous predator. No. They would have killed it and left it where it fell, or maybe, sent an animal control truck for it later. Something ominous had occurred, something that meant big trouble.

Kelly pulled away from Nick. He watched her, a frown turning his lips downward. He wondered what she was up to, especially when her hips started to sway gently and she stopped in front of a different MP. She said something that brought a smile to the young man's lips and they laughed together at some private joke. Her laughter tinkled above the din. Then she flipped her glorious hair behind her ear in a provocatively seductive fashion. A sharp stab of jealousy sliced through Nick like a Samurai's sword.

Fierce animal instinct coiled in the pit of Nick's stomach. He struggled to regain his control. He knew she was desperate to find out what was happening inside the closed circle. Too desperate. He feared for her safety.

Still, he didn't like the dark feelings enveloping him. He clenched and unclenched his fists stealthily, coming up behind her to catch her words.

His gaze was fixed on Kelly and he didn't see the colonel and his elite guard approach. He jumped when the colonel bellowed his name.

"Bradley. Kerrigan. My men are searching for the two of you."

Kelly spun on her heel coming face to face with the colonel.

Nick lifted a quizzical eyebrow. "You found us, Sir. What can we do for you?"

"Oh, I think you and your tigers have done enough. More than enough." The colonel frowned, crossing his arms over his chest. His fingers drummed his sides impatiently.

"What did my tigers do Colonel?" Kelly asked. She joined Nick, standing in front of him. Nick saw Kelly square her shoulders and tilt her head ever so slightly.

Nick put his hands on Kelly's shoulders. He directed a level gaze on the colonel.

"Darned right I'll show you what your carnivorous beasts did to one of my men." The colonel stomped around them. The MPs lowered their rifles, permitting the colonel and his contingent entrance. Medics fell back in deference, giving wide berth to the colonel and his group.

Nick followed Kelly who paced herself a few feet behind the colonel. His sharp eyes took in the scene. It looked as if a landing pad were being cleared - for a medivac helicopter most likely. Several military personnel bearing medical insignia on their lapels stood on the far side of a single stretcher where a soldier lay, bloodied, delirious. They awaited the colonel, standing more or less at attention. Medical personal were never in one hundred percent regs, but then who cared, they weren't real army, just weekend warriors.

The closer they moved to the stretcher, the better Nick could see the soldier's face. It wasn't a pretty sight. Someone, or something, had really mangled the boy. He looked like he had been in one hell of a fight—rather one sided from the looks of it—and he wasn't on the winning side.

God help him, but Nick didn't know if he could get closer, if he could look the wounded man in the eye. He closed his eyes briefly, trying to block memories that usually only haunted him in the dead zone of his nightmares.

Battle scarred comrades in arms shot down in the Gulf War superimposed themselves over the soldier's baby face. This soldier was a mere child, despite the fact that he wore the uniform of a guard. He was most likely a poor kid who'd enlisted to get the new GI bill. Most of his time was probably spent in his campus frat house chasing girls and studiously *not* cracking the books. Like most recruits, he probably thought the most difficult part of enlisting would be awaking before the sun to run four grueling miles and playing mind games with his drill sergeant for six weeks. He'd never figured on being called into real action to combat lethal danger.

Beneath his hands, Kelly stiffened. She had probably never seen such carnage. He wished she didn't have to witness this. He wished he could protect her from this even if he wasn't surprised. Wasn't this exactly what he had dreaded?

Nick couldn't bear to deal with the other image torturing him. Not now, not here. It would haunt him forever, but he had learned how to push it to the back of his mind during his waking hours. It loomed ultimately more painful than fallen friends and soldiers—men who risked their lives to protect their country and their loved ones. It had almost been the death of his soul.

Yet, his mind teased unmercifully, this is how his Ashlea looked inside her tiny casket...

He pushed the thought away refusing to deal with it now, refusing to deal with his shattered heart. Danger lurked in dawn's mist, so thick, it hung in the air like a shroud.

The colonel stood over the soldier for countless moments, shaking his head almost imperceptibly. His shoulders hunched slightly. Nick could tell he was a leader who cared greatly for the men in his command. Yet, when the colonel turned around, his gaze shot flames through Kelly like heat seeking missiles.

Nick felt the urge to protect her, to save her from the scorching fire which could burn, scar and sought ultimately to destroy.

The colonel propelled Kelly to the stretcher. She stumbled over a rock and lurched forward.

Tiny hairs on the back of Nick's neck bristled. His muscles coiled primitively, ready for battle if necessary. Still, he held himself back, the law officer inside him holding tight reign.

"I want you to see what your tigers did to my soldier, Kerrigan! Look closely. They mauled him. What am I supposed to tell this boy's parents? *If* he survives, he'll be scarred for life!" The colonel's voice broke in a near sob. "Tell me what I'm supposed to tell them!"

The colonel was taking this too far. He had to be stopped. When Nick stepped forward menacingly, MPs restrained him. He struggled but his arms were held tightly.

Kelly turned just enough so that Nick could watch the play of emotions on her profile. Anger, bright and furious glowed in her sunburned cheeks and flashed from her eyes. Nick could see her muscles tense, her shoulders rise and square themselves. She flicked her hair behind her shoulders. Her breasts protruded proudly. She was ready to do battle and she looked magnificent.

Then she composed herself, the color fading as her face became a silent mask not unlike that of a law enforcement officer forced to deal with an irate citizen demanding twisted justice. Nick noted, however, that her stance remained poised, flexed and waiting for the unexpected. Her aura reminded him of a cornered animal, ready to turn on an unsuspecting aggressor.

"Were there any witnesses to this attack?" Kelly asked. "Did he tell you what happened to him?"

He watched fascinated, wanting to intercede, supremely frustrated that he could not.

Kelly leaned over the baby-faced soldier. Nick presumed she was looking for hard irrefutable evidence that her tigers were responsible for this carnage. Nick, however, felt 99.9% certain that Kelly would never believe her tigers capable of such a violent act unless she were witness to it. Nick knew what the beasts were capable of. He wondered if his worst nightmares had just been realized—again?

Kelly straightened and turned around. She met the colonel's gaze with steely resolve. "With due respect Colonel," Kelly said, "I don't see any evidence linking my tigers to your soldier. Any..."

"You don't see what those monsters did to that boy? You don't see how they mangled his face?" Infuriated, the colonel stomped to the wounded soldier and flung the protective sheet off him. Several gasps escaped from the crowd. Heads turned away. Sympathetic moans whispered on the almost silent breeze.

By rights, Nick thought, the boy should be dead. But he was starting to awaken, to thrash his head and move parched lips. Screams of agony ripped through Nick, chilling him more than the night breeze. One of the doctors bent his head to catch the boys' words A second medic injected him full of something that mollified his agony. The writhing stopped. The boy fell into merciful, fitful sleep. Nick watched fascinated as the boy's fingers twitched, almost as if in a dance of death.

Kelly and the colonel seemed oblivious to everybody around them, including the wounded soldier. They were locked in mortal combat.

"As I was saying, if you let me finish, Colonel," Kelly said. Nick didn't like the attitude lacing her words like arsenic. One didn't speak to a military man in those tones, especially not a high ranking official like the colonel—even if the speaker was a civilian. It just wasn't done. Obviously, Kelly had no experience with the military or military protocol. "Any large animal could have done this. If I'm right and it wasn't my tigers that mauled your soldier, you'll be looking for the wrong suspect - and you'll give the predator that did this free reign to ravage and maul."

"How dare you speak to me so disrespectfully Kerrigan. I'll have you fired for your insubordination!" The colonel strode forward, jutting his face within an inch of hers.

Kelly did not back down. "I'm giving you my professional opinion and if you don't take it, further injury and deaths will be on your head. Besides," Kelly paused. Her eyes narrowed and her lips thinned. "You don't have that kind of authority over me, Mister!"

Nick had to intercede, even if he believed the colonel could be right about the tigers. He couldn't be allowed to treat Kelly roughly. Nick yelled over the din to be heard. "Colonel!" When the old soldier didn't turn, Nick raised his volume several notches. "Colonel! She's not one of your soldiers. She doesn't know the rules! Go easy on her!"

The Colonel advanced on Kelly as stealthily as a panther on the hunt and she stepped backward, stumbling over the littered ground. Kelly's feet slid out from under her and her head hit the ground with a thud, landing on a sharp stone. A trickle of blood oozed from her forehead where a sharp edge had sliced soft flesh. She looked dazed, hugging herself, rolling on the ground in agony.

Medics rushed to her aid, kneeling over her. A nurse was shining a miniature flashlight in Kelly's eyes. Another held her wrist, seeking a pulse.

Nick struggled violently, wrenching free of his captors with a guttural growl. Primitive anger exploded in his veins. He was beyond reason, beyond caring. His mate was being threatened and he had to protect her.

Three MPs were no match for him and he broke free. He dove for the colonel, his arm arced back ready to land a blow in the colonel's face. He swung with all his might and when his fist connected with the colonel's nose, he felt bone crunch and blood spurt between his fingers. Just getting warmed up, Nick wrestled the old soldier to the ground. The man was incredibly lithe and he fought as a warrior whose honor was in danger of being besmirched. Still, he was no match for a man protecting his woman.

Suddenly, several pairs of hands lifted Nick and put him on his feet as if he had levitated.

"Arrest these two!" the colonel shouted. "Put a guard on them." The major and captain rushed to the colonel's side and helped him to his feet. Staggering, the colonel held his nose, glaring daggers over the ridge of his knuckles.

"Are you okay, Sir?" the major asked, gushing concern as he dusted off the colonel. The captain took a handkerchief out of his pocket and handed it silently to the older man.

The colonel glared at the major. "My nose is broken. I have to call McMurphy's parents. Man-eating tigers are mauling my men. Do you think I'm hunky dory, soldier?"

"No, Sir!" The major snapped to attention.

One MP dragged Nick's arms behind his back while another handcuffed him. Nick suffered the indignity in good grace. "Colonel," Nick spoke quietly. "You will need to call my base in West Palm."

The colonel spewed a mixture of blood and spit on the ground by Nick's feet. "I don't have to do anything, Boy. I ain't no policeman. You're under military arrest."

"If I may have permission to speak, I'm a..."

"I don't care what you think you are. You and that tiger lover are a pain in my backside. And I want you out of my sight." Two nurses took the colonel to a second stretcher and made him lie down From the stretcher, he yelled, "Get them out of here. I want them out of my face!"

Nick's attention riveted to Kelly as an MP put a matching pair of handcuffs on her, forcing her to march to his side at gunpoint. She staggered and he feared she would faint. Her forehead was bandaged where the medics had cleansed her wound but her eyes were still dilated.

Eight MPs in all escorted Nick and Kelly to the guard tent. How ironic, Nick thought, that only yesterday, he had asked the guard to bring Kelly to this jail for her own safety and now he was being held prisoner.

One of the MPs pushed Nick into the tent with the barrel of his gun. Nick fell headlong, his nose landing inches from a pair of pointy toed hard leather boots. His head hurt when it hit the ground with a thud. His head throbbed and he felt dazed for a moment but nothing permanent seemed damaged. When the ringing in his ears subsided he could hear sinister laughter. It slithered down his spine like a rattle snake. Nick twisted his neck to look for the sound of that maniacal laughter. Rafael grinned menacingly at Nick. Teeth gleamed like crystals in the dark tent. Rafael's eyes narrowed and Nick felt extreme malice slice through him.

# Chapter Nine

What in Hades?" Nick cursed loud enough to be heard in West Palm Beach. He struggled to stand without aid of his hands. Digging his elbows in the dirt, he put his full weight on them. His knees strained. The small of his back felt like a rubber band about to pop.

"This is nothing but murder, pure and simple," he told the guards, his nostrils flaring. He moved to the opposite side of the tent away from the youth where he lowered himself onto the ground.

Kelly recoiled violently when she spied Rafael and his friends. "You can't leave us with them!" Kelly pleaded to the MPs. "They want to kill us!" She stretched on tiptoe to glare in the MP's face. Green eyes flashed emerald fire.

The MP bestowed a supercilious gaze upon Kelly. "You're safe here. They're handcuffed."

Nick spoke up, disgusted, although not completely surprised. "You know darned well we're not safe with them. They tried to kill us last night." He kicked his toe in the dirt at the foot of the MP in charge, a tall lanky Tech Sergeant. "At least move the girl..."

"We'll be right outside. The girl's safe," the sergeant spoke in a dead pan voice. He spit in the dirt next to Nick's boot as if challenging Nick to combat.

When Nick opened his mouth to protest further, the sergeant shoved his gun barrel in his face. "I don't want any trouble. Understand? I don't want to be in this alligator pit any more than you do."

When Nick remained defiantly silent, the sergeant bent toward him, raising his voice like a drill sergeant. "Understand, pretty boy?"

"Understood," Nick muttered, narrowing his eyes. Perspiration trickled down his neck to his back. Gnats buzzed around his face.

The soldiers pivoted on their heels starchly. They ducked outside the tent. Nick presumed they stood guard just outside. "Good riddance!" he muttered. If they wouldn't help they might as well go.

The youth remained silent, reverent even, until the MPs stepped out of the tent, except for a faint smirk twisting Rafael's lips that matched the sinister glint in his eye. One couldn't be arrested for a facial expression but if they could, Nick thought, that would be paramount to murder.

Despite the fact that the youths were handcuffed like himself and Kelly, their presence filled Nick with dread.

"Are you all right, Cincinnati?" Nick jerked his head, motioning for Kelly to sit by him. She hurried over to him, stealing covert glances at the youth. She lowered herself gently, squatting first, then putting her legs out awkwardly.

"Except for bearing a remarkable family resemblance to Quasimoto, I'll survive." She spoke lowly, wincing. "How about you? You bumped your head." Her voice oozed sympathy and concern.

"I'll survive," he lowered his voice to a mere whisper. "But we've got to check out of this hotel before our friends figure out their steel toed boots are lethal weapons." Lowering his lips, he brushed hers briefly.

"Isn't that so sweet? The lovebirds are all lovey dovey in the corner!" Rafael taunted, his black eyes glittering. His friends laughed, guffawing. Rafael showered dirt across the tent with the toe of his boot.

"Ignore them. The less said the better." Nick didn't want Kelly's anger to flare up.

"What's wrong, cat got your tongue, gringo?"

"Like he got yours?" Kelly retorted, flashing a mischievous smile, flicking her sun kissed hair behind her shoulder.

Rafael screamed an obscenity, his face contorting terribly. The other youth chuckled, apparently enjoying the joke.

Nick rolled his eyes Heavenward. "Keep your cool. Just because they're handcuffed, don't think they can't kick, bite and stomp the living you know what right out of us."

Kelly's eyes glittered like emerald treasure in the dim light. His arms ached to hold her. He settled for a kiss.

Lowering his head, he captured her lips in a lingering kiss. They tasted sweet, like honeysuckle, felt soft as a newborn's tender skin.

Kelly pulled away, biting her lower lip. "What are we going to do? If I scream loud enough someone's got to get us out of here..."

"Don't count on it. The colonel is hoping someone will finish the job he started. He probably put us in here on purpose."

"Don't be so stuck up over there. We want to talk too." Rafael jeered. He strained to stand. He paced back and forth like a caged panther, glaring at them. His expression looked puzzled as if he were trying to figure out a collegiate equation—probably how he was going to get pay back from them with handcuffs on. It wouldn't take him too long to figure it out.

"Listen carefully, Cincinnati. We may only get one chance and we'd better make it darn soon."

"You got a plan to get us out of here?" she whispered in his ear. Her warm breath tickled his sensitive inner ear but he steeled himself not to kiss her again.

He nodded his head once. Then he leaned closer to her so he could speak in her ear. "My keys are in my front right pants pocket. You'll have to reach in and get them out. Maybe my handcuff key will unlock these."

"King wouldn't like it if he knew I were sticking my hands down a man's pants..." she quirked a lascivious eyebrow, grinning like a hyena.

"King isn't here," Nick murmured, heat suffusing his veins, despite his resolve to remain cool as an ice cube. "And as you keep telling me, you're a big girl now. Do it!"

"I told you to stop whispering over there!" Rafael screamed. He stomped his feet. "You're making me real nervous!"

"How can I reach them?" Kelly whispered, keeping one eye on the boy.

"We'll have to twist around a bit, but you have to do it. Put the keys in my hands. Keep your hands by mine so I can unlock you. Then unlock me." Nick scooted around. "Try to be inconspicuous. I don't think our friends will keep our secret."

"They'd sooner kill us," she agreed, a smile frozen on her lips.

"I'm going to turn now and you reach in my pocket. That guy's like a lit powder keg."

"I oughta kick the crap right out of you gringo. You think those guys are gonna stop me?" He stomped his feet in a temper tantrum. "They don't care if I beat you up. Maybe I should come over there right now..."

"No need, man. Look, I'm sorry..." Nick said, wanting to appease the youth. To Kelly, Nick whispered, "The kid's spoiling for a fight. It's going to happen unless we escape soon. Hurry up and get the keys and give them to me."

"You ain't sorry gringo. You ain't sorry one bit. Rich bastards don't care for poor kids like us."

"I care," Nick assured him.

Good. The kid seemed distracted. He was still talking and he could feel Kelly getting close to the keys. It shouldn't be much longer. He had to ensure they had enough time.

"Then why'd your woman throw that monster in my face? Why am I scarred up?"

"You scared her man. You scared the cat. She can't help it if the cat jumped up and scratched you. If she'd held onto it, it would've clawed the both of you."

"You expect me to buy that? She knew what she was doing. You'd better keep a leash on that wildcat." He paced back and forth. Nick could see his hands clench and unclench. "Is she good in the sac, gringo?" Rafael's eyes glittered. The end of his lips crooked up.

Kelly blushed, turning her head away. She had the keys, even though she had contorted herself to do it. He felt her bristle at Rafael's last remark. He didn't know how long she could hold her tongue. So far so good.

"That's none of your business, man." Nick turned slowly so that his back was to the wall. "Can you control a cat? They do what they want to do.

"You drew knives on us," Kelly murmured accusingly. Her finger nails raked Nick's open palm.

Shivers chased down his spine but he schooled himself to remain stock still. Years of survival training paid off.

She fumbled with the keys. A click sounded like a sonic boom. The cuffs popped, falling off. He waited for the clang when they hit the ground, but it never came. Kelly must have caught them.

"Smart girl," he murmured, praising her. The tension on his arms relaxed immediately. He felt her dangle the keys over his outstretched hands. He grabbed for them. On the third try, he snagged them.

Unlocking Kelly took mere seconds.

"Now what? How do we escape? Crawl under the flaps?" Kelly suggested hopefully. "Do you think the guards left? They seemed pretty confident we're secure." Kelly turned her back to the tent hurriedly. She leaned against him.

"I don't know, Cincinnati. Maybe we can slip away in the dark."

"That'll be hours! They'll catch us before then," she reminded him urgently. "We've got to go now."

"I thought I told you two to stop whispering! Something funny's goin' on gringo. I don't believe you." Rafael stomped over to Nick and stood over him glowering down. "I think my friends and I ought to teach you two some manners."

"Oh yeah?" Kelly said. "First, you gotta know what they are." Kelly jumped to her feet, sticking her neck out like a Bantam fighting hen.

"I told you to put a leash on her man! I ain't gonna take this talk from no woman. My mother doesn't dare speak to me this way!"

"Who are you kidding? You don't have a mother. You were hatched!"

"Cincinnati!"

The other youth stood, encircling Nick and Kelly. Their expressions from mildly amused to maniacal. A death squad.

Kelly didn't seem to care. She fumed like a hot spring.

"Are you calling me chicken?"

"If the shoe fits..."

"Get them!" Rafael yelled. He let out a wild scream, then swung his leg back for a kick. "Get those..."

"Nick! Watch his feet!" Kelly warned, ducking out of the way.

Nick rolled out of the way just in time. Rafael's foot whooshed by him with enough force kill a grown man. Instead, Nick grabbed the youth's leg, felling him, jumping lithely to his feet, swirling to land a karate kick to another target. He got two youths in one kick.

"Bull's-eye!" he murmured, grinning.

The fourth circled Kelly menacingly. When he lifted his leg to kick, she side stepped and grabbed his leg as she'd seen Nick do to Rafael. But she had no technique and it knocked her off balance. She sprawled on the ground.

Nick leapt in the air, feet and hands out in perfect karate position. He landed on the youth with all his weight, knocking the kid out.

"Nick, behind you!" Kelly yelled.

He turned just in time to see Rafael running at him like a battering ram, head lowered into ramming position. Nick sidestepped again, then lowered a karate chop on Rafael's neck when he passed. Rafael crumpled to the dirt, out cold. The other youth struggled to rise. Nick flung one over his shoulder. He rammed his head into the second's stomach, doubling him over.

"I didn't know that you're a regular one man fighting machine."

"What's the commotion in here?" one of the guards yelled. Nick stood with his back to the front of the tent, blending into the canvas with his camouflage fatigues.

The small guard entered, his gun pointed inside. Nick kicked the gun out of the guard's hands. A shot rang out. When the guard tried to pull back out of the tent, Nick lowered a well aimed chop on the soldier's neck before he knew what hit him. Grabbing the mans collar, he dragged him inside, heaving, grinding his teeth in supreme effort. "You're heavier than you look," he mumbled under his breath.

Kelly ran to get the gun. She pointed it at the opening of the tent, waiting for the next guard who dared enter.

Two more guards plunged in like an unsuspecting tourist into a nest of alligators. Nick kicked the guns out of their hands and felled one with a punch to his stomach.

But Nick was no match for two trained soldiers at once. The other held his own and the men circled each other, their arms arched, looking for weakness in their enemy.

"Hold up your hands or I'll shoot!" Kelly promised, her aim unwavering, her expression deadly.

The last guard froze. He obviously hadn't seen Kelly in the shadows.

"Stay right where you are. Lift your hands above your head." Kelly chuckled mirthlessly. "I always wanted to say that!"

The guard obeyed, not moving one muscle the wrong way. Nick reached in his pocket where he had put his handcuffs and pulled them out. "Lower your hands slowly."

"No funny stuff, or I'll shoot!" Kelly said, her tone Machiavellian.

"Let's make like a tree and leave!" Nick snapped the handcuffs on the guard sounding like a steel prison door slamming shut. "You won't get away. This place has tighter security than Ft. Knox."

"Oh, no? Watch us," Kelly said, flipping her hair regally.

"Let me go or I'll scream," the guard said.

Nick looked at Kelly. He smiled. Then he brought the butt of his gun down on the guard's neck. The guard slumped over slowly, unconscious.

"What do we do now? We can't just walk away," Kelly whispered, her eyes shifting right to left. "Can we?" she enveloped him emerald fire.

"If we look like the guard we can. We're already in fatigues," Nick said.

"I'm beginning to like the way your mind works." Kelly walked to the small guard. She looked down at him for a few seconds. "Help me roll him over. His clothes should fit me. I'll look like an MP.

"The prettiest MP in the service," Nick chuckled. "What about me?" Nick undressed the man hurriedly.

"You'll be my prisoner this time. Only make believe."

Nick raised an eyebrow. "That might work. But we have to hurry. Who knows when they'll awake or reinforcements will show up?"

Nick threw the clothes in Kelly's face. "Pay back, wench! Put them on now."

Kelly slipped into the man's uniform quick as lightning.

Nick slid the MP arm bands over her wrists and slid them up her arms. "Perfect. Grab the rifle. Let's go!"

Kelly started for the door.

"Not that way!" Nick stooped and retrieved the man's hat. "Stick your hair under this. And keep your face straight. Act like you know what you're doing."

"What am I doing?" Kelly furrowed her brows together, lifted her small chin.

"Escorting your prisoner to your jeep - to transport him downtown."

"Cool!"

"Maybe I should be the MP and you be my prisoner."

"Uh-huh. It's my turn. Anyway, we don't have time to waste. I'm already dressed for the part."

Kelly stepped out of the tent, scouting the area. The coast loomed clear. "Come out."

When Nick came out, Kelly put the gun in his back. Sunlight glinted off the steel barrels.

"Go easy on that Cincinnati. Is the catch on?"

"Of course the catch is on. I know what I'm doing," Kelly asserted, smiling devilishly. "I've been shooting longer than I was in school."

"I really hope you know what you're doing, Cincinnati."

"Stop worrying. The catch is on." Kelly prodded him with the tip of the barrel. "Do you wanna talk and get caught or move and get outta here?"

"You'd better not shoot me in the back, Cincinnati."

"Are you threatening a woman with a gun in your back?" She laughed.

"Point taken!" Nick started walking, watching for any hint of movement, anything out of the ordinary. "Let's go! Walk until you see an abandoned jeep then act like you're making me get in. I'll pretend to have handcuffs on."

"Good idea."

A few people looked at them curiously, but no one stopped them.

"Keep your eyes peeled for a deserted jeep. One with keys in it preferably." His gaze darted back and forth. "If necessary, I can hot wire it."

"You're full of surprises, Lieutenant." She chuckled. "I thought you were too straight arrow to steal a jeep."

"I learned a few tricks in the Air Force." Nick admitted only as much as he had to. No one knew the extent of his real training. Only those with Top Secret Security clearance could ever delve in his records...

He did his level best to forget most of that training, to block it from his conscious memory.

"Jeep at three o'clock," Nick murmured. "Point me in that direction."

Nick shifted his path. Kelly followed. "Keep your eyes open for trouble."

Nick looked around. "Okay, hop in," he instructed, jogging to the driver's side.

The major stepped out of the tent and strode purposefully for the jeep. The captain followed like a trained watch dog, speaking in the major's ear.

Nick froze, uncertain what to do. Would it be better to take this jeep and run? And possibly have the entire guard chasing them, shooting? Or keep walking and hope they went unnoticed?

Nick was torn till the last moment. He had just about decided to jump in the jeep when he veered slightly to his right and kept walking.

"Carry on, soldier," the major greeted Kelly, tilting his head. He hopped into his jeep and drove away. Mud churned beneath wheels that groaned, hissed and slipped.

"That was close!" Nick whispered, wiping perspiration from his brow. He rubbed his stubbled jaw line, pondering their next move.

"I don't know if this is such a good idea. Maybe we should just walk out of here." Kelly shook her head.

"If we don't get out of here fast, and a set of wheels is the only way, they'll catch us quicker than you can say Rambo." When Nick felt Kelly hesitate, he reiterated, "It's our only chance. If they catch us again, they won't jail us in a tent. There'll be cement walls so high you won't know if it's day or night."

"Over there at 7 o'clock."

"Move quickly. Let's get this one."

"What if it doesn't have keys?"

"Then I'll have to hot wire it."

"Won't that take a long time?" she bit her lower lip.

"Not long." Nick smiled devilishly, his fingers twitching.

Nick looked around him, pleased when he saw no one else in sight. "Go for it!"

They ran the last few feet to the jeep, mud sucking their boots under, trying to prevent escape.

Nick hoisted himself over the side, landing in the hard seat with a loud thump.

Kelly struggled to climb in. She slipped in the mud, clinging to the door, her knuckles white.

Holding out his hand to her, he hauled her inside.

She fell unceremoniously, sprawled all over the seat. Her hands clutched thin air. Her feet kicked the wind.

"Sit up before someone notices you." Nick fumbled to hot wire the jeep. "Damn!" he mumbled, struggling to get the wires to spark.

"Won't it start," she whispered, a worried gleam in her eyes.

Nick's lips turned down. "Take those MP arm bands off and pull that hat over your eyes. Don't look anybody in the eye. And keep your mouth shut! Maybe we can pull this off yet."

Suddenly, the engine purred to life. "Good girl." Nick patted the dashboard. He moved the jeep out, turning a corner at the next intersection in case the owners came out and saw it had been *borrowed.*

"Are you implying that I have a big mouth?" Kelly arched one finely shaped brow. Her lips twisted.

"If the shoe fits!"

"I oughta teach you some manners..."

"Shush! We're coming up on the exit. Let's try faking it through." Nick looked studiously ahead, a bland expression on his face. Compared to crossing enemy lines in the Gulf War, this would be a piece of cake. Hopefully.

"And if we can't?" Kelly whispered. She pulled the brim of her hat further over her eyes. Her beautiful face lay in shadow. Her soft lips pursed in a straight line.

"We might have to barrel through," Nick murmured looking for other escape routes, spotting none.

Kelly slumped in her seat, her chin touching her chest.

"Sit up Cincinnati! They'll know we're hiding something for sure if you act that way."

"I don't like this," he gritted through tightly clenched teeth, barely audible. He fixed his gaze straight ahead, looking out the corners of his eyes as he'd been taught by the military.

"Neither do I." She swatted a pesky mosquito away from her face.

"We're almost to the gate. Act nonchalantly."

"We might get shot and I'm supposed to be nonchalant?"

"That's right. But hold on tight."

"You don't have to tell me that," Kelly chuckled, clutching her seat.

"And Cincinnati...."

"Yeah?"

"If bullets start flying, duck!"

"That, you don't need to tell me," she concurred, turning her face toward his.

Nick pursed his lips. "We're almost home free. Maybe you won't have to"

A guard checked incoming and outgoing vehicles. Randomly. He inspected ID cards, comparing them to the vehicle's drivers.

Only one vehicle remained in front of them then it would be their turn to pass through. Nick didn't recognize the man. Good. Maybe he wouldn't notice something amiss about them either.

The soldier left the truck in front of Nick's jeep to answer a cellular phone. He spoke into it then turned his back to Nick and Kelly. Then he turned, looking around him, his gaze settling on Kelly who sat in her seat frozen.

"I don't like this." Nick had a bad feeling. He checked his rear view mirrors then looked around him, trying to act casual. He caught movement out of the corner of his eye. Soldiers crept upon them, guns drawn, their expressions bleak.

"They're onto us. Hang on tight!" Nick revved the engine. Stomping the gas pedal, he forced the jeep to move. It lurched forward, almost hitting the truck ahead of him.

"Wrong way!" He swore under his breath. Backing up like a bat from hell, he swerved around the truck, plowing down loose wire fence. The jeep jumped into the air, landing with a thud.

"Ouch!" Kelly crouched in her seat. Her rifle almost flew off the seat, out of the jeep. She grabbed it at the last second, as it tilted toward the ground. A shot exploded next to Nick's ear.

"Crikes Cincinnati! I thought you put the safety on?"

"I did!" When Nick turned an accusing gaze on her, Kelly shrugged her shoulders, smiling, "Sue me."

"Point it the other way before you kill me with that blasted thing!"

Gunfire exploded from behind.

"Why does everybody try to kill me?" Nick muttered.

"Everybody?" Kelly asked, her brows lifted, a question in her green eyes.

"Yeah. This pretty much happens wherever I go," he admitted. Putting the pedal to the floor, he coaxed the jeep to give him everything she had. He swerved in a criss cross pattern to avoid bullets flying thicker than a mosquito storm in the Everglades.

Kelly's hat flew off and her hair blew in her face. She fought a losing battle to put it and keep it behind her ears.

"Can you shoot that thing?"

"I'm a crack shot, remember? But I've never tried to aim a gun from a flying car before." She pushed hair out of her face again.

"This is your chance. I hope you're a quick learner."

"Why?"

"I want you to shoot out their tires. Do you think you can do that?" Nick slid what he hoped was his most serious glance at Kelly. "Remember, if you shoot one of them, we're good as dead."

"You really know how to apply the pressure."

"Just trying to keep us alive. And aim low. Try now. They're gaining on us."

The guards shouted something at them. But Nick couldn't hear.

Probably "stop or they'll shoot". It might as well be "stop and we'll shoot." No way.

"Can you hear what they're saying?" Nick yelled.

Kelly shook her head. "I can't hear them in all this wind. I can barely hear you!"

Crawling up in her seat, she crouched low. She aimed the gun, ducking down when gunfire whizzed by her cheeks so closely she could feel the burn of gunpowder. She cuddled her singed cheek. Behind her, the windshield shattered into a billion slivers of glass. She brushed them off her clothing and the seat.

"Try again, Cincinnati."

Kelly raised her head, leveled the rifle, then peered down her sights. Then she squeezed the trigger. The force of the gun's kick knocked her back into the dashboard.

"Are you okay?"

"Just winded. I'm not finished yet." She cracked a mischievous smile.

"Try again. Brace yourself."

Kelly hefted her rifle to her shoulder, squinting one eye, peering down the barrel. Gunfire shot out like a Roman Candle, a bright flash of light nearly blinding him at this close range, acrid smoke tickling his nostrils. She checked her cartridge. "We're almost out of bullets."

More gunfire rang out. Nick swerved, throwing Kelly against him. Kelly's gun fired into the air. Nick ducked.

"Are you okay? Sorry about that. How many bullets are left?"

"Two."

"You've got to make this count. They're gaining on us!"

Again, Kelly aimed her rifle. Her expression was one of intense concentration. This time, when she squeezed the trigger, her bullet sailed into the air, landing true.

A huge explosion rocked the jeep, pushing it to the road's shoulder. He held the wheel with all his might, keeping it from whipping out of his fingers, sending them into oblivion. Skidding tires screeched like demons on Halloween night. Peering into the rear view mirror, he smiled when he saw that Kelly's bullet had indeed blew out a front tire of the first vehicle.

"Yes!" she yelled, hopping up and down in her seat. Her hair, brighter than fully bloomed marigolds, bounced buoyantly on her shoulders.

The jeep skidded to a halt. A second, followed closely by a third jeep followed.

"You only have one bullet left?"

"Yep. What now, Nick?" Kelly's eyes grew wide again. Her fingers clutched the butt of the powerful rifle.

"Don't know, Cincinnati. I just don't know. We'll try to lose them. If you can shoot out a tire in the next jeep that would only leave us one to lose. Do you think you can do it?"

"Those are pretty astronomical odds and I'm not a betting woman."

"Luck had nothing to do with it. Try again." He smiled what he hoped was a reassuring smile.

Kelly turned, her jaw set determinedly. She aimed carefully. She concentrated so long this time he wondered if the trigger had frozen solid. As she squeezed the trigger, gunfire rang out from behind. It would only be logical that the guard would try to shoot out their tires as well. he swerved to avoid being hit. Jerked against his shoulders, Kelly missed.

"Damn! That was our last chance."

"This is going to call for drastic measures."

"How drastic?" Wide green eyes clashed with his gaze.

"Whatever escape presents itself, we've got to take. I'm usually at the other end of this chase." He gritted his teeth.

"Usually?"

"Always - except maybe when I was in the Air Force." Nick glanced at Kelly quickly. He shot her a reassuring smile. "And one or two other times."

"What if nothing presents itself?"

"We'll have to make our own. I have a few tricks up my sleeve," he admitted, hoping he wouldn't need too many more tricks.

"Someday, I want to hear what you did in the Air Force. If we get out of this alive..."

"We will, if I can help it."

"They're getting closer Nick. If you've got an idea or some

black magic you'd better use it now."

Nick looked around. He forced himself to think. What options did they have? Mighty few. That's what. The only thing he could think of might just get them killed...

Nick glanced in his rear view mirrors. The guard bore down on their tail. Unless he did something to prevent it, they'd catch them in a few moments. What was to stop them from saying they'd shot Nick and Kelly in the chase? If he didn't take chances, they might be dead anyway.

He had to take the chance.

"Hang on for your life, Cincinnati!" Nick grimaced, intent on his plan. Suddenly, he swerved dead right, almost throwing Kelly out of the jeep.

She struggled to sit right, bracing herself against the dashboard.

"I hope you can swim," he muttered, his eyes straight ahead.

"What are you planning?" she asked, her tone hushed, deadly quiet.

"See that canal?" He inclined his head slightly, his eyes still fixed straight ahead. From the corner of his eye, he saw several expressions flit across her expressive face.

"What canal?" she peered around.

"Straight ahead."

"The one without a bridge?" she exclaimed, her eyes widening further. She clutched his forearm, her finger nails digging into it .

"Uh huh."

"You can't!" Kelly gasped. "You'll kill us for sure."

"No choice. I couldn't stop now if I wanted to."

"What are you going to do?"

"Jump that canal. It's narrow. If I can hit that little incline just right, we'll make it."

"If? That's an awfully big *if!*"

"People I've chased have done it to get away from me."

"And you jumped it?" Kelly's eyes narrowed to mere slits. She dropped her hands to her lap, clasping them together in prayer position.

"I wasn't that desperate. Let's hope they aren't either."

"So you've never done it before?"

"There's always a first time... Hold on!" Nick grinned, enjoying the game. Why didn't women get a kick out of this? Nothing had been this exhilarating in longer than he could remember.

She screamed when the tires left solid ground.

# Chapter Ten

"You're crazy! Do you hear me? Completely certifiable!" Kelly screamed into the wind. She wasn't sure he heard her.

She watched Nick's knuckles turn white on the steering wheel when the jeep left solid ground. She bit her lip to stop herself from screaming and held onto her seat with all her might. The wind whipped her hair around her face. Although it bothered her, she didn't dare let go of her seat. She couldn't if she wanted to. Her fingers felt paralyzed like the rest of her. Had she ever been so scared?

Well, maybe once or twice since she'd met Nick, the lunatic.

When she glanced at Nick, he was still grinning like a cat in a chicken coop. He was having fun! The man had no sense. Then, she softened. She felt sure her brothers, especially Kevin, would behave exactly the same. Danger seemed erotic to men like moonlight to women. They thrived on danger. Maybe, just maybe, a tiny voice teased in the depth of her mind, that's what attracts you so much to this man... She shook her head to make the unwelcome voice disappear.

"The jeep's pointing up and out. That's good. It's not a far jump...just a little canal." Nick's voice battled the wind.

"*Just* a little canal?" She looked down into the swirling murky water. Her reflection looked distorted, almost ghostlike. It looked anything but *little*. Dangerous. Frightening. Pure death. They were all synonyms that popped into her mind. She knew that if they fell into it, they'd be sucked down so fast, so deep that water would become their eternal grave.

Her gaze riveted to the far bank. She knew it was crucial that he keep a good grip on the steering wheel so that the jeep land right side up and keep going. There were so many *ifs.* If they didn't fall, if they didn't land just right, if the guard didn't shoot them, if the guard didn't jump the canal after them... Her head pounded with the capital letters I F, over and over like some ancient, evil mantra.

"Are they following us? Are they still shooting?" Nick's thoughts mirrored her own. He didn't sound the least bit scared.

Finally, after what seemed an eternity of flying through the air, wondering if the jeep would drop straight into the water, the jeep landed on the opposite shore with inches to spare. The back wheels spun, trying to clutch solid ground. Just when she feared they were slipping backward to their doom, the tires grabbed and propelled them to solid ground with a bump and grind.

The impact almost threw her out of the jeep like a roller coaster that loop-de-looped at that wild amusement park between Dayton and Cincinnati. They always had to have the largest, most thrilling ride in the country but she doubted they could top this ride.

She felt herself sliding like melted butter on a hot skillet, a sickening lurch rising in her stomach, a scream stuck in her throat. Then Nick grabbed her hand in his large, strong one and yanked her to safety just before she fell.

"We're alive! We made it!" She flung her arms around his shoulders, squeezing him with all her might. She kissed him square on the lips, thrilled to be alive. Her emotions road a Ferris wheel—twirling higher and higher, whipping around. Pure adrenaline scorched her veins. When she came down from this ride from hell, she'd land with a thud.

He shrugged loose. Untouchable like her macho brothers when they were doing one of their *guy things*. "We'll wreck for sure. Later." He struggled to regain control of the jeep as it swerved like a drunken sailor on his first shore leave in a year.

"I thought I'd never see Kevin or Dad again. Don't ever do that to me!"

"It was just an itty bitty jump..." He smiled, feigning innocence. He shrugged his broad shoulders as if to say "Oh well."

"There you go again!" Kelly punched him in the shoulder playfully. "It looked like the Grand Canyon!"

She turned in her seat, squatting on her knees, keeping an eye on the guard. Nick sped away, keeping one eye trained on his rear-view mirrors.

"Oh God, Nick. They're jumping too. Get us out of here!" Those IFs were getting larger, more ominous by the moment.

Nick stomped the gas pedal and sped away as fast as the abused jeep would permit. Tires spun in the mud like an old mixer in thick fudge brownie mix, threatening to hold them captive.

"Hurry, Nick!" She grabbed Nick's arm imploring him to soar like an eagle.

"They're not going to make it," he said with glib conviction. He pursed his lips and the scar on his cheek pulsed.

"How do you know?" Her eyes remained glued to the scenario unfolding behind them. The bright Florida sun shimmered in the dense haze, casting an ethereal glow over this unbelievable scene. She dare not breath until she knew their fate. Her brows furrowed together.

"They're not headed for the incline. They're going for a swim," he said as sure as if he promised. Or maybe he possessed some magical powers that would ensure his words would come true. Maybe he had a touch of Indian blood in his veins.

"It's diving in. They're jumping into the water," Kelly murmured watching the scene unfold in horror. They looked like the barrel full of monkeys she'd played with as a kid. Just like that little barrel, seemingly tons of soldiers flipped out in several ludicrous positions, arms and legs sprawled, clutching at nothing but air.

"Look at the way that guy's flipping in the air! He's going to be one sore puppy tomorrow." He laughed dryly. "Ouch! What a belly flop!"

"Oh God, Nick. Are there alligators in there?" She shivered, remembering her own close escape. Visions of the horrible monster filled her with dread. Those men didn't deserve that fate. After all, they were just weekend warriors far from home, leaving loving wives, girlfriends, mothers and little babies behind waiting for their safe return. They should be home drinking mint juleps on their Carolina verandahs, enjoying a pleasant Saturday afternoon.

"Could be. Sometimes I get calls about gators wondering into the city through the canal. Chelsea might have driven a few more in than usual."

The jeep stayed afloat for barely a moment, giant bubbles like a witch's brew boiled up around the jeep before it started sinking into the murky depths. Men scrambled ashore as if a nest of alligators snapped at their heels.

As if that weren't enough commotion, brakes squealed. Men screamed obscenities. Chaos erupted full force. It looked like a television newscast in slow motion.

"Another one's going in," she said. Her fingers clutched the back of the seat. Her hair whipped behind her. The third jeep stopped on the edge of the canal, its front tires hanging over the edge.

Soldiers scrambled to the back of the jeep to balance it until everyone climbed to safety. Then the jeep slowly somersaulted into the canal, barely missing the first jeep. Water plumed out of the canal, a fissure suddenly bursting forth.

"Would you look at that! They struck oil!" Nick laughed. He scratched his stubbled jaw. His Adam's apple throbbed.

Nick turned the jeep onto the road. It grunted and groaned, straining to stay in one piece. The frame shimmied beneath them.

"You think they'll follow?"

"They'll have their units watching for us." Nick cut his eyes to meet her astonished gaze. "We're not out of Cutler Ridge yet. Remember the barricades?"

"You mean we'll have to run another barricade?" She shook her head. "This can't happen a second time."

"I hope not. But it's possible. We'll have to ditch this jeep and these fatigues fast."

She thought she recognized this street. Then, again, all of Miami looked pretty much the same at the moment - totally, utterly destroyed. One gigantic nightmare. Yet, there was something very, very familiar about this particular street. That garage door spray painted with the bold red word ALLSTATE, triggered the connection.

"Isn't that Mattie's house Nick? The one where you saved the little girl?"

"The house of terror?" He furrowed his eyebrows. His ears wiggled.

"Look. Over there." She pointed to a pile of rubble, hope flaring in the pit of her belly. It tingled all the way down to her fingertips and her toes that curled inside her boots.

"There's my sedan, all right."

"We can ditch the jeep and get away clean!"

"You've been watching too many cops and robbers on television, Cincinnati. As long as the guard didn't contact my base and get my license we might make it... Still, even if they did, it'll be a lot less conspicuous than riding around in this wreck of a jeep. The bullet holes would give us away for sure."

"For sure," she said dryly, smiling tightly at him. "If it didn't rattle apart first."

"Hold on, Cincinnati!" Nick swerved to his right, into the grass and pulled behind the rubble that had been Mattie's house.

"It looks clear. I'll meet you at the car in a moment," he promised. He ran his fingers through his ruffled hair.

"Can't we go together?" She glanced around her expecting to see the guard, the police or another gang heading for them. Instead, the street seemed eerily deserted like a ghost town.

"I want to hide this baby a little better. A few palm fronds here and there outta do the trick. Then we won't be as conspicuous."

"If you say so," she murmured, not totally convinced she'd be safe without his protective presence. She'd really come to depend on him.

"Go on. I don't know how much time we have." He jumped out of the jeep and started leaning palm leaves and broken lumber against the sides, not wasting a motion. The muscles of his strong shoulders rippled beneath his green T-shirt. They reminded her of poetry in motion and at any other time, she'd have loved to stay and watch, but today, time seemed to be pressing in on them.

Still, she hesitated, uncertain of leaving his side. "You said you don't know if they'll be watching for your car..."

"Go! Act natural," he persuaded, his chest heaving. Perspiration beaded his brow. It soaked the back of his T-shirt.

"Hurry," she whispered wishing she could elicit a promise, knowing she didn't have the right to any such convention. Still, she lifted a silent prayer for his safety and well-being—and her own while she was at it.

It was hard to walk naturally when adrenaline pounded through her veins like a racehorse. She inhaled deeply, trying to calm herself, whiffing the scent of wet grass and acrid smoke. Every house in the neighborhood must have barbecue grills flaming with chicken, ribs and steaks grilling. Her mouth watered and her stomach grumbled. They'd hardly had a bite in more than forty eight hours, if stale candy bars even counted as a bite. Right now, she'd kill for a burnt hot dog or well done hamburger.

Nick opened the door and hopped in. His boots sounded like a hammer against the floor board. His knuckles looked skinned where he must have grazed them on broken boards and debris.

Nick tore off his shirt and flung it over the seat. His neck looked brick red and sore where the sun had beat mercilessly upon it. She wished she had some sun block and aloe gel to soothe him.

"I don't believe we jumped that canal! My hands are still shaking." She held her hands under Nick's nose. She grimaced when she saw how badly chipped her nail polish had become and quickly withdrew them. She eyed his bare chest where blonde hair coiled tightly, feeling the absurd desire to run her fingers through it.

"Are you trying to seduce me, Lieutenant?" She openly admired his bronzed skin.

"Can I?" Nick's voice turned husky. He pulled Kelly onto his lap, encircling her with his arms. She snuggled into his warmth, nibbling his earlobe. "Hmmm. That feels good."

Nick buried his face in Kelly's neck, flicking his tongue across the sensitive hollow of her throat. The stubble on his chin tickled her, making her squirm deliciously. Exquisite torture taunted her, awaking desires low in her belly. She allowed her hands free reign to glide over Nick's smooth back.

He lifted his head, then captured her lips, but not before she saw that his eyes had darkened to deep molasses, their intensity almost frightening. She opened her lips to his and drank deeply of his strength.

Warm experienced fingers kneaded her back. His thumbs rubbed in concentric circles sending her adrenaline soaring. They moved higher and higher, moving to her front then grazed the bottom of her full breasts.

She gasped and the pressure of his lips increased, his tongue thrusting deeper into her mouth.

Sharp tapping on the window dimly penetrated her consciousness. Slowly, she pulled away, looking at Nick knowing Heaven could not be better than being held in his arms but that Hell was nipping at their heels. It took every ounce of gall she possessed not to jump when she saw a face peering in the window at her. A face framed by fatigues. She wouldn't have been more alarmed than if she'd come face to face with Beelzebub himself, fiery red face, pointy horns and pitch fork.

"Follow my lead, Cincinnati. Don't panic," he whispered, his face a mask of jocularity. A seasoned thespian couldn't have changed expressions faster. His hand clasped hers and squeezed in reassurance. Maybe he was a chameleon.

She slid off Nick's lap and moved to her side of the seat. She allowed her hand to stay laced in Nick's like a tight corset. His strong fingers comforted her more than being crushed against her aunt's ample bosom.

Nick rolled down his window partially. "Did you need something?" Nick met the man's gaze squarely and sincerely. If she didn't know better, she would swear he was as genuinely honest as Ozzie Nelson.

The man looked inside the car before he spoke. He reminded Kelly of a cop who peered flashlights into cars on lover's lane in the dark to catch under age kids in illicit clinches. She felt heat creep up her cheeks remembering the sole time she'd been caught and her daddy had been called to come and get her from the police station. King Kerrigan hadn't been happy that night and the whole household had gotten an earful at two a.m.

She held her breath. Could he see the uniform shirt she'd flung on her floor? Or the green military T-shirt? The dark green should blend into the shadows like a thief in the night.

"This is a dangerous place to get intimate. And pretty public," he drawled in a thick Carolina accent.

"Yeah, I suppose it is," Nick chuckled. "I just came down from Virginia to get my bride and take her home. We were just so happy to see each other..." Nick laid on a thicker southern accent than normal. He could pass for a good old boy.

"Don't you have Florida plates?" the soldier asked. He walked to the back of the sedan and peered at the plate. Any moment Kelly expected it to burst into flames beneath his x-ray vision.

When he came back to the window, Nick drawled, "I flew down to Orlando and rented a car. I was anxious to get her home."

"We're newlyweds," Kelly said. She scooted next to Nick and kissed his stubbled cheek. It felt rough against her soft flesh and it fired unnamed desires in the pit of her belly.

Nick put his arm around her again and she could feel his warm breath on her neck. She snuggled close, wishing she could stay here forever.

"That's a good idea," the guard said. He lifted his gaze and looked around the neighborhood. "I wouldn't let my wife stay in this forsaken place either. All hell's breaking loose. You need to get her out of here now, before you get caught in crossfire..."

"Crossfire? As in bullets?" she feigned shock, using the excuse to snuggle closer to Nick. Her eyes widened. She looked up at Nick and implored, "We've got to leave now!"

"Settle down, honey. I'm sure you misunderstood."

"No sir, she didn't. Somebody stole one of our jeeps and there's a chase. Just go straight down this road and you'll get out of Cutler Ridge. Ah heck..." the soldier straightened to his full height. Kelly couldn't see his head any longer. "I'll show you the way. Follow me. Are you ready to go now?"

"The sooner the better," she said, shivering. She might not be surprised but she sure as tooting felt the urgency to get away from here.

Nick nodded his head. He found the T-shirt where it had fallen on the seat and he slipped into it. Turning the key in his ignition, he coaxed the engine to start. It purred to life. He slid into the road, following the military jeep like a sheep following a sheep dog.

"I don't like this, Nick. Do you think he's leading us into an ambush?"

"Naa. The military doesn't work that way. If he were suspicious, he would've arrested us on sight or called in reinforcements. You were pretty convincing back there, you know," he drawled, cracking a smile. His knuckles grazed her cheek in an endearment that caught her off guard.

"So we're safe?" She felt heat stealing up in her warm cheeks. She hadn't been exactly acting...

"I didn't say that exactly."

"What d'you mean? *Not exactly?"* She wrinkled her nose and bit her lower lip.

"I mean, that until we're clear and gone from Cutler Ridge, the guard and ditch this car, we could get picked up like that." Nick snapped his fingers. He turned a deadpan expression on her. "You're pretty hard to hide with that flaming red hair."

It was the most ominous snap she'd ever heard, the most serious face she'd ever seen. She stared, her mouth agape.

"Close your mouth. Our friend's probably got an eye on his rear view. Maybe, you should, uh, cuddle up to me. Make it look good," his voice dropped an octave, deep and dark, completely disorienting her.

"I can do that. To make it look - uh- good."

She snuggled close, draping her arms around Nick's neck. She let her fingers play with the hair curling behind his ears. One long finger traced his scar. She laid her head on his shoulder. He felt so warm, his hair felt so soft, his heart cantered in his chest evoking an answering response from her own.

"We're almost out of Cutler Ridge, Cincinnati." She felt his lips touch her forehead. They felt soft and warm. The corners of her lips turned toward the Heavens.

"Any sign of trouble?" she crooned, dropping kisses along his cheek, flicking the scar with her tongue.

"None yet. But if you make this look too good, we'll wreck for sure."

"Don't look in the mirror, then."

He chuckled, turning eyes full of merriment on her. "Did you just say what I thought you said?"

"Probably."

"You're incorrigible!"

She didn't cause trouble. Trouble just sort of followed her wherever she went. Her brothers laughingly referred to her as a trouble magnet.

Nick grinned, flashing a dazzling smile at her. He dropped another kiss on her forehead.

Her stomach somersaulted. This man drove her crazy!

The jeep honked and the sergeant motioned for Nick to stop and roll down his window. Nick did as he was bade.

"You headed to the airport?" The sergeant smiled at her and winked.

"Yeah. Which way do I go?" Nick pushed an unruly lock of hair out of his eyes.

"Take this road to the second intersection, then go left. Then follow the signs to the Palmetto Expressway. Get on going east. There'll be more signs. Just follow them. Can't miss them."

"Thanks Sarj!" Nick gave him a lop-sided grin and tilted his head in a friendly manner.

"Anytime, Sir."

Nick rolled up his window. He held up his hand in final farewell.

The sergeant saluted back touching the tip of his fingers to the brim of his fatigue cap.

Nick pulled out, following the sergeant's directions. When he got to the highway, he turned west.

"Where are we going?" She lifted her head from Nick's shoulder.

"Where any self-respecting tiger would go. To the Everglades."

She looked around her, awed at the destruction everywhere. Palm trees that only two days ago lined the highway like proud soldiers lay torn and broken at the side of the road. Gutted houses spray painted with messages to be seen by aircraft and helicopters lay open to the rain and relentless sun of noon day. Animals could roam in and out at will.

"Promise me you won't shoot Kenga or Rama," she said, pulling her eyes back to Nick.

He pursed his lips, remaining silent.

"Nick? Did you hear what I said?"

"I heard, Cincinnati."

"Well?" She hung on his words.

"I can't promise you that," he said in a dead pan voice.

"You must!" Disappointment flared and she sat back.

"I won't hurt them unless it's absolutely necessary," he muttered. "Tigers aren't known to be the warm, fuzzy type."

"But you think it might be necessary?"

"I don't know. I hope not." Nick turned to look at her, his eyes anguished.

"I told you they're harmless."

"Whatever got a hold of that boy wasn't harmless," Nick said, his eyes glued to the road. He swerved to miss half a roof blocking the left most southbound lane.

"You think Kenga and Rama did that?"

Heat shimmered up from the road in steamy tendrils. She supposed the August sun tried its damndest to dry Chelsea's tears but it looked like Hell's fires flamed extremely close to the surface.

"I don't know. It's possible." He leaned across her and opened the glove box. It fell open on her knees with a gentle whoosh. He dug around inside and pulled out dark sunglasses.

"Do we really know that's where Kenga and Rama are?"

"Turn on the radio. Let's take a listen." He slid the sunglasses on, shading his expression from her.

She shaded her eyes with her hand from the bright glare wishing she had a pair and leaned forward and flicked on the two-way radio.

Few cars ventured to brave this mouse maze and she could certainly understand why. If she had her choice, she'd have steaks and corn grilling on her balcony while she lounged around reading her newest Danielle Steel book. Let the Highway Department rack up a healthy dose of overtime getting the byways unclogged.

"Is this what the Eve of Destruction will look like?" Kelly mumbled, half to herself, half to Nick.

"We won't know the whole extent of Chelsea's destruction for a few years..."

"A few *years*?" Years seemed incomprehensible, like the equation for pi that stretched into infinity, never ending.

"We're still just discovering some of the ramifications from Andrew back in '94."

"How so? That's so hard to believe," she said, awestruck. Nothing seemed real in this tropical hell. It was topsy turvy as if the world of the Hobbits had suddenly become reality and Miami were underground and hidden from all but the most perceptive eyes.

"Last time, like this time, several zoo animals, as well as exotic pets escaped. Many were never recovered. Many mated in the wild with our local species." His voice became deathly quiet. Ominous like Rod Steiger announcing *And this is the Twilight Zone...*

"So species from all over the world, never meant to meet, are suddenly mating..."

"A regular melting pot. The biological diversity could be staggering. We don't know what our gene pools are anymore, what we have to contend with..." Nick swore when he swerved suddenly to miss a piece of debris tossed into the road like a tumbleweed by a strong gust of wind.

"What have you found so far?" she whispered picturing a Godzilla alligator that would make the one they wrestled look like a hatchling.

"A lot of weird looking birds. Reports of strange monkey and reptiles..."

"Reptiles," she whispered, chills chasing down her spine.

"Imagine if two poisonous snakes from different sides of the world mated... Their venom could produce the most deadly toxin known to man."

"Is anyone looking for them?"

"Rounding up the carnivores have to be our immediate priority," he murmured. His glasses slid down his nose and he looked at her over the rim of the glasses. "Do you propose we turn over every rock in the Everglades and take blood samples of every snake we find?"

"No-o-o," Kelly sighed. That would be impossible. "You still think Kenga and Rama mauled that soldier? That they might...?

Nick's sharp gaze cut to Kelly like a sharp knife. "It's entirely possible. I can't take the chance. Tigers are the largest carnivores known..."

Suddenly voices interrupted. Kelly jumped. Then she realized it was just the radio.

"...male and female suspects escaped from tent city near Cutler Ridge. Names are Lieutenant Nick Bradley of the Florida Fresh Fish and Wild Game Commission and Kelly Kerrigan. They may be driving a white Florida Highway Patrol sedan. They are armed and dangerous. Approach with extreme caution. Repeat. Suspects are armed and dangerous. Approach with extreme caution."

"Oh God, Nick. We're fugitives. They're looking for us!"

"Yeah and we're sitting ducks on the highway." Nick swerved, cutting across four lanes of traffic without warning, barely making the exit. Tires protested, squealing like a wounded gator. Kelly tossed about the cab like a bean bag. Her body ached from all the abuse that had been heaped upon it today and it screamed from this further indignity.

"What're we going to do?"

"Ditch this car and hide that red hair of yours. It's like a beacon. Put the hat back on and stick your hair up inside it."

"Where are we going to ditch the car? You mean we're going to *steal* another car?" Kelly groped in the back seat till she found the hat she'd been wearing.

"We *borrowed* the jeep. We gave it back, remember?" Nick grinned. Kelly's heart somersaulted again, leaping up and down in her chest.

"So we're going to *borrow* another car?" Sarcasm dripped from her lips. "We'll top the list of America's twenty Most Wanted for sure."

"Not even close, trust me."

"We'll end up like Bonnie and Clyde," she whispered watching a flamingo tiptoe across a dead end street, its wings flapping open.

"Now, you're exaggerating, Cincinnati."

"Which hat should I wear? The camouflage hat that screams "army"?" Kelly stuck the fatigue cap on her head and turned back and forth, wrinkling her nose. "Or your Mounties hat?" Kelly put Nick's highway patrol hat on. It engulfed her like a mixing bowl, hiding her eyes. Kelly pouted.

Nick snatched his hat away and tossed it behind him. "We'll

chance someone seeing your hair. Try to be inconspicuous for once."

Kelly folded her arms under her breasts and sat back in her seat. "Is this better?"

"Much." Nick checked his rear view mirrors. "I think I know someone who'll let us borrow her car..."

"Your girlfriend?" A man this fine couldn't hide in the Everglades all the time and if he did, he must have a few Indian maidens taking care of his needs.

"My mother."

"She lives nearby?" Kelly asked, surprised.

"Yep. On the edge of the Everglades, at the end of civilization. We're almost there." Nick's eyes darted back and forth watching for any signs of trouble. "If I hadn't had to leave the highway, we'd be there by now. We'll just have to use the back streets."

"What if they spot us?" Kelly's eyes roved as well. Her heart lurched every time she saw another car, even a shadow. She didn't know where she found the energy to be so jumpy. Her limbs felt so exhausted, she could sleep for a month and still be tired.

"We can always jump another canal." Nick chuckled.

"That's not funny..."

"Lighten up. My base is trying to straighten out this mess..." Nick reached over and squeezed her hand. His touch infused warmth into her chilly veins like a match to a cold camp fire.

"We'll be fugitives. My brothers will have to bail me out of jail..."

"We are fugitives, but not for long... with any luck. That colonel should be brought up on brutality charges. He forced us into an incident..."

"Incident?"

"If we're caught, stay silent. I've told my base this is an *incident* in progress and that the guard falsely imprisoned us after the colonel assaulted you."

"You're good."

"It's the truth. The trick is..."

"Trick?"

Nick looked at Kelly, his expression very solemn. "We have to stay alive long enough for my base to bring charges against him and get us absolved. It may take awhile seeing we fired at military personnel."

"They started it!" Kelly felt the warmth drain from her face.

"Precisely. They started it. They endangered our lives. We were acting in self-defense."

"But you think they may shoot us before we're cleared?"

"I don't know. I don't want to take any chances. We'll hide the car at mom's house, take hers and go."

"What if they're waiting for us there?" Wouldn't they think you'd hide out there?

"Hmmm mmm." Nick seemed to ponder that. "Maybe. But it should be several hours before they have that kind of information. "I know of a deserted barn where we can hide it."

"If Chelsea didn't tear it down."

"We'll see. It's just down this road."

"Is this the way to the Everglades?" Kelly asked. She looked about her at the thickening foliage. Houses stood further and further apart. Animals dared to play near the road. A pair of frisky deer ran and leaped over low bushes. Delighted, Kelly laughed.

She spied a speck in the distance that she couldn't quite make out even though she squinted her eyes. The afternoon sun proved just too bright. "Is that it?" She lifted her arm and pointed at the black dot.

"One and the same. It looks intact." Nick pulled into the old gravel drive, barely discernible as weeds covered it like a thick shag carpet. A few yellow and lavender wild flowers poked their heads out of the weeds, oasis of beauty on a barren plot of land.

Kelly eyed the dilapidated structure warily. "Are you sure it's safe?"

"It's sturdy enough. I used to swing from the rafters like Tarzan. It's built like a fortress"

"Or George of the Jungle?" She smiled and batted her eyelashes.

"Can you open the door and hold it while I drive in?" He ignored her sarcasm.

Kelly hopped out of the car and skipped to the door. It opened easily and swung wide without any prompting from her. After Nick drove in, she closed the door behind him and bolted it. It was dark inside, save for some light streaming in a high window.

Mold and musty hay tickled her nose. She put a finger under her nose to stifle a sneeze until she grew accustomed to the odor.

Nick turned off the sedan's engine, then hopped out. He strode to the trunk and popped it open. "Are you hungry, Cincinnati?"

"Starved! What d'ya got in there?" Kelly strode to Nick's side and peered into the trunk hoping for a miracle and settling for a sandwich. She stood with her hands on her hips.

"Warm water. Warm soda. Stale crackers. Potted meat. And melted candy bars." He waved a candy bar in her face that looked like it had been nuked in a microwave on full blast.

"No thanks." Kelly grimaced, shaking her head, passing on the whatever the chocolate had mutated into. "Warm water, crackers and potted meat, I s'pose." Not quite the miracle for which she'd hoped. Not even the sandwich. But safer than that rancid candy.

"Good choice. That's what I'm having." Nick leaned inside and rummaged around. "Hold this." He passed out the food and Kelly grabbed it. He leaned back inside the trunk. "Voila!" He pulled out a blanket and strode with it to the far corner of the barn.

"Where are you going?"

"We're going to have a picnic," he stated as if they didn't have a care in the world. He spread out a small pile of hay then waved the blanket in the air as if to form smoke signals.

"Here?" She peered at him to make sure he hadn't slipped off the edge of reality. He looked sane enough. But who was to say she retained enough sanity to be a judge of that?

"Sure. Take off your shoes. Make yourself at home." He lowered himself to the blanket and stretched his legs before him. He patted the blanket next to him. "Sit down."

Kelly passed the food and water into Nick's outstretched arms, then crossed her legs Indian style beside him.

"I'd give an arm and a leg for take-out Chinese right now," she mumbled, eyeing the cracker sandwiches dubiously. She grabbed a bottle of water, cracked the seal and took a long swig of hot, horrible water. She choked and coughed then spit it out.

"Take it easy on that stuff. It's more potent than hundred year old Scotch." Nick pulled the tab on the potted meat. "Hand me a cracker, Cincinnati."

Obediently, Kelly opened the air tight package of crackers and handed one to him.

"Thanks." Nick spread a mound of meat on it and handed it back. Kelly nibbled it tentatively. Not half bad, she mused, considering she hadn't eaten in hours and her stomach grumbled like a grouchy old man. Silently, she passed two more to Nick which he fixed for himself and another for her.

Nick sprawled out on the blanket and rolled onto his stomach. "Could you rub my back, Cincinnati? I must've strained a muscle. It's sore as the dickens." He cushioned his cheek on crossed arms, peering at her through drowsy, half-lidded eyes.

Kelly's throat constricted when she met his gaze. If that wasn't a sultry "come hither wench" sort of look he was giving her, what was? Of course, she didn't have much experience with men, not mature, drop dead gorgeous men like this one, anyway. But the look in his eyes sizzled like hot steaks on the grill.

She stuffed the cracker she held into her mouth, then wiped her sweaty palms down the legs of her fatigues. She stood on her knees and hobbled over to him. She tucked her hair behind her ears, then tentatively touched his shoulders as she towered over him. She kneaded his lower back gently, putting the heel of her hand just above the triangle where the bottom of the spine met his buttocks. She closed her eyes, reveling in the feel of his tautly coiled muscles beneath her hands.

Nick moaned. "You have magic fingers. Can you rub under my shirt?"

Kelly sucked in a deep breath, wondering if he had looked into her heart and read her deepest desire.

Last night when he had held her in his arms so tenderly and masterfully and kissed her in places only a lover should know, she had felt so exquisite, so alive, she thought she'd died and gone to Heaven. Pure primitive pleasure had burst within her like the formation of a new star, blinding, wild and very, very dangerous.

"Okay," she whispered huskily. Her toes curled and the little hairs on the back of her neck prickled. Gingerly she lifted his shirt letting her fingertips glide from the small of his back to the cleft between his shoulder blades.

Nick shivered against her fingertips. She felt the electric connection as sure as if she had heard a modem connect.

Growing bolder, Kelly kneaded his shoulders, then his neck, them permitted herself to play with the soft hair on the nape of his neck. His fair fascinated her, so blonde it emitted the sun's rays even in this darkened barn. She wanted to run her hands through his hair, to feel it's thick texture through her fingers.

When Nick moaned again, Kelly realized she was actually caressing his head. His obvious pleasure dissolved any lingering trace of nervousness and she leaned over and kissed his neck, just below his ear. Her breasts brushed his back bare of everything except the bandages she'd administered. His touch ignited sun bursts in the core of her belly.

She leaned over and kissed the side of his neck, letting her lips linger on an erratic pulse.

Slowly, Nick rolled over. His arms caught Kelly to him, pulling her hard again him, trapping her. She couldn't escape if she tried. She didn't want to.

Caught in a web of sensual pleasure, Kelly trailed kisses along Nick's throat, along the scar on his cheek, on his closed eyelids, reveling in the sound of his moans. His hands roamed her back molding her to him. One lifted her shirt, sneaking inside, raising it higher and higher until his fingers found the snap of her bra. He fumbled for a few moments, then sighed pleasurably when the little hooks came undone for him.

She felt wonderfully free and lifted her head a few inches to look into his half-lidded eyes.

"You're so beautiful. So soft..." Nick put his hand to the back of her head bringing her lips to meet his. He kissed her gently, playfully, sucking her bottom lip. His five o'clock shadow brushed her lips and her cheek. Then he grew more demanding. His hand slid to her breast, shoving the bra aside. He cupped her full breast in his hand, his fingers caressing in a hypnotic rhythm. When he started rubbing the nub between his fingers, she moaned into his mouth and writhed helplessly against him.

Nick pulled her slightly away from him and Kelly missing his warmth, gazed at him questioningly. His eyes looked like bottomless pits, dark and dangerous.

"Sit up so I can take off your shirt," Nick said huskily.

Kelly pushed herself up, still straddling his legs. His manhood bulged against her thighs igniting her desire. She raised her arms above her head and he lifted her shirt off and tossed her bra behind him with a quick jerk of his arm.

"So beautiful." Nick sat up putting his arms behind her. He bent his head, capturing her nipple between his lips. The stubble on his chin and upper lip tickled her. "I wish we had some coconut gel so I could spread it all over you—and lick it off." He suckled her breast. "Would you like that?"

Kelly moaned, feeling scrumptious. "That feels so good. So wonderful." She arched into him and he opened his mouth wider, suckling her breast. Her arms cradled him to her fiercely. Bending her head, she leaned her cheek against his soft hair.

After an eternity, or was it a brilliant sparkling second, Nick lifted his lips. Her breast felt cold and wet from where his tongue had bathed it. Flicking his tongue along her soft flesh, he trailed hot kisses to her other breast. He caught her extended nipple with his teeth playfully. Then he took it deeply into his mouth, moaning. His hand unbuttoned the button on her fatigues while his other hand slid inside caressing her bottom.

Kelly bent her head further and nibbled his ear. Her tongue lathed his earlobe with warm, wet kisses. When she delved her tongue inside his ear canal, Nick writhed against her.

Coconut gel would be nice, but definitely not necessary.

"Stand up. Take off your slacks."

While Kelly peeled her fatigues off, Nick lifted his hips and tore his own pants off, tossing them into whatever twilight zone her bra had disappeared into. His underwear followed faster than a speeding bullet. Their eyes never left each other. His sizzled with passion. Hers melted from the desire pulsating in the depths of her womb.

"Come here," he commanded seductively. Nick slid flowered panties down her legs. She stepped out of them impatient to be rid of the suffocating garment. She kicked them up in the air like a

Can Can dancer, laughing gleefully.

Reaching up, Nick's hands encircled her waist, bringing her down on top of him. "Touch me." He grabbed her hand and brought it to his gloriously hard shaft, clasping her fingers around it.

Feverishly hot, his pulsating shaft burned her hand. His hips moved up and down. His gaze never left hers. His hands cupped her free swinging breasts, kneading them, squeezing them, driving her to the brink of delicious insanity.

"Come here," he murmured huskily. His chest rumbled with his heavy breaths. A slick sheen covered him like gold dust.

Kelly nodded, unable to speak. Without hesitation, his hands slid to her waist and lifted her as easily as a feather. Large hands encircling her hips, he guided her on top of him. She slid down his shaft until finally, he completed her.

# Chapter Eleven

Kelly awakened groggily in a strange place that smelled damp, musty and musky. Somehow she felt warm and cold. Warmth flowed into her where something firm and hard, yet very soft lay against her. Cold penetrated where the faintest of breezes tickled her bare flesh sending tiny shivers dancing over her bare skin.

She opened her eyes wider. Memories flooded her. An arm jostled her and she slid her glance to Nick who snoozed beside her. His arm flung over her, his sleek with the night's perspiration, his body still molded to her. A contented smile played around the edges of his lips.

She hoped he dreamed of her. A smile played on the corners of her lips and she stretched like a cat awaking from a long nap.

What time was it anyway? How long had they slept? Was she dreaming all this?

Dream or reality, she never wanted these new sensations to end.

She snuggled closer to Nick, fitting herself to his long, lithe form, reveling in his warmth. She rubbed her cheek against his firm chest, listening to his steady heart beat. Her movements, slight as they were, stirred him to consciousness.

"Hmmm." His arms tightened around her, his head dipping, his lips seeking hers. The hair on his upper lip teased her. His lips captured hers languorously, lacking their earlier passion, yet seductive as wine and roses on a moonlit summer's night.

Fountains of light poured in through tiny cracks in the warped barn walls. Morning birds sang the songs they'd sung since the dawn of creation. Honeysuckle mixed with the smell of hay, tickling her nose.

She snaked her arms around his neck and pressed closer to him never wanting to let go or move out of this position.

He released her lips and lifted his head. His eyes blazed with unrequited passion. "You taste wonderful. I could drown in your lips." His voice sounded deep and rich and just a bit gravely. He kissed her again, sucking her lower lip into his mouth. Surprising her, he slapped her bare bottom resoundingly.

Her head snapped up. Puzzled, she searched his eyes, one brow lifted. "What was that for?"

"We've got to get up and get dressed."

"Do we have to?" She groaned languorously, not wanting to move away from his warmth. She cuddled closer against him and nipped his masculine nipple. When he shuddered against her, she smiled at her power over him.

"Yes. If we want to find your tigers." He lifted her off him then stood. She gazed at him appreciatively. God he looked so fine. So chiseled. So tanned. So very sleek. Even the Greek God Apollo could not possibly be so beautiful or so tawny. She let her gaze drink in his leonine beauty and grace. She ran a finger down the side of his sinewed leg.

He bent and held out his hand to her. She took it and he pulled her up against him for one more quick kiss. When she started melting against his lips, he captured one pert nipple in his mouth in a languorous suckle.

Her head arched back in pure ecstasy. Her silky hair tickled the small of her back.

"Get dressed or we'll never leave," he said against her lips. He turned so suddenly she stumbled. Their clothes lay tossed helter-skelter on the hay and he had to search to find all the pieces.

Her bra hung from an old pitchfork. Her panties had flown into the rafters. This seemed like a game of hide and go seek and Kelly loved every minute of it.

He picked hay from his slacks with a grimace before sliding his legs inside.

She took immense pleasure from the way his muscles rippled

when he bent and stretched, how he filled out the seat of his pants.

"Help me pack up. You grab the water and crackers. I'll get the blanket."

Within moments, all traces of their *picnic* had disappeared. He stowed the goods in the trunk then rooted around until he pulled out a shotgun. Taking out several magazines of extra ammunition, he placed a box of shotgun shells on the rear bumper, removed two, expertly sliding them into the rifle chambers. The remaining shells quickly disappeared into his various pockets. He searched the trunk again and this time came away with a long-barreled tranquilizer gun which he deftly slung a look over his shoulder.

"Are you planning all out war?" She leaned against the barn door chewing on a piece of straw. She liked the way he filled out his pants when he leaned into the trunk.

"Here." He turned suddenly, thrusting a rifle in her arms. "Only if necessary," he mumbled under his breath. "I'm hoping communication stays down for awhile and we can get in and out before they figure out how to read a map."

Eyeing him speculatively, a worried frown creased her forehead. Slinging the gun across her back, she adjusted the straps so it fit snugly. She felt like Clint Eastwood in an Italian western.

Was he still hell-bent on shooting Kenga and Rama?

Oh, she knew the rules. Very well. Too well. Public safety remained the bottom line, the absolute, non arguable rule. It's just that she knew her tigers. She and her family had coddled them from tiny cubs. She'd bottle fed and bathed them. They were completely domesticated and would not, could not hurt anyone.

Could they?

She'd wear the gun just in case they ran into one of the million and one other predators she didn't feel sure were so safe.

Of course, Nick and the rest of the world didn't know this. Not too long ago, a zoo keeper in the West Palm Beach Zoo had been mauled by a tiger and one of Nick's colleagues had had to shoot the creature. The press had had a field day with the attack, especially when the lieutenant—the strong, silent, masculine type—had started crying on national television.

"She won't mind your bringing an unexpected guest?"

"One thing you'll learn about Mom is that she loves visitors. Just watch out she doesn't talk your ear off. She spends way too much time alone with her animals."

She looked pointedly at the puke green fatigues that accentuated her curves better than a Wonder Bra and grimaced before she glanced up at him. Putting sugary sweetness into her voice, she asked, "She won't find it strange that we show up in Army fatigues, carrying enough ammo to blow up Miami?" As used as her Aunt Meghan was to her family's eccentricity, such a sight might throw her into a coma.

"There's not much I do that surprises her anymore." He slid his insidious silver sunglasses over the bridge of his nose and he transformed from the warm, teasing Nick to the cool, aloof lieutenant. He turned those vacant orbs on her and she wondered what he was thinking.

"Like jump canals with your jeep?" she asked dryly. She rubbed her sore rear end with the flat of her hand. It tingled as if to tell her it never wanted to see a jeep or car chase or it would disown her. "I won't underestimate you again."

Without warning, he leaned forward and stole a kiss. She couldn't hide her surprise when he backed away as fast as he'd captured her lips.

"Like that?" Traces of laughter mocked her and she glowered at him.

Tilting her nose in the air, she play acted at studiously ignoring him, even if every nerve ending in her body stood at attention longing for more contact. But he didn't deserve her attention after that crack, even if it meant depriving herself of his.

Not that he dwelled on her abrupt change of mood. He pushed the heavy barn door open then shut it behind her.

She turned and walked backwards several steps, perusing the old barn, it looked out of place, even out of its century so close to ravaged Miami. No one would think to look for Nick's car in there, would they? Rotting wood, peeling, faded paint and most of all, it's precarious lopsidedness made it an unlikely candidate for asylum. It looked more like an Edgar Allen Poe nightmarish house than a sanctuary. Or a motel.

She couldn't suppress the heat that climbed in her cheeks at the memories of last night in that barn. And now she was going to meet the man's mother looking like G .I. Jane. She shook out her hair, finger combing it in case tattle-tale straw stuck in it.

"What are you doing?" Nick backtracked and peered at the top of her head. "Did a wasp land in there?"

"No. Just checking..." She almost told him what for, then caught herself. It wouldn't do to let him know her thoughts were still with him last night – or his mother. *The Rules* would crucify her. Then of course, they would anyway.

A knowing grin swathed his too handsome face. His chest seemed to puff out in his green T-shirt.

She felt a sprig of hay and tugged at it self-consciously. Several fell out at her feet. Twisting, she brushed some off her shoulders to the sound of his snickers.

He laughed the first real laugh she'd heard out of him and she stopped and glared. "It's not that funny."

"Afraid my mother will guess?"

The heat in her cheeks increased fifty degrees, maybe one-hundred. "I don't know what you're talking about." She turned around, chin held high, eyes straight forward, shoulders squared. Schooling her thoughts to behave themselves, she trudged forward through the high wet weeds, her toes tingling when dampness enmeshed them.

Heavy hands fell on her shoulders, slowing her step. Hot breath rasped her neck and he nipped her ear. "Yes you do. You're completely transparent."

"Thanks." She twisted away from those hands that were sending electric charges through her. "Most men think I'm the mysterious type." Absurdly mad at her hair for causing this conversation, she french-braided it, almost enjoying the pain when she tugged her hair to get it tight. When she finished, she tucked the stray ends underneath the braid to hold it.

"Most men haven't seen you in..." His glanced raked her up and down and her blush crawled like a thousand tiny spiders to her chest.

Both eyebrows lifted as she waited for him to finish his sentence. If he feared for his life, he'd better not complete it the way his mind was working.

"Fatigues." He grinned slyly. Why, oh why did he have to wear those glasses. It wasn't fair that he could read the expression in her eyes while she couldn't read his. But the twist of his lips told their own story and she he laughed at her without a doubt.

Had she imagined their closeness last night? Or had she been dreaming?

As they hiked through the hot sun, perspiration trickled between her breasts and down her back. She swabbed at her forehead with the back of her hand. She couldn't have felt hotter in a Brazilian rain forest. She dreamed of wintry days and precious snow. She'd never complain about icy roads or arctic temperatures again, *if* she got out of Miami alive.

"Pass the water," she said, holding out her hand for the canteen strung around his neck. Bending over, she rested her hands on her knees, waiting for him to do as she bid.

"You okay?" he asked, a twinge of concern in his voice. "Do you need a break?" He glanced over her shoulder as if looking for uninvited guests and she knew he didn't want to stop.

"Is it much further?" Stretching to her full height, she accepted the canteen graciously, tilted her head back and took a long swig of warm water, the best she'd ever tasted, even if it was probably Miami tap water. Although she could have drained the receptacle, she made herself stop after a few swallows. Drips of water beaded on her lips where she let them stay to cool her lips where the relentless Florida sun burned them. She suspected she'd be bright pink by noonday, if she wasn't already. By dinner time, she'd be lobster red even if she felt almost as boiled now.

"Not much. About half a mile as the alligator runs."

Without hesitation, she punched his shoulder. "I can't believe you said that, after..." She held herself and shivered as if she froze. Visions of the monster flashed in her mind and chills filled her.

Suddenly, the tall saw-grass looked sinister and she wondered if any gators hid in their depths, laying in wait for them? And what other creatures hid in the fields? She twisted the canteen lid back on and passed it back to him. "Let's go." She made sure she kept pace with him instead of lagging behind as she had before.

Her over active imagination worked overtime, the trek getting to her. The scene from Jurassic Park where the raptors plucked unsuspecting men from the benign looking field reeled across her mind's big screen. She shuddered, feeling foolish. Nonetheless, she kept her eyes peeled for the slightest sign of movement and stayed glued to Nick's side.

Risking his snickers, she held the butt of her gun, ready to shoot if necessary. Fine safari hunter she'd make, scared of a gator. She was glad her father couldn't see her, now.

Pesky insects buzzed around her face and she swatted at them ineffectually. When she got out of this mess, she swore she'd buy stock in the insect repellent companies. Tons of it.

She tried to ignore the insects droning in her ears to listen for any unusual menacing sounds, especially voices, engines and alligator grunts. She didn't particularly feel like meeting up with any of the gator's long lost relatives.

"We're almost there." Nick took her arm and tossed her a grin that made her heart throb. Did he have a clue what he did to her when he did that?

"What will she think of us arriving on foot?" Another thought, much more disturbing than merely meeting his mother's expectations made her pause.

He slowed and looked at her. "You mean what if the guard's waiting for us?" He scratched his chin where at least a day's growth of dark blond whiskers stood at attention. She was close enough to count about thirty-seven before she realized he'd asked a question to which he awaited a response. She looked askance at him.

"We'll scout her property out first. That means we'll have to walk around it in concentric circles and spiral our way in." He switched his rifle from his left to his right shoulder. "Can you make it? Or should I leave you here while I check it out?"

Tired as her feet were from the abuse heaped on them in the past two days, the adrenaline pumping through her veins made her assert herself with fervor, "You're not leaving me here alone."

The scent of honeysuckle and wet grass wrapped around her and much as she appreciated it, she longed to smell even one burned hot dog. Hunger gnawed at her stomach something ferocious.

After what felt like a one hundred mile trudge through the jungle, Nick turned into a small drive way. A little farmhouse stood back from the road, next to a large red barn, several animal pens and a gray tool shed. A reddish brown golden retriever lolled on the front stoop impervious to the kittens swatting at its bushy tail. Shingles, boards and a few garbage can lids littered the lawn. A palm tree lay upended next to the barn. All in all it appeared the old homestead had fared well.

"What is she like?" Kelly shaded her eyes from the sun with her hand so she could read Nick's expression. She lifted her heavy hair off her neck to let the cool breeze wash over her.

"She's an animal lover, like you. She loves to cook - makes the best cheese and mushroom omelets you ever tasted. Do you like omelets?"

"Right now, that sounds like ambrosia." Kelly's mouth watered at the thought of real food. Gooey cheese and luscious mushrooms tossed together in creamy eggs would fill the void that gnawed at her belly.

"Maybe, if we play our cards just right, we can talk her into making us one. Compliment her on her flower garden and she'll do anything you ask."

Kelly's stomach rumbled at the mention of food.

Then she spied a tangle of plants uprooted and trampled next to the porch. "It looks like Chelsea leveled it." She pointed to the garden.

Nick grimaced. "I guess I'll be spending the next few weekends with the mulcher."

The porch door swung wide. A short woman with straight iron gray hair that fell to her shoulders peered out. When she spied Nick, her face split into a sunny smile.

"Nicky! Where'd you come from?" She bustled out the door, carrying a fluffy, squirming puppy in her arms. The pup looked like a bandit with black rings around his eyes and black spots on his otherwise white body. But he wasn't a Dalmatian. She couldn't quite tell what he was. Probably All-American mutt. The best type of dog.

The puppy writhed, then jumped down, squealing as his chubby legs carried him to the barn where he squeezed under a rabbit hole. Just the tip of his wagging tail stuck out the hole. It looked like a finger beckoning her to the barn.

Nick met her half way and he swung her in his arms. He planted a big kiss on her cheek before he set her down. "Hiya Ma! Generator working? House still standing okay?" His glance looked around the whole yard. "I see you didn't blow away to Kansas."

"The generator's an absolute Godsend! I have television. I have refrigeration. And I even have air conditioning - and *ice*. This is so much better than after Hurricane Andrew. I'm not sweatin' like a pig in a tin can."

Kelly kept a respectable distance although her ears were perked to catch every word, every nuance of dialect. Although Nick's mother looked friendly, she felt awkward so she stayed put, watching and assessing. She didn't have much experience with mothers unless you counted Carol Brady or Harriet Nelson.

The tiny woman seemed to be a bundle of energy. She certainly loved her son. He towered over her and she had to throw her head back to look at him. Anyone who loved animals the way she seemed to must be all right.

Still, Kelly held her breath. She knew she looked a wreck in Nick's T-shirt after everything she'd been through today. Perspiration lines trickled down her back where the gun lay and she could feel damp hair clinging to her cheeks. Her lips must be swollen from where Nick had kissed them unmercifully. Her nerves were frayed. She felt jumpy as a cat on a hot tin roof listening for the sound of engines, watching for soldiers, waiting for someone to grab them.

No. This was not the way she'd wished to meet Nick's mother.

Then Nick's mother turned to Kelly and bestowed upon her the sunniest smile she'd ever seen. The knots in Kelly's belly dissipated and she forgot why she'd been so nervous.

"Ma, I'd like you to meet Kelly Kerrigan," Nick said. He took his mother by the elbow and led her over to Kelly.

"Kelly, this is my mother, Joan Conway."

"Pleased to meet you Kelly." Joan took Kelly's arm and propelled her to the house. "You two look all tuckered out. Did your car break down or something?" Joan looked pointedly at the shotguns Nick and Kelly carried. Her eyebrows lifted but she didn't say more.

"Pleased to meet you Mrs. Conway."

"Call me Joni. I don't cotton to being called Mrs. Conway no more. Conway's been gone a long time."

"I'm sorry to hear that..."

Joan chuckled, exposing a large dimple. Her eyes twinkled, so like Nick's yet not. They were full of heart and soul. Somehow, Nick's were usually wary and guarded. "I'm not. Last told, I heard he was whooping it up in Vegas on somebody else's money. Good riddance to him! Where's your car?"

"It's a long story, Ma. I'll tell you all about it when we're in the air-conditioning, from the sanctuary of my favorite chair."

"Get yourselves inside then. Would you like something to drink?" Joan asked. Their heavy boots clomped on the old porch deck.

"Ice water would be heavenly," Kelly said. Her cheeks felt flushed from the hot Florida sun. It must be over 100 degrees in the shade! Miami was sweltering and all those poor people trapped in the city had nowhere to shelter or even get ice water. Could hell be any worse?

Thank Heaven for generators and Nick's insight to install one!

Nick held the door for the two women. Air conditioning hit Kelly like an arctic blast and she tossed her head back in pleasure letting it wash over her and cool her fevered flesh. She'd never take air conditioning for granted again!

"Sit yourselves down and I'll get your drinks," Joan said, bustling off to the kitchen. Kelly couldn't help but smile after the perky little woman. She was so...cute, for lack of a better word. Warm. Friendly. Appealing.

"We're mighty hungry, Ma. Can we raid your fridge?"

Joan paused, turning. "I just baked some banana bread last night. Can I warm you up a couple of slices with butter till I fix something that'll stick to your ribs?"

"Please Ma." Nick plopped into his favorite chair and let out a long sigh. "Can we have a big glass of milk with that?"

"Can I help you, Mrs... I mean Joan?"

Joan waved her hand nonchalantly. "It won't take but a moment. You can freshen up in the upstairs bathroom while I get this ready. Take a shower if you like. And there's clothes that might fit you in my closet you're welcome to, Kelly."

"Thank you. That sounds wonderful." She writhed against the wet T-shirt that showed her every curve like a second skin. It couldn't be more uncomfortable if it were raw wool against bare skin.

"Nick, show her where it is, will you?"

"Sure, Ma." Nick stood, stretching his arms above his head reaching for the stars. He tried to stifle a yawn and failed. He looked in dire need of another back rub, but now wasn't the time or place. Kelly blushed thinking of the one she never quite finished...

"It's just up the stairs, second door on the left," Nick called behind him as he bounded up the stairs taking two at a time.

Kelly followed leisurely. The house was filled with so much memorabilia that she was busy looking at everything, trying to piece together Nick's early life and figure out this enigma she was falling head over heels in love with.

The pictures were especially intriguing. Nick's face stared back at her from the gallery lining the stairwell. There were the obligatory baby pictures of Nick in a diaper. Nick in a bath tub. Nick in a christening gown. Then Nick as a chubby toddler, followed by Nick in baseball, soccer and football uniforms and then Nick in his high school graduation gown.

Kelly came to a dead stop when her gaze found a picture of Nick in his *wedding* tuxedo? She blinked her eyes, trying to clear them. Maybe it was just someone that looked like Nick. She stood on tippy toes to peer at it close up. Unless he had an identical twin, that was Nick.

She brought her attention back to Nick beaming at a beautiful blond-haired, blue eyed angel in a gossamer wedding gown that seemed to trail behind her forever and ever. The woman, his wife obviously, gazed at him with absolute adoration. He looked like the cat that had just swallowed the proverbial canary, proud and puffed up with pride.

Kelly gaped at it, still not sure her mind wasn't playing tricks on her. Then she realized that she didn't know Bradley except perhaps in the Biblical sense. But she didn't *really* know him. What did she know of his past, his relationships, his dreams, fears and desires? Nothing. Absolutely nothing. Of course, the niggling voice of truth at the back of her mind spoke up to defend Nick - *you only met him three days ago. How could you know anything about the man?*

Still, shouldn't he have mentioned he was married before he made love to her? Just a little casual hint would have sufficed.

Or maybe he was divorced? It happened. It happened all the time. Maybe he hadn't thought to tell her he was married anymore because he wasn't.

That must be it. But the look of love on those faces looked like the forever kind of love. One that wasn't split apart because of some silly spat over bills or even in-laws. Kelly tortured herself with a million possibilities of what could be. She forced herself to tear her gaze away from that picture and move slowly up the stairs. Next thing she knew, Nick would come looking for her and this was the last place she wanted him to find her. She needed more information.

More baby pictures followed, but this time of a little girl dressed in frilly pink dresses and big beautiful bows. She was a stunningly beautiful child whom the photographers had adored.

Lots more pictures followed depicting the child as she grew till they stopped at around age 5. So Nick had a five or six year old daughter? There were several pictures of Nick holding a baby, Nick playing with a mischievous toddler, Nick, his mother and the child opening presents around the Christmas tree. There was even one of Nick wearing an Air Force officer's uniform holding the girl. There was a sleek fighting plane behind Nick. Was he a pilot?

She had so many unanswered questions swirling in her mind. She felt dizzy.

"Did you get lost down there, Cincinnati? Should I send out rescue teams?"

"No. No, don't do that. I'll be right there," Kelly yelled up. She gave the pictures one last perusal, pursed her lips and sprinted up the stairs to the second door on the right where Nick was pouring through his mother's closet looking through her clothing.

"Some of these things might be a bit baggy on you, but not too bad." Nick threw a few outfits on the bed. "They'll be better than putting what you've got back on."

Kelly walked to the bed, straining to wear a normal expression on her face. She didn't want him to read the turmoil boiling inside her. She sifted through the clothing and selected two outfits. "I'll try these after I shower." She pointed to a door at the back of the room. "Is this it?"

"Right through that door." He walked over to her and put his arms around her. "Maybe I can join you?" he asked in a sultry, seductive voice. He dropped feather light kisses on her neck. His warm breath sent shivers down her spine.

She felt so good, so right in his arms, she wanted to melt against him. Yet, she couldn't get those pictures out of her mind. In a husky voice, she said, "I don't think you should with your mother downstairs. What if she came up and found us?"

"I guess it's not such a good idea," Nick agreed, sounding almost sulky. He let her go. "I'll take mine after yours then. Don't use all the hot water." He plopped on the bed, stretching out, looking so inviting, so tempting, her resolve almost crumbled.

Kelly crossed the room to the bathroom, strengthening her resolve not to give into him yet again. This man had gotten into her blood and he might not even be free. She paused at the door, needing to know, yet dreading the answer. "Nick?"

"Hmmm?" He turned towards her, propped his elbow on the bed.

"Who was that woman with you in the wedding gown? And the little girl?"

Nick's expression immediately went blank as if a shutter had been drawn. He rolled onto his back and stared at the ceiling as if the answers to the universe lay there.

"Nick? Who are they?" Kelly asked softly, walking back to the bed, staring down at him. Lightly, she trailed her fingers down his arm and pulled back perplexed when he stiffened at her touch.

"They're my wife and daughter. Melissa and Ashlea." His voice was devoid of emotion, as if he were barren inside. Yet his eyes turned dark and brooding, as if demons tortured his soul. Deep lines etched around his mouth and he suddenly looked much older.

Alarm pierced her heart, mixing with the shock that made her feel ice cold and clammy. It had never occurred to her that he might be married. Her gaze drifted to his hands. They were barren. There wasn't even a white wedding band line on his ring finger.

"Your *wife*?" Kelly sank onto the bed beside Nick, stunned at his revelation. She'd never guessed he was married throughout their adventure. He'd never said a word. He certainly hadn't *acted* like a married man.

"She *was* my wife," he said morosely, his voice so low she had to strain to hear it. Without looking at her, he mumbled, "She died in childbirth."

Her glance shot to his face and she caught the sheen of tears behind his eyes.

"Oh!" Kelly muttered, surprised. She hadn't expected this. Tears, hot and sudden, threatened to choke her. A plump tear splashed down her cheek then fell to the bed. She stretched out beside him on the mattress and cradled his head to her bosom, stroking his soft hair. "I'm so sorry, Nick," she crooned soothingly. "I never dreamed...I never thought... Oh, I didn't mean to be so, so..." She hugged him and buried her face against his broad shoulder. The remainder of her words were lost, muffled against his chest.

His arms stole slowly around her, squeezing her tightly to him. His tears wet her cheek. "She was so young, so innocent. And I couldn't save her."

She'd never seen darker eyes. Never had the term *eyes were the mirror to the soul* rang truer. Nick's eyes radiated his deep loss, his sadness. Nothing had ever pierced her soul as his obvious anguish.

She'd lived a carefree life, her mother dying when she was too young to remember, her father, Aunt Meghan and older brothers filling her life with sunshine and laughter so that she barely noticed the void, other than a curiosity she seldom admitted to.

"Shhh," she murmured, pressing her lips to the side of his mouth, stroking his hair away from his forehead. "Don't torture yourself, Nicky. It happened a long time ago..."

"You don't understand." He massaged her back. "You can't understand," he repeated over and over. "She was so young. So innocent. So beautiful."

Tears stung Kelly's eyes. She didn't know whether she was crying for his pain or her own. The depth of his love for his young wife echoed in his deep voice. After all these years, he still tortured himself. He didn't seem ready to love again. Perhaps he'd never be ready. Maybe he was a one-woman man.

How long they lay like that, Kelly didn't know. She cradled him in her arms, absorbing his pain at her own expense. She wondered where the girl was. She'd be six, right? At least five. As much as her curiosity pushed her to ask, something held her back. There would be time for that later when Nick felt stronger, less vulnerable. She'd probably be downstairs with her grandma when they went down to eat.

"Are you two alive up there?" Joan yelled up. "The bread's done and waiting. I'm making some omelets for you too."

"Are you going to be okay?" Kelly asked, cupping Nick's cheek in the palm of her hand. She gazed into his eyes. "I'm here if you want to talk... if you need me." She struggled to sit up, immediately at a loss without his warmth.

"I'm a survivor," he said, his voice devoid of emotion. "The Iraqui's couldn't get me, and neither have the poachers..."

"That's not the same thing," she protested gently. She knew her heartache must shine in her eyes and she lowered her lashes to veil her vulnerability from him. "I think I'm beginning to understand you. You're a daredevil because you're not afraid to die. Your heart died with her, didn't it? And you're a loner, because you don't want to be with anyone if you can't be with *her.*"

"Don't try to psychoanalyze me, Cincinnati," he said, sitting up, crossing his long legs Indian style over the rumpled quilt. "You can't understand and I'm not ready to explain."

Kelly reached for his hand resting in his lap and covered it with hers. "I'm here. Your mother's here. You're not alone."

"Nicky! Do I have to come up there and drag you downstairs?" Joan threatened, her voice sounding closer.

"She'll do it," he warned. "Never underestimate my dear mother. She doesn't make threats she doesn't keep."

"I'll remember that," Kelly said, smiling tremulously, trying to compose herself. "I'm glad you brought me here. I'm beginning to understand what makes you tick, Lieutenant."

"You don't understand the half of it." He lowered his voice so low she wasn't sure she heard the next words correctly. "You don't want to know..."

"Well, I'd better hop in the shower," she said hesitantly. She leaned over and pressed her lips lightly to his in a kiss of commiseration then nuzzled her face against his. "Will you be okay?" She felt loathe to leave him like this, even for the five minutes it would take her to shower. She gazed deeply into his eyes and tried to read his thoughts. But he'd effectively concealed his pain and returned her gaze steadily.

"We'll be down in a jiffy, Ma!" He swatted her on her bottom. "You'd better get ready. We still have a long way to go today."

Kelly swung her legs off the bed, stretched to her full height then sashayed to the shower. Although the warm water felt wonderful sluicing off the day's perspiration, she didn't linger. Her mind was too preoccupied, too worried about Nick. She didn't even feel hungry anymore.

When she came out of the shower, dressed in a green pantsuit that fit fairly well, Kelly dropped a light kiss on his lips. He had fallen asleep. "Wake up sleepy head. Your turn."

Delicious smells wafted upstairs, a rich cheesy aroma that beckoned to her and gave her second thoughts about how hungry she really was. "I'll be downstairs helping your mom."

Nick sat up and rubbed his eyes with his fists as if he were a little boy. "Okay. I'll be down in a few minutes." He swung his legs over the side of the bed and watched silently as Kelly left.

Kelly glanced at the picture of Nick and Melissa on the way down the stairs. What a tragedy! Nick's wife had died so very young and she'd never known their adorable daughter, had probably never even held her baby. Tears threatened to choke her again. What an emotional roller coaster she'd been on the past two days. She couldn't wait for the ride to stop so she could get off. Except, she didn't know if Nick would still be around afterward and that thought bothered her more than she was willing to admit.

That wonderful aroma beckoned to her from the kitchen. Her stomach growled reminding her that she hadn't eaten anything substantial since before the hurricane ripped through Miami and shattered her life. Perhaps she was hungry after all.

But she was even hungrier for information. Could she possibly pump Nick's mother for information about Nick? She wasn't sure, but she could test the waters and see just how forthcoming Joan would be.

She kept her ears perked for sounds of a child - anything at all. A small voice, a giggle, toys clashing, a tiny footstep. Anything that would suggest there were anything but adults in this farm house.

Of course, a thought struck Kelly. The girl could be staying elsewhere. Nick might employ a baby-sitter at his house. Hadn't he mentioned that kept an apartment in Miami? It was possible...

Kelly opened the swinging kitchen door carefully. "Hi Joan," she called to alert her hostess so she wouldn't sneak up on her and startle her like her brothers loved to do when they were in one of their devilish moods.

Eggs and bacon sizzled on the stove where Joan danced and hummed a snappy little show tune. Several thick slices of banana bread layered a plate in the middle of the table. Tall glasses of milk sat next to it. Kelly eyed the spread ravenously.

Joan turned in time to read Kelly's rapt expression of pure, undiluted hunger. She chuckled. "Go ahead and grab a piece but it's a might cold by now."

Kelly sat down at the table and helped herself to a thick slice of bread and one of the glasses of milk. "It looks wonderful. Anything would be great after stale candy bars and boiling soda."

"Is that what you've been eating?" Joan bustled about happily, transferring her masterpieces to big man-size plates. "No wonder you're eyeing my bread like one of my St. Bernards. You must be starved."

Kelly took a dainty bite and found herself closing her eyes in rapture. "It's the food of angels. Are you sure I haven't died and gone to Heaven?"

"Just plain old country cooking. Nothing at all fancy about my banana bread nor my omelets." Joan carried a plate and plopped it down in front of her. "There you go."

A plateful of the biggest, cheesiest omelet she'd ever laid eyes on winked up at her. Steam rose, swirling into the ceiling fan. Mushrooms still sizzled. There must be three thousand, perhaps even three hundred thousand calories on that plate and Kelly planned to consume every last one.

First she had to take a swig of that milk which is exactly what she did. It felt so cool and refreshing going down, nothing at all like the boiling water or soda she'd had to put up with for the past three days, or was it two decades? It certainly felt like the latter.

Joan pulled out a chair on the opposite side of the table and sat down. She took a glass of milk and slice of bread for herself. Holding out the bread, Joan gave Kelly a speculative look. "I don't like to meddle in my son's life, but I have to know why the two of you showed up here toting shotguns and looking sorrier than Tom Turkey on Thanksgiving morning."

Kelly regarded Joan critically. Just how much should she divulge? The less she told Joan, the less she'd have to hide if authorities showed up here looking for them. If she knew nothing she couldn't be considered an accessory to their crimes—or harboring felons. But it was obvious that Joan suspected something amiss. Who with half a brain wouldn't? Of course, everybody looked ragamuffin and war torn since Chelsea hit. No one would be doing their laundry or even washing their hair for several days, perhaps several weeks. In one swift attack, Miami had been thrown back to the stone age, except the population was way too high to bathe in the same stream the way cave men used to. Few people were blessed like Joan with a generator and their own well.

After much contemplation, Kelly decided the best thing to do was to tell the truth—a very abbreviated version of the truth. Joan's bright eyes were too alert to accept lies, even tiny ones. "I'm a zoo keeper at the Miami Metro Zoo and I'm searching for two escaped tigers. Nick was looking for them too, so we decided to team up."

Joan's mouth gaped open. That wasn't the reaction Kelly had expected from this woman. At least not without telling the rest of the story. This was the tame part of it. Joan, however, stayed introspectively quiet for so long that Kelly started to worry.

"Are you okay, Joni? You're not scared are you?" Kelly asked, forgetting all about her food, delicious as it was. "I assure you my tigers are harmless. I raised them from cubs..."

Finally, Joan snapped out of her daze. She peered at Kelly. "How is Nick taking all this?"

Now it was Kelly's turn to stare. She tucked her unruly hair behind her ears. "Taking what? Oh, you mean escaped tigers?" She took a drink of the milk and kept her eyes glued to Joan.

When Joan stayed silent, Kelly continued. "Well, he's very worried about the public safety. He doesn't believe me that they're harmless..."

"Of course, he wouldn't!" Joan stated vehemently. She slammed her fist on the table and it sounded like a cannon ball had fired.

Kelly stared blankly at Joan. She must be missing an important puzzle piece here.

"Don't you know?" Joan asked, her voice very low, very quiet.

"Know what?" Kelly asked, perplexed and growing more concerned by the minute. Joan looked like a woman about to reveal an ominous revelation. The air in the room was so thick, Kelly was afraid she'd choke. She leaned forward in her chair, letting her fork clatter to her plate.

"You don't know, do you?" This time, Joan made a flat statement, her bright eyes going suddenly dull. She turned and gazed unseeingly out her kitchen window.

Kelly shook her head slowly. She leaned forward, coaxing Joan to reveal her secret.

"My granddaughter was mauled by a panther, right out there by my barn. I heard it. I heard the terrible growls, her screaming and crying, calling out for me. By the time I found her, it was too late."

"Too late?" Kelly hadn't realized she spoke her thoughts aloud until Joan turned agonized eyes on her.

"That monster killed my little Ashlea. My baby's baby. I let her down. I let him down."

"Oh no!" Kelly whispered, horrified. "Are you sure it was a panther?"

"Sure as I know my own son. I got down here in time to see it ripping into her. In time to see it rip the last shreds of life from her little body." Joan bent her head in her hands. "And I couldn't do a thing to save her. I was too late. Too late."

Kelly stood without volition and crossed to the other side of the table. She wrapped her arms around the tortured woman and held her as she sobbed against Kelly's bosom. Kelly couldn't tear her gaze from the barn. She imagined the horrible scene, wondered what it felt like to lose her own child and shed a few tears of her own. Finally she understood why Nick thought of her tigers as monsters.

Tigers weren't so far different from panthers, not at all.

It was amazing that Nick hadn't crawled into some deep, dark hole and covered himself up. Instead, he was out saving other people's children from horrible fates.

Yet, Kelly surmised, maybe he had hidden away. Hadn't he mentioned that he practically lived out of his car? That he spent much of his time in the Everglades chasing poachers?

In his shoes, wouldn't she feel the same? Wouldn't she fear, and even hate the creature and his kind that had killed her child? Probably so.

Kelly gave what comfort she could until Joan's tears subsided. When Joan lifted her head, she sniffed back stinging tears and dabbed ineffectually at her eyes with trembling fingers. She smiled at Kelly tremulously. "Maybe you're an answer to my prayers ..."

Kelly tilted her head. "Now what makes you say that?"

"My son's been so lonely. So determined to bury himself ..."

The kitchen door swung wide, creaking on rusty hinges. Nick sauntered into the room, looking considerably refreshed from when he had withdrawn from Kelly on the bed. "Hmmm. I guess it's time for the Pennzoil." Without missing a stride, Nick grabbed a glass of milk and slid a plate of omelets to a vacant place at the table and straddled a chair.

"Are my ears burning?" He shot a sizzling look at Kelly. The glint in his eyes softened when his eyes alighted upon his mother. "Are you all right, Ma?"

Joan smiled tremulously. She squeezed Kelly's hand which lay gently on her shoulder. "I'm fine." She leaned over the table and buttered a thick slice of banana bread then held it out to Nick. "Have yourself a piece of my bread. It's a might cold, but it'll hit the spot."

"Thanks Ma." Nick stuffed half the bread in his mouth, his Adam's apple bobbing out when a big chunk protested going down his throat. Kelly's eyes widened at the spectacle. She knew he was hungry, but what a display! Then the corners of her mouth softened, tilting upwards. He was a typical man, just like her brothers, every last one of them, enjoying good home cooking. Trouble is, she'd been the only woman in her house for as long as she could remember and they'd gone without a woman's cooking until her aunt had taken pity on her and taught her a few culinary skills. The few Kelly had sat still long enough to learn. Kelly had never been the indoor, domesticated type, and she'd felt stifled and more than a little bored trapped inside four walls on perfectly sunny days when she'd have rather been outside running with her dogs or riding her horse.

Still, she admitted frankly now, it would be more than a little nice to bring that look of exquisite pleasure to a man's face. At least to Nick's face.

"Have you tried this, Cincinnati? Ma's won grand prizes at the Dade County Fair three years running for this bread. Old Lady Jenkins over in Florida City keeps trying to top Ma, but the judges love this bread almost as much as I do." Hungrily, Nick stuffed the rest of the bread in his mouth and rolling his eyes in ecstasy as he savored it slowly.

"When you're done eating, Nick, could you take a look around outside for Sugar? I haven't seen her all day and I'm getting worried." Joan twisted in her chair, darting furtive glances out the back door.

Nick licked the crumbs off his fingers, then plunged into the omelet, dicing it with his knife and fork. "Maybe she's out chasing rabbits."

"In this heat?" Joan shook her head, her forehead creasing in a frown.

"Who's Sugar?" Kelly asked. She took a slice of bread and bit into it. Her teeth cut a chunk of banana that hadn't been mashed to pulp.

"My best dog. Little Sheltie. A might arthritic now, so I doubt she's chasin' any rabbits. Curled up on Old Man Fogarty's sun deck dreamin' about rabbits more like it."

"How is her back doing?" Nick asked. He piled omelet into his mouth, and she enjoyed his healthy appetite. She'd always enjoyed watching her brothers eat at home and was amazed how her father could pay the food bill month after month the way they could empty out the refrigerator in record time.

Nick's voracious hunger reminded her she'd barely taken a bite herself. Her stomach grumbled in protest. Squeezing Joan's shoulder in silent support, Kelly returned to her seat and took a bite of the creamiest, fluffiest eggs this side of heaven, dripping with so much cheese the American Cancer society should put a warning label on them but Kelly didn't care. To heck with cholesterol and fat grams. She was enjoying the best meal of her life.

Joan beamed from Nick to Kelly, apparently pleased they were enjoying themselves. Her tears were dry and Kelly wondered if they had ever really been there. "Not too good, then she's gettin' to be a senior citizen like me. We're a matched set."

"You're not old Ma," Nick protested, scraping the last of his eggs off the plate. "Aaah, that was great!" Nick took a swig of the milk, then wiped the white milky mustache from his upper lip with the back of his hand. Then he leaned forward in his chair, balancing on two legs. He rested his head on the arms that lay atop the chair.

Kelly finished up fast, assuaging the hunger that had gnawed at her belly for most of three days. Pushing her chair back, she stood and collected her dishes. Out of old habit she collected Nick's dirty dishes and carried them to the sink.

When she turned on the tap and adjusted the water for washing, Joan picked up the remaining bread. "Wait a minute, Ma. I want another piece."

Joan held out the plate and Nick swiped a piece as if it were stolen treasure. He chomped on it happily, watching Kelly perform the womanly duties.

"Here, I'll do those," Joan commanded, her tone brooking no argument.

Still, her dad had taught her it was only polite to help with the clean up, so Kelly protested mildly. "I don't mind..."

Joan bustled her way into the sink, stopped it up and poured a generous glob of liquid soap in the sink. Soap bubbles ballooned up. A few escaped, tickling Kelly's nose. "Actually, I have an ulterior motive. I wasn't lyin' about being worried about my Sugar. She's not as spry as she used to be." Joan looked up from where she scrubbed egg yolk off a plate. "Would you help my son find her and bring her in? I'd feel much better if she spent the night inside with me."

Nick stood so suddenly, his chair toppled to the ground with a large bang. "We'll look now before it gets dark and we have to get going..."

Joan turned eyes full of surprise on her son. "Just what kind of trouble are you in that you can't spend the night?"

Nick's expression turned into a solid mask.

Heaving a sigh, Joan turned an accusing gaze on Kelly. "I'm not gettin' any information out of my bullheaded young son. Will you tell me why the two of you showed up here with so much fire power and why you feel you have to get going so soon?" She finished the last dish then grabbed a dish towel that hung from her refrigerator door and dried her hands. Leaning her back on the kitchen counter, Joan looked from one silent face to the other, hers full of exasperation.

Silence hung ominous in the air. "Well?" Joan finally broke whatever spell bewitched them, crossing her arms across her ample bosom. "Is someone going to tell me?"

Kelly shot an unhappy look at Nick. His eyes squinted in a don't-you-dare-say-a-word glare that would have frightened a lesser soul. Little did he know that she was quite adept at dealing with men in all their moods—it was women that scared the bejeevers out of her.

"We're kind of expecting a little trouble to follow us here," Kelly finally admitted, drumming her fingers lightly on the table top.

"A little? Those guns look mighty big to me," Joan said "What kinda trouble you expecting?"

"The National Guard and the Police are looking for us..."

"You *are* the police, aren't you?" Joan heaved a big sigh. She pursed her lips resolutely.

"We had a little difference of opinion with the Guard. You could say we borrowed one of their jeeps and got it a little shot up..." Kelly said.

"The Colonel thinks Kelly's tigers mauled one of his men and he got rough with her and locked us up. We escaped, there was a... chase... "

"...and here we are," Kelly finished, plastering a smile to her face that felt totally alien to her mood at this moment.

"Soooo," Joan surmised, "some soldiers may come looking for you here. Am I right?"

"That's about the size of it. If you see G .I. Joe toting a gun in your yard just tell them you never saw us." Nick grimaced. He crossed the room and looked out the window, his head turning one way, then the other as if looking for visitors. "We'll take a quick look around the place for Sugar then we have to be moving on. I don't want you caught in the middle of this."

"Don't you worry none about me. But you two had best be getting out of here," Joan said. She dried the dishes with an old dish towel and stuck the plates in an upper cabinet.

Nick glanced at his watch, then looked up. "It'll take them a might longer to figure out where you live. Cincinnati, you look around the yard, in the barn and in the tool shed. I'll take a look at Old Man Fogarty's place and around the woods a bit."

Nick ambled to the back door and swung it wide. Pivoting on his heel, Nick turned. "Cincinnati..."

"Yeah?" She leveled a forest green gaze at him, her smile soft, questioning.

"Don't go crawling under the house or anything like that," Nick warned.

"Why not?" She pushed herself off the kitchen counter where she'd been leaning comfortably.

"Sometimes there's snakes under there. One year, I pulled a whole nest of water moccasin out of there..."

Kelly shivered. "Snakes?" Her voice came out like a squeak.

Nick chuckled, smiling a lopsided grin. "If you don't go under the house, you'll be just fine."

"Thanks," Kelly gulped, trying to keep her composure despite the fact her hands turned clammy. "I'll remember that."

"I'll look in the house again, in case she's playing hide and go seek with me. Sometimes she sleeps the days away," Joan said. "I've been thinkin' of changin' her name to Lazy Bones."

"I'm going now, Ma. Don't worry. We'll find her. Sugar knows where she gets her eats."

Kelly ambled to the door, her thirsty gaze drinking in the view of Nick's well shaped backside sauntering away from her in his well worn jeans. He must have looked magnificent in his flight suit decorated in his Captain's bars, with his officer's smirk melting every heart for miles around before he flew into the wild blue yonder, one of the last of a breed of true daredevils.

She was startled by a hearty chuckle just behind her. She shifted her gaze, pretending to be scanning the grounds for the dog. What kind of dog was she looking for again? A schnauzer? No. A miniature Lassie dog, wasn't she? A sheltie. Thoughts of Nick had cleared her mind of her mission.

"You like my son, don't you?" Joan stated matter- of-factly.

Kelly turned to her, slowly nodding her head. "Is it that obvious?"

"To me. I don't know about him though."

"What do you mean?" Kelly couldn't help herself. She was thirsty for every tidbit of information she could learn about this enigma of a man. And this woman knew him better than anyone.

"I'm just afraid there's so much ice around his heart it may never melt. He locked it up when Ashlea died and no one's gotten near him since." Joan leveled a very serious gaze upon her. "I think you'd be good for him, despite your misguided views about those tigers of yours. I want you to promise to be good to my son."

Kelly's mouth gaped open. Was Nick's mother giving them her blessing, before she even knew how Nick felt? Oh, he was attracted all right. He'd not tried to hide that fact. But he'd not mentioned one word about a lifetime commitment, not even so much as asking if he could see her again when this ordeal was over.

Joan's finger closed Kelly's mouth gently, but firmly. "You'll be catchin' flies if you do that, Miss Kelly. Run along now and bring my Sugar home safely. I'd never forgive myself if something happened to her."

Kelly nodded, smiled and bent to give Joan a peck on her cheek. "Don't worry. We'll find her."

"I know you will. Now get."

Kelly looked around the yard, peeked under the steps but minding what Nick said she didn't go any further into the dark recesses under the house. Her too vivid imagination conjured up all sorts of snakes and creepy crawly things that made her skin tingle and caused the flesh on her arm to goose bump.

Every few steps Kelly stopped and whistled. She put two fingers in her mouth and whistled as long and hard as she could, something she remembered from one of her favorite childhood shows. Was it Lassie, or The Andy Griffith Show where the little boy be bopped down the old country lane whistling for his dog? If she kicked off her shoes and rolled up her pants legs she could double for Opie, she thought, laughing at her own joke. Then she called out, "Here Sugar. Here girl."

No response. She frowned.

Next she checked out the barn even climbing to the hayloft even though she knew an arthritic old Sheltie couldn't climb a ladder. But she wanted to be thorough. To be absolutely honest, she wanted to take a peek at what was probably one of Nick's favorite childhood haunts. It was even better than her old tumble down tree house with the tattered curtains that her brothers had moaned and groaned were women's stuff. This place had a strong aura. She just bet Nick had brought his wife up here before she was his wife, when his Ma was nowhere around. He seemed to have an affinity for afternoon delight on top a soft pile of fresh hay...

Her dad would have gone crazy if he'd had to chase her brothers out of here with all their girlfriends. She giggled when she pictured him in farmer's overalls sporting a pitch fork. Her brother, Kenny, the missionary, had been the biggest flirt in the history of Milford High and she could just see her dad chasing Kenny with one of his blonde bombshells against the backdrop of a full moon and a baying hound.

Slowly she climbed down the ladder, taking in the rest of the barn. It was pretty much a shell. No cows, no goats, no chickens or pigs—no real farm animals in here. Not even any farming instruments. She guessed it hadn't been a working farm in many years.

Again she whistled then called, "Here Sugar. Come here girl." Her voice echoed in the almost hollow barn, a little eerily. Suddenly, the shadows loomed large and the air felt stale and suffocating instead of sweet, country and fragrant.

She backed out of the barn carefully, looking over her shoulder so she didn't stumble into any rabbit holes or trip over any of the puppies that she heard yipping and yapping outside. Thoughts of snakes came unbidden to her mind and she wondered if any slithered under the hay, ready to raise its serpent's head to strike...

Sunlight struck her full in the face, warming her deliciously. Again she whistled. Well, she decided, Sugar had probably gone down to Old Man Fogarty's place to sunbathe. If she weren't on this mission this would be a great day to sunbathe. Angry clouds that had swirled overhead had finally lifted leaving a sky that was clear cerulean blue and a sun that kissed the country side like mountain mist. She bet that Kenga and Rama had found a big rock somewhere and lay stretched out enjoying the sun too.

Her mission accomplished, she turned to the house then spied the tool shed out of the corner of her eye. Was it even worth looking inside? Dogs couldn't open latched doors. Walking towards it anyway she noted the door swung slightly ajar. Well, this was the country. Most country folk didn't bother with locks, especially on an old rusty tool shed on a non-working farm. If someone wanted to steal the weed eater and garden hoe bad enough, Joan would probably say good riddance to them. Maybe Sugar had nosed her way into the old shed looking for a little shade instead of a little sun.

And maybe snakes liked dark musty places like tool sheds too, the thought came unbidden. Maybe she didn't have to go inside the shed, Kelly decided. If she whistled at the door and called Sugar by name, surely she would come out if she were inside. Surely...

Kelly put her fingers into her mouth and whistled as loud as she could two feet from the door. "Sugar. Sugar, are you in there?"

No sound. Kelly spun on her heel to leave when she heard rustling from within?

If it were Sugar, she could push her way out the door herself, couldn't she? It was just a flimsy aluminum door after all.

Then Kelly remembered that Sugar was arthritic, old and having back problems. A real senior citizen. She had probably nosed her way in, fallen asleep and been woken up from a wonderful dream where she chased rabbits or cats like a teenager again just to be rudely awoken by some stranger whistling in her sensitive ears. The poor thing might be disoriented, unable to find her way out of an open pasture.

"Okay, girl, I know you're in there. I'm coming into get you."

Kelly swung the door wide, looking low to the ground for Sugar.

Instead, sunlight bounced off highly polished steel glinting in the bright afternoon sun.

## Chapter Twelve

*A* white and brown spotted rabbit hopped out the open door, clipping her foot in its hurry to escape the sweltering shed that had imprisoned it.

She jumped back, her hand to her throat, her pulse racing at the base of her neck. "You scared the living daylights out of me Peter Cottontail," she murmured.

Wondering what it was that had looked like the steel barrel of a gun, she poked her head further into the shed, relieved to find only a long handled shovel and some garden implements.

She sank against the old shed till she regained her composure, the hot sun pouring upon her.

"Any luck, Kelly?" Joan called from the back door. "Did you find Sugar?"

Kelly straightened and shielded her eyes from the harsh sunlight. She peered towards the door and made out Joan's short, stout silhouette through the mesh screen. Shaking her head, she said, "No. No trace of her out here. Nick probably found her."

"Come on in and talk to me. Once she smells my cooking, she'll come begging for her share."

There was so much Kelly wanted to question Joan about. Mainly about Nick. He was so complex she didn't know if a lifetime would be enough time to understand this man. But she held back, not wanting to say the wrong thing again or appear too anxious. So, she sat back and let Joan lead her into small talk, describing the scenes of destruction they'd witnessed around Greater Miami.

Joan shook her head and exclaimed over Kelly's stories.

In the distance, a dog barked and Kelly turned her face toward the back door. Joan dropped the dish towel she held next to the sink and plodded to the screen door. "He found Sugar," she exclaimed, clapping her cheeks with her hands. She pushed the screen door open and bustled outside.

Sugar ambled next to Nick, her gait slow and rolling, a slight limp in her hind legs. She yipped excitedly when she saw Joan and her bushy tail wagged.

"You've been a bad girl, scaring me the way you did," Joan admonished, scooping the hippy dog into her arms. She clucked, shaking her head and nuzzled her face into Sugar's fur.

Sugar licked Joan's face with her sand-papery tongue, then panted.

"Yeah, I'm glad to see you too," Joan confessed gruffly. She smiled at her son. "Thank you for bringing her home. Where did you find her?" She climbed the stairs to the kitchen and Kelly swung the door wide and held it open.

"Sunning herself on Old Man Fogarty's porch like you predicted. If I wasn't in such a hurry today, I'd have been inclined to join her. It's a dandy day to sunbathe." He squinted at the bright sunlight. When he lowered his gaze, his eyes flickered a knowing glance at Kelly.

She lifted her eyebrow and tilted her head.

Lowering his lips to her ear, he whispered, "I found tiger tracks leading towards the Everglades. Get the gear so we can move out. They're fresh."

She stopped dead in her tracks. The hair on her arms prickled. "You mean we're close?"

"I can smell them," he promised knowingly, a glint of excitement in his eyes.

"What are we waiting for?" Kelly said in a hushed voice.

"What's all the whispering about?" Joan demanded to know, Sugar nipping at her heels. "Are you planning on deserting me already? You just got here."

"You don't want us here if the Guard tracks us down. Trust me," Nick promised. "Give me a hug for the road, Ma." He opened his arms wide and enveloped her in a bear hug, dropping a kiss on the top of her head.

"In that case, what's holding you up?" Joan clasped him to her bosom and patted him on the back. "You be careful. Don't be a hero."

Nick smiled slyly and checked his pistol for bullets, then loaded the empty chambers. "I'm just doing my job."

"They don't pay you enough to get yourself killed." Joan pulled away and shot a stern gaze at her son. "What would I do without you? Watch out for those tigers..." Her voice lowered to almost nothing, but Kelly caught her last words and bristled. So they were back to the tigers. Always the tigers coming between them.

"Get the guns from the living room while I hook up the trailer to the truck," Nick commanded. "Be quick about it. We've been here far too long. The rule of survival is to keep moving."

Kelly felt twin apprehension. She kept expecting the Guard to rumble up the drive, thus, she ran back in a flash, putting her feelings aside, at least until they got the job done. Then she'd think about this issue that loomed between them like an albatross. Later would be much better. Right now, she had to save Rama and Kenga and elude the Guard.

"You be careful too," Joan told Kelly, giving her a hug at the back door. "Don't let my son goad you into any stupid heroics."

"We'll be careful," she promised, crossing her fingers behind Joan's back. If her father were here, he wouldn't have wasted his breath on such warnings. He'd know that Kelly couldn't help from getting into trouble to save her life. She'd always been a magnet for trouble. Perhaps not such big trouble, but nonetheless. Joan didn't have to know this, not yet anyway.

Nick grabbed Kelly by the hand and yanked. "Were you planning to come now or did you want to wait till Christmas? I thought you were as anxious as me to find those tigers."

"I am!" She kissed Joan on the cheek. "Goodbye. Thank you."

"Be careful!" Joan yelled, watching them from her stoop. Sugar rubbed against her legs and Joan dropped a hand to her head and scratched behind her ears.

Kelly waved as she slipped into the car.

Nick threw the car in gear and sped away no sooner than she

closed the door. He covered her hand lying on the seat with his large one and squeezed. "We're going to find them."

"I know." Kelly smiled tremulously, turning her hand, entwining her fingers with his that felt so warm, so strong and inspired her to greater heights. She marveled at the thick mat of dark blond hair curling over his strong forearm. "I know we will."

She stared open mouthed at the piney woods, tangled with hammocks, ferns and vines, carpeted alternately by saw grass prairie and thick underbrush that enveloped the car. Pines and mangroves lay ripped from their roots, some in the middle of the road.

Nick swore when he stomped on the breaks to avoid hitting a deer that sprinted into the road, and the truck swerved violently.

"Are you all right?" Nick asked.

She shook her head, watching the deer leap gracefully over scrub on the other side of the road. Its flanks strained with fluid grace, its ears bent backwards against the wind.

"Andrew and Chelsea wiped out a lot of the tree canopy and did one helluva number on the ecosystem, out here," Nick shook his head. His lips curled down. He slid his sunglasses and slipped them into his shirt pocket. Daylight stretched behind them. Dancing shadows beckoned ahead.

A sign stating *Chekika entrance to Everglades National Park* swung precariously in the wind, dangling from a wire by one screw.

"What does *Chekika*? mean?" She turned to Nick, leaning her arm across the seat. She ran her fingers down his arm, delighting when he shivered beneath her feathery touch. So she did effect him like he effected her. She felt suddenly breathless in this magical world.

"Chekika's a park named after a great Indian chief." Nick's gaze slid sideways to Kelly. His eyes twinkled mischievously. "If we weren't on a mission, we'd visit the swimming hole that's fed by an artesian well. It spews sulfuric mineral water into the hole."

"Do alligators go there?"

"Sometimes they sun themselves below the observation tower in Shark Valley. I guess no one told them about the dangers of skin cancer."

"I can hear the forest's voices," she whispered in awe. Cicadas chirped. Gators grunted. Tree frogs burped. Even the wind whispered through the pines.

Nick pointed to a grassy area. "See over there? The Indians call that grass that looks like shimmering water *pa-hay-okee.* It covers the forest."

This magical, albeit dangerous world, swallowed them whole. She felt like they'd left the last traces of civilization behind. For all she knew, they could have traveled back in time as well.

"Welcome to the Everglades, Cincinnati." Nick pulled the grumbling truck to a halt, parking behind lush shrubbery.

"I took the liberty of throwing together a couple of back packs for us." He jumped lightly out of the truck and ambled around to open Kelly's door. When she stood on the ledge to alight, Nick grasped her waist, his hands encircling it easily. Their eyes met and held. Kelly searched his deeply, a hard knot forming in her belly when his dilated to huge round disks.

Kelly sniffed appreciatively. Woodsy, slightly salty, sulphurous, piney aromas delighted her. The recent rains liberated the scents of freshly cut lumber and grass. A man's scent. Nick's scent. Pure, outdoors, authentic. The signature of the deep, wild forest.

Kelly cleared her throat, voicing the niggling thought she'd been trying to push to the back of her mind unable to keep quiet any longer. Her brows furrowed together. "What will happen to us after we find the tigers?"

Woodstorks, egrets, spoonbills and other birds harmonized with the cicadas and frogs in a beautiful lover's concerto.

Absently, Nick's thumbs caressed Kelly's waist. His strong sensuous hands made her yearn to give herself up to pure passion, throwing everything else to the winds. She wanted to give herself to him on that velvety shimmering water as Indian maidens did before the white man stepped foot on this wild, forested peninsula.

"I'll find a way to clear us of any charges - if there are any. Then, I guess we go back to our real lives." Nick gazed at her steadily, but his voice dropped.

"Will I see you again?" she struggled to utter the words threatening to choke her. Her pride demanded she keep silent, but her errant heart won the inner battle.

"If your tigers escape again, I promise I'll be right on the scene Ma'am," he said, smiling up at her.

Darts pierced her heart. Did he mean this was it? Or was he teasing her? She couldn't be sure. "I'm serious, Nick." She put her hands on his shoulders and stared at him unblinkingly. Her heart pounded so hard she was sure he could see the rise and fall of her chest and hear her uneven respiration. "I want to see you again. Do you want to see me?"

There, she'd said it! She'd just trampled her pride to bits if he didn't feel the same way about her. Worse, she was letting herself in for a broken heart.

It felt like an eternity that Nick regarded her. In reality, it lasted only seconds.

"I ..." A truck rumbled down the path on the other side of the bushes that hid Joan's old Chevy. Nick's gaze cut to the road, his attention diverted to the intruders. Without really looking at her, Nick lifted her to the ground and released her. Stealthily, he crept to the bushes, glaring at the truck. "Damn! Yancey and Billy Ray. They can't be up to any good," he muttered.

Kelly, who had crept behind Nick, caught his last words. "What do you mean?"

"Poachers!"

Her jaw dropped. Her worst nightmare. Her gaze riveted on the truck that screeched to a stop. She grabbed Nick's arm, her fingernails digging into the firm flesh. "Why are they stopping? Did they see us?" Kelly whispered in a stage echo.

"I don't think so. The trail ends there. They're going to hike." Spinning on his heel, Nick propelled her before him. Their boots scrunched the wet saw grass under their heels, sounding impossibly loud. "It's high time we get our gear on and follow."

"Spray this on me, fast!" Nick tossed a can of insect repellent to her. She obliged, then Nick took it from her hands and sprayed her down. She covered her mouth so she wouldn't gag on the aerosol fumes that threatened to overwhelm her. A few small coughs escaped anyway.

When she could finally breath, she whispered, "They'll smell us coming!"

"Would you rather get eaten alive out here? I've seen mosquitoes out here so big you can strap a saddle on them."

She shook her head slowly mouthing, "No."

"Besides, they're probably wearing it too and the scent will simmer down in a moment anyway." Nick hoisted a pack onto his back then helped her adjust hers. "Strap the tranquilizer gun on your back and carry this. Just don't shoot me!"

Nick paused, a contemplative gleam lighting his eyes. He pulled a pearl handled knife out of his pocket, turning it in his palm. Surprising her, he tossed it to her without warning. "Put my spare in your front pocket."

"Why?"

"You never know when you might need it out here." Nick snapped the bullet cartridge off his rifle and replaced it with a full case. He tossed a full cartridge to her to follow his example. "Never turn your back on Yancey." His eyes narrowed, shadows flitting across them. Then his expression changed to one of rapt attention.

"Get down, Cincinnati!" He pushed her to the ground, his weight on her back.

Wings rushed by. The wind felt sinister. High pitched squeaking hurt her ears and she covered them with her hands.

"What's happening?" Her lungs burned.

He rolled off her and she gulped fresh air. "Just bats."

Finally, after an eternity passed, the flapping wings disappeared. Eerie silence loomed.

He stood, stretching to his full height, towering above her.

Wet leaves and grass clinging to her, she struggled to sit up. He held his hand out to her.

She took the proffered hand, straightening beside him, dusting herself off. Her eyes only reached his shoulder level, forcing her to look up at him.

Peering into the darkness, she strained her ears to listen for more wind disturbance. Their winged visitors seemed to be gone. All she could hear were bull frogs croaking and birds chirping.

Nick's cellular phone shrilled, making her jump. In the technologically silent forest, it sounded like a three-ring alarm. Even the frogs and katydids paused their nightly symphony in deference to the high-pitched whine. "Damn! I forgot to turn that off. It's a sure bet Yancey knows we're here now."

She glanced around her apprehensively, expecting poacher contingents to ambush them. She chided herself for being paranoid, knowing it wasn't foolish to be careful with so much at stake.

Nick sprinted to his truck to stop the siren. "Bradley here," he spoke sotto voce, cupping the receiver in his hands.

He listened silently for a few moments, hauling the rifle off his shoulder, squinting down the barrel. Then he checked his supply of ammunition. When he took it out, moonlight glinted off it like bauxite. He peered at the cartridges, his lips twisting into a grim line, then snapped them back with a bang.

"Yeah, we're okay. We just had a close call with a couple of bats. Tell the guys in pest control they'd better be on the lookout for vampire bats in Chekika Park. Dispatch a squad as soon as you can. The last thing we need is a rabies outbreak."

She strained her ears to catch Nick's words, the phrases *rabies, biological diversity* and *poachers* not sitting well with her. She did her best to ignore grunting alligators and rustling grass, erasing images of Jurassic Park from her overactive imagination as fast as they appeared.

She inched toward the truck. Shadows loomed larger and night creatures would be on the prowl shortly, if they weren't already. It seemed as if yellow eyes stared at them through the long grass and once again, she chastised herself for her musings.

"Yeah. Uh-huh." Nick regarded her surreptitiously, the expression in his eyes shadowy. Turning his back, he ambled a few feet away from her, mumbling into the phone so she couldn't catch further snatches of his conversation.

She stared at Nick's broad back wondering what could be so bad he didn't want her to know. He'd already told her there were poachers in the area. What could be worse? Every few moments, he looked over his shoulder, presumably to ascertain that she was okay, then he'd turn away again. His eyes were as inscrutable as if he still wore those damned sunglasses.

After what seemed an eternity, he tossed the phone in the truck, pivoted on his heel and strode to where she stood.

"Well?" She stared at him accusingly, straining her neck to look up at an almost ninety degree angle, getting a bird's eye view of his stubborn stubbled chin.

"Well, what?" he countered, irritatingly, divulging nothing. His Adam's apple stood out in his throat, her only clue he wasn't too happy about something.

"What happened? What's going on?"

"You're not going to like it." He gazed over her shoulder again, his eyes narrowed to mere slits. His stony countenance was back and he looked like an animal listening for its prey—or its enemy. She'd seen that exact same expression on Kenga's and Rama's face many times and she respected it.

"So tell me already." She clutched his forearm, her gaze burning into him, imploring him to confide in her. Electricity passed between them, sizzling beneath her fingertips where they touched. She did her best to ignore it, but it was like closing her eyes and ears to a nuclear explosion.

"The Guard is playing hardball. They're looking for us." His gaze bored into hers, his expression dead serious. "They've got to have a pretty good idea we're in the Everglades. They called the office from Krome Avenue demanding to know our whereabouts."

"Did anyone tell them?" Her voice sounded husky, almost breathy and she swallowed a lump in her throat. Now what would become of them? Of her tigers? Not that she was honestly surprised by this turn of events. It was only a matter of time.

"No. Garcia owes me. Besides, he doesn't like the Guard coming down from South Carolina, interfering in our business..."

Faint gunshots sliced through the night.

Tigers roared.

Alligators growled.

Birds squawked.

Her head snapped in the direction of the sounds, instantly alert. Her ears twitched. Her muscles clenched. Her nerves coiled as tightly as wire springs.

She vaulted toward the gunshots, all thoughts of the Guard vanishing, her adrenaline pumping urgency into her steps.

"Cincinnati! You'll get killed. Wait for me!"

Although she heard his urgent commands on a base level, his words fell on deaf ears. Her entire focus lay on saving her tigers. No one, nothing, would get in the way of her mission.

The moment sprung upon her. The end lay in sight. The exhaustion claiming her body vanished as the morning mist and she felt re-energized as surely as if she'd been recharged.

Running through the boggy swamp was difficult enough without the absence of light except for fountains of moonlight and her flashlight's minuscule beam. Muck pulled at her boots. Twigs caught at her shoe laces. Broken branches and even splintered trees barred her path. They scratched her arms and legs, but she barely felt the pain. What she felt, she pushed away into the far recesses of her mind, to the irrelevant. She'd think about it later when she had the luxury of time. They presented a mere nuisance, like the horde of mosquitoes trying to make her into a pincushion.

Grimly, she persevered, forcing herself to continue despite her breathlessness, pain and sheer exhaustion. Kenga and Rama needed her. They depended on her. Sure enough no one else would protect them.

More gunfire rang out and she thought she heard a roar of pain and fury.

Behind her, Nick pounded through the bushes. He'd stopped calling her name but she heard his raspy breath. Occasionally, he blocked the moonlight streaming over her shoulders, lighting her path. In those moments, the swamp seemed darker than the outermost stretches of the universe. Still, she pushed forward with grim determination.

She ran like the wind, glad her track training hadn't deserted her, even if she was a little out of breath. She blanked her mind to the impending danger as best she could. Heaven only knew that if she thought about what she was doing, she'd turn and hightail it back to the truck. There must be alligators and other night creatures about that thought she looked tastier than a mere turtle.

No, she couldn't let herself stop and think about that. Kenga and Rama were out of time. She couldn't stop now when she was so close.

So close she could hear loud voices.

So close she'd never forgive herself.

Suddenly, her foot caught in an exposed root. She fell headlong, her rifle discharging loudly as a Roman Candle. The wind rushed out of her lungs in one long whoosh.

Panicked because she knew the poachers heard her and would be searching for her, she struggled to free her foot that was bent awkwardly. Sharp, throbbing pains shot through it, stinging like a shot of flu serum as she tugged at her calf. When she grazed her ankle, pain shot through her. She prayed it wasn't broken, sure she had at least sprained it. She had to get out of here—fast. She could hobble on a sprain if she had to. And she had to. Surely, she'd find a stick she could use as a crutch. Meanwhile, she'd use her rifle.

Twisting up, she pulled and tugged with all her might but she couldn't free herself. But that was irrelevant unless she could get free.

"Where are you, Bradley?" she mumbled under her breath shakily. Her fingers dug into her flesh, leaving bruises.

A long shadow fell over her, looming like the Swamp Thing, diffused and swimming in leaves that covered the ground. The moonlight haloed the outline, but it looked anything but angelic. She looked up hoping to see her very own forest ranger come to rescue her once again.

Instead, hope turned to nameless fear. The shadow didn't belong to Nick but to some hulking figure of a man that grinned at her lasciviously. Evil pulsed around him and she froze like a wounded animal trying to fade into the foliage.

"Billy Ray! We got ourselves a lady cop!"

A burly young man who looked to be in his mid twenties, sporting a tattoo of a Cobra hood on his bulging left arm, crashed through the bushes. He pushed a teal Marlin's baseball cap up on his head and swiped away a band of perspiration. "What's she doing here, Yancey?"

Yancey cuffed the younger man in his head, making him take a backward step. "What do you think blockhead? She's another fed. They're thick as rats diving out of the sewer in a flood." His lips curled, surly.

*She* was the *rat*? He had things backward.

"What are we gonna do?" Fear rimmed Billy Ray's wide set eyes. His hand shook and she wondered if he'd shoot her and she sat very, very still, lest her movement twitched his finger on the trigger.

"Keep that thing pointed on her, boy," Yancey said. Yancey jerked her to her feet, jerking her foot from the root.

Searing pain lightning-bolted through her and she stifled a yell only by biting on her bottom lip so hard she tasted salty blood. Her ankle throbbed, electrifying pulses shooting up her leg. But she wouldn't give Yancey reason to laugh in her face or gloat.

Violently, he whipped her around, pulled her arms behind her back and tied her hands behind her back. Obviously, gentility and sensitivity weren't in his make-up. Rough-hewed hands grated against her flesh like burrs. Vice-like fingers bit into her arms.

She glared at him, tempted to spit venom in his vile face, while she stiffened her spine. But she pulled the reign in on her temper as he commanded the man who held the gun on her. She might have a quick temper but she also had a quick mind.

"Take her back to camp. I'll set out those steaks for bait." Yancey turned to leave. Billy Ray shoved her forward, none too gentle himself. But then, he'd taken lessons from the pro.

"You'd better listen to Uncle Yancey. He's got a mean streak that runs the Red River wide when he's riled. And believe you me,right now, he's mighty riled! He don't like no feds sneakin' around our camp." He spat out a brown wad of juicy Skoal not a foot from her feet. He wiped the dribbles off his chin on his shirt sleeve then grinned at her with tobacco stained teeth, not all that different from the gator that had tried to have her for breakfast.

"I'm not a fed," she said with as little expression as possible. She chuckled to let him know how ludicrous his assumption sounded.

"You look like a fed." His eyes slid over her, lingering in the usual places. "You're wearing a uniform."

"I'm a zoo keeper." She glanced down at her soiled clothing and grimaced. Since when did pantsuit scream uniform? The fatigues she'd worn earlier would rightfully lend that impression, but this? But then, she didn't think her captor was driving with all his lights on.

She stumbled over a fallen tree. Billy Ray caught her as she was falling and she recoiled from his touch as she would a viper's embrace.

Billy Ray snorted. "I never saw no zoo keeper that looked like you!" He leaned forward until his hot breath rasped on her neck. "Maybe I should take out a zoo membership if you come in the bargain."

"Membership is closed," she said between clenched teeth, twisting her face away. *Anytime now, Lone Ranger.* Where was Nick? Had Yancey found him? Heaven help them if he had.

"Anything you say, Red. I just want to get those tiger hides and get out of here. These woods are more crowded than Flagler Street on Saturday night! I'm getting nervous."

When they reached the poacher's campsite, Billy Ray motioned for her to sit on a sleeping blanket that was stretched out by the cold ashes of a dead fire. Empty beer bottles, cigarette butts and twinkies wrappers littered the ground. "You stay right there while I attend to some private business." Obviously feeling overconfident, Billy Ray lay down his rifle across the clearing and disappeared through the bushes.

The glint of moonlight on that rifle barrel mesmerized her. It lay so tantalizingly close, her fingers itched. Yet it might as well be on the moon with her hands tied behind her. Frustrated, a guttural growl rose in her throat.

Something was straining in her back pocket. The knife Nick had insisted she carry for emergencies dug into her tail bone! If she could get it, she could free herself and escape. But how?

Staring at the rifle as if it were a crystal ball, she considered her options and her chances. Her glance flicked Billy Ray's way, but not so much as a leaf twitched.

She twisted her wrists, struggling to loosen the rope as she'd seen James Bond and any number of television super spies do. She felt it slacken a notch which encouraged her to try harder. After twisting and turning, struggling so hard she could hear her teeth grind, and her wrists felt raw and stinging from rope burn, the rope loosened allowing her ample space to work the jack knife out of her pocket. Carefully, she popped the blade. She sawed at the rope at a snail's pace, careful not to slit her wrists, her nerves jumping every time she heard so much as a twig snap. Finally, the twine slithered to the ground at her feet.

Wasting no time, she dove for Billy Ray's rifle. She grabbed it just as he came crashing through the bushes. Rolling, she came up with the gun pointed wildly in the air, struggling for accurate aim.

"What are you doing!" With a wild gleam in his eyes, Billy Ray dove on top of her, grabbing for the weapon. His weight nearly suffocated her. His stench nearly knocked her out. They rolled in the mud as they struggled for control of the deadly weapon.

Her strength was no match for his, but her determination served her well. She dug her finger nails into the sensitive underbelly of his throat and twisted and jammed her fist into the bottom of his nose as her policeman brother had taught her in self-defense.

He howled with pain as blood spurted from his nose. Instead of doubling over, he grabbed her shoulders, twisted her around and slammed her to the ground with a primitive snarl.

Wind whooshed from her lungs and she started to black out as her fingers found the trigger.

Both barrels exploded. Gunpowder singed her nostrils.

# Chapter Thirteen

Kelly's eyes squeezed opened slowly. Yancey's foot stomped not two inches from her face and he yanked the rifle from her grasp before she could catch her breath. Everything still looked fuzzy and shadowy and she squinted.

That was one terrible nightmare. She shook her head to clear her mind, but the man's face came into focus and she froze. She wished it were merely a nightmare.

"You're too much trouble." Yancey's words came out more as growls than words.

"I'm bleeding! Red shot me!" Billy Ray yelled when Yancey returned to camp. He clamped his hand ineffectually over his oozing wound. Blood oozed through his fingers.

"Stop whining. We'll make her pay. All we wanted was a little fun and a few fur pelts. She'd no right to do what she done to you, boy." Yancey struck a match and lit a cigarette. Inhaling deeply, he glared at her, his eyes as soulless as the devil himself.

"No right." Billy Ray wheezed, coughing. "You'd better get me to a hospital, Uncle Yancey, afore I bleed to death."

Yancey exhaled, smoke filling the air. "We ain't parading into no hospital with a federal marshal after us. We might as well wear a neon sign around our necks telling the world we're poachers."

"Get me a bandage or something, at least," Billy Ray said on punctuated breaths. Blood seeped through his trembling fingers.

Yancey waved his arm in an exaggerated sweeping gesture encompassing the Everglades, the ash falling off his cigarette. "Ain't got no bandages. Does this look like Jackson General to you?" He exhaled an exasperated sigh.

"Cut the crap. Help me tear off a piece of my shirt and tie it over my leg, like a tourniquet." Billy Ray struggled to rip his shirt.

"Oh, all right, crybaby. Looks like a little scratch to me. We're still gonna make Red pay," Yancey said, a dangerous glint in his eye that scraped shivers up her spine. "First, I got to tie her up again and I'll do it right. Then I'll settle the score with that red haired bitch before dark settles and she escapes again." He licked his lips.

"I get first crack at her. She maimed me for life."

"Stop whining, Billy."

Sudden crashing in the bushes grabbed her attention. Hope flared in her heart. Was it the Lone Ranger?

Yancey seemed to forget all about Billy Ray, cocking his rifle. "Shut up, something's coming. Might be them tigers," he whispered loudly, harshly, brooking no argument. Excitement gleamed in his eyes. "Jamaica, here we come. They'll fetch a pretty penny on the Black Market."

"What if it's Bradley?" Fear twinged Billy Ray's voice.

The gleam in Yancey's eyes glowed brighter. "I'm ready for him. Let him come."

Hope died, suffocated by fear. Nick wouldn't rush in without scouting them out first, would he? He was brighter than that.

Yancey crouched low, his rifle aimed at the bushes, laying in wait for whatever was coming. Heavy beads of perspiration dotted his brow.

A deer bounded through the clearing and she let out a sigh of relief, her shoulders slumping. The handcuffs cut into her wrists again, chafing them.

Yancey fired his gun wildly and the deer veered to the right, straight at her in its fright. She pitched to her side, it's sharp hooves narrowly missing her as it bounded through the far bushes.

The bullet whizzed by Nick's cheek from where he watched in the bushes. His military training served him well. He ducked and rolled in the opposite direction, trying to scramble away into the cover of the bushes away from danger.

Yancey's head snapped up and he peered into the bushes. He

reloaded his rifle and cocked it.

She followed his gaze and spied movement and the glint of gold. Her breath left her and her chest tightened. She knew it was Nick. And she knew Yancey knew it, too.

Before he reached cover, Nick felt the cold unrelenting steel of Yancey's rifle barrel jabbed in between his shoulder blades, like a long pointy bayonet, pointed directly at his heart. One false move and he'd be speared like a kingfish.

"Freeze, or you're gator bait." Yancey poked the rifle deeper into Nick's shoulders, laughing maniacally.

Nick didn't need to be told. He always froze when Yancey stuck a gun in his back, he thought sarcastically.

"Billy. Lookit who we got here! It's Pretty Boy warden. Get his gun."

"You know I can't walk over there Yancey. My leg's bleeding." Billy Ray clutched his leg for emphasis, his face contorted with pain.

"What'd you rather have? A bleeding leg or his bullet through your heart? Get that gun!" Yancey yelled.

Billy Ray stood as best he could. The saw grass rustled and bushes parted as Billy dragged his injured leg behind him, whimpering like a wounded dog.

Yancey just shook his head, mumbling. "Why do I put up with that idiot nephew of mine?"

When Nick thought he'd collapse from exhaustion, he felt the gun ease off a bit.

"When I tell you to, stand up real slow, Pretty Boy. Put your hands up in the air real high."

Yancey stuck the gun in Billy Ray's hands. "Cover me."

"Don't move, Bradley," Bill Ray warned.

Yancey stuck his hand in Nick's pant pockets lifting out his keys, knife and handcuffs. "Lookit what I found here. All kinds of neat police gadgets." Yancey snapped the switchblade open. Waving it under Nick's nose, Yancey got right up in Nick's face. "No funny stuff. Remember when I gave you that?" Yancey traced the scar on Nick's cheek with the tip of Nick's knife.

Nick watched Yancey stoically, not moving a muscle. Kelly's face lay in shadows but he could feel her rapt attention on them. This wasn't the moment for heroics. It was a time to watch and wait. Now would be a good time for the Guard to appear if they were planning to anyway.

"What you looking for?" Yancey demanded.

"I though I heard a gator growling." Nick lied, quick on his feet. "I was running from one when I happened upon you fellows. Thought for sure by now it'd caught us."

"Sure you weren't looking for some pretty red head?" Yancey scowled. He pressed the knife closer.

Nick's heart quickened a few beats. This guy suspected he was with Cincinnati?

"What red head?" Maybe if he pretended he didn't know her, she'd be released.

"Just that piece of fluff over there that caused us a mite of trouble. We've got scores to settle with both of you." Picking up a long piece of grass, Yancey chawed on it thoughtfully, still holding the knife on Nick. "You know, Billy Ray. I bet she's with Pretty Boy here."

With a ferocious gleam in his eye, Yancey turned to Nick. He bounced on his haunches gleefully, then spat in Nick's face. "We're gonna have a little fun with your girlfriend while you watch. Then we're gonna take care of the both of you so that you don't get in our way again."

"Yeah! Then we'll use you for gator bait. Serve her right for shooting me." Billy Ray grumbled, daggers shooting from his eyes.

"I don't know what you're talking about. I came out here with a contingent of federal agents. I wouldn't bring a woman out here." Nick lied, hoping they'd let Cincinnati go.

"I ain't seen no one except you and her, Pretty Boy. Where's all your friends, if they're here?" Yancey smiled broadly, his yellow teeth dripping with tobacco juice.

"Holy Jesus, Yancey! What if there are a whole bunch of feds out here? They'll lock us away for sure. Maybe we should let them go and get the hell out of here."

"Shut up." Yancey grimaced. "He's bluffing. He's alone except for the girl."

"They might be surrounding us now." Nick worked on Billy Ray's insecurities. He might be able to split the loyalties if he played it right. "It'd go better on you if you let me go unharmed."

"Jesus, Yancey! What if he's telling the truth? Let's get out of here! Those cats aren't worth going to jail for."

"I ain't gonna tell you again. They're bluffing. We're going to Jamaica as soon as we get those cats. Keep your rifle on him. Shoot to kill if he moves." He turned to go, then threw over his shoulder. "Don't you be listening to any of his lies, Billy Ray. He's just trying to fool you. All the Feds are too busy having a shooting match in Cutler Ridge to care about two cats in the swamp. We're all alone except for these two troublemakers."

"You'd better be right, Yancey, you just better be." Billy Ray pointed his rifle at Nick. Muttering under his breath, just loudly enough for Nick to hear, he said, "And those cats had better fetch a pretty penny. They sure better."

"Nobody will buy those tigers, Billy Ray. You know that, don't you? Nick told him. "They'll be too hot to handle. I made sure of it before I left. I told all the TV and radio stations before I set out. *Everybody* knows those tigers, Billy Ray. There aren't many white tigers around. You're shivering and your ghostly pale. Infection's setting into your leg. Why don't you let me doctor it before you have to have it amputated. There's lots of nasty germs out here."

"One more word," Billy Ray threatened between shivering clenched teeth, "and I'll shoot. Swear to God, Pretty Boy."

The rifle shook in Billy Ray's feverish hands. Nick didn't doubt the truth of his words. What a rattlesnake's nest he'd stumbled into! What had ever possessed him to let a woman tag along? A red-headed, hot-tempered, trouble-maker at that?

He was beginning to feel like a cornered animal. Now he knew what went through their minds when he had the drop on them. Should he risk getting shot, maybe killed, by rushing Billy Ray, or did he wait docilely and let Yancey finish him off? Billy Ray *did* have the drop on him, but he wasn't feeling too good.

If he were to rush him suddenly, Billy Ray'd only get one shot off at best. Unless he got very lucky and killed him with that bullet, Nick could overpower him. Wounded, Billy Ray was no match for him. It was his best chance, probably his only chance, and Cincinnati's only chance.

Watching Cincinnati, Nick knew he had to try. She was no match for Yancey. That guy was a keg of dynamite ready to explode, just like her mouth. Hopefully, Billy Ray would look away, if only for a second. Then Nick would strike—hard.

It wasn't long before Billy Ray glanced away. An animal roared, perhaps one of Cincinnati's tigers, and Billy Ray looked nervously at the bushes.

Nick pitched himself forward and rolled to the side, kicking the gun out of Billy Ray's hands. He'd forgotten that he was tied up and couldn't use the gun even if he managed to get it. Nor could he use his fists. That left his feet. So he kicked like a mule, aiming for Billy Ray's stomach and injured leg. One of his kicks must have connected for he felt intense pain and through the haze, he thought he heard Billy Ray's agonized scream.

"If you want the lady to live a little longer, pretty boy," he heard all of a sudden, chilling his blood, "you'll crawl back to your corner and sit real nice and still."

Damn, Yancey was back, his rifle poked into Cincinnati's back.

"Why don't you just kill us now and be done with it?" she screamed at her abductor. "You're going to shoot us anyway. Why prolong it?"

"Well," Yancey said, acting like he considered her question. "Billy Ray and I figure you owe us something."

"Owe you?" Kelly growled, like one of her tigers, claws unsheathed, teeth bared. Her cats eyes flashed fire. "The only thing I owe either of you is a kick in the teeth, or the ba..."

"Kelly!" What was she trying to do? Get them killed? They needed time, time for the backup he'd called to find them, to rescue them. It felt like hours ago that he'd radioed for help. They might be close by now, maybe just around the bend. And she'd get them killed just before they were rescued. He didn't want anything to happen to her. He wanted a chance to explore his love for this feisty, red-headed termagant. Even if they only had a few more moments together in this lousy swamp, he wanted it. He might be selfish, but he wanted every single second he could get.

Yancey either didn't see the fire flash in her eyes, or he didn't care. He probably figured he had the upper hand and there wasn't a thing they could do to change it, Nick grimaced. He was probably right. "I ain't had a woman in a *long* time and I reckon you're as good as any."

"I love that sweet talk!" Kelly gritted sarcastically through clenched teeth. Her emerald eyes flashed fire more brilliant than the sun.

"And it will be even more fun making your Pretty Boy boyfriend watch and there ain't a damned thing he can do about it," Yancey grinned a devilish smile, baring his yellowed dirty teeth, getting right in her face. "And while we're doing it, I'm gonna tell you exactly how I'm gonna skin those tigers."

"No!" She screamed, ignoring Nick's warning. Spinning on her injured leg, she swung her good leg behind her, kicking with all her might, aiming to make Yancey an eunuch.

Nick watched in dread fascination as Yancey side stepped her feeble attempt and caught her leg, flipping her to the ground with the ease of a karate master. She landed with a thud, her eyes closed.

"No!" It was Nick's turn to scream as he struggled up. "Are you afraid to fight a real man? Only cowards bully women!"

Yancey raised his rifle, aiming it at Nick's head, cocking it. "You'd better pray the Lord have mercy on your soul, Pretty Boy. I'm tired of your games."

An exploding gunshot rang in Nick's ears, deafening him. Fear gripped him, but not for himself, but for Kelly. They couldn't shoot her. He couldn't lose her like he'd lost Melissa and Ashlea. He struggled against the chains that bound him like a caged animal, intent on protecting Kelly.

He breathed a sigh of relief when he saw the bullet miss its mark. Still, he bristled, waiting for his chance to teach Yancey and Billy Ray a lesson they wouldn't forget.

Suddenly, ferocious growls from the pits of hell bellowed in Nick's ears and his heart slammed against his ribs. The gunfire had probably scared them to death, prompting them to strike back. Vivid images filled Nick's mind and churned his stomach. He struggled to put the Technicolor images from his mind and regain his composure. He'd be worthless to himself and to Kelly if he lost his nerve.

Shrill screams reverberated in the air. Nick couldn't tell if they were Cincinnati's, their abductors or the tigers. But they were eerie, horrific.

He sought the tigers in the dimming light, waiting to meet death bravely. He steeled his soul for the inevitable, expecting to see gnashing teeth baring down upon him or Cincinnati, perhaps both.

Instead, he couldn't believe his own eyes. He blinked, not believing what he saw. Two white Bengal tigers leapt from the bushes in a graceful arc. Their sinewed bodies stretched in a perfect dive, their faces round and full. They wrestled Yancey and Billy Ray to the ground with barely a struggle.

Billy Ray screamed, inciting the tigers further who growled and gnashed their teeth.

A shrill shriek ripped from Yancey's throat.

Cincinnati pulled herself up groggily, her eyes cloudy and dazed. But her voice rang firm. "Kenga, Rama, stop! Heel!"

To Nick's amazement, the tigers stopped immediately, lifted themselves off Yancey and Billy Ray, and ambled to Kelly's side. They lay down on either side of her like trained dogs, licking her hands as she tried to pet their heads. "Good boy. Good girl."

Billy Ray and Yancey were crawling on their bellies through the slick saw grass like GI soldiers in the Viet Kong, heading towards their side arms. "Cincinnati, look out! They're going for their guns."

"Kenga. Rama. Attack!" Her eyes flashing severe warnings.

"No!" Yancey and Billy Ray yelled in unison, covering their heads under their arms. "Not that, we'll stop. Don't let them eat us," Yancey pleaded. His lanky frame trembled. His eyes darkened.

"Please stop them." Billy Ray quivered uncontrollably, losing control of his bodily functions. A growing wet circle stained his pants.

"Guard!" Hearing her command, Nick watched in amazement as Kenga and Rama each sat on a man. They didn't harm him, unless their immense weight on the smalls of their backs crushed them. They just stretched out on the men as if they were taking a leisurely Sunday afternoon nap. They yawned, their jaws dropping wide open, their huge tongues lolling down then curling back up like a New Year's whistle. They even made that loud whining sound that kitty cats make when stretched out in the afternoon sun, but much louder.

Crashing came through the bushes. Nick pivoted on his heel, looking for the new source of danger, expecting to come face to face with the black, beady eyes of a hungry gator. His heart lurched, and he scooted best he could into the clearing away from the bushes, hoping the tigers didn't take a mind to *guard* him instead of Billy Ray or Yancey.

Voices followed the rustling of the brush. What if this was more poachers? Tiger hides fetched a pretty penny. There were bound to be other poachers aiming at this grand prize. He knew for a fact that Yancey and Billy Ray weren't the only money grubbing poachers in these parts.

"Bradley? Kerrigan? Is that you? Where are you? Identify yourselves," a stern voice said.

"God, Nick. That's Colonel Messenger. He found us!" she whispered theatrically, her eyes wide and scared.

"We're saved Yancey!"

"Stop whining Billy! It's more feds." Yancey breathed harshly, barely able to speak with the weight of the tigers pushing in on his lungs.

"Identify yourself or I'll shoot!" the Colonel yelled.

"It's Bradley. Glad you could make it," Nick drawled sarcastically. "To your right, about one hundred yards," Nick added when they stumbled in confusion.

When the soldiers, led by the colonel arrived in the clearing, they stopped dead in their tracks, unsure what to do when the saw Kenga and Rama sprawled over Yancey and Billy Ray, their tongues lolling out the sides of their mouths. They looked afraid, as if the tigers would perceive them as new danger and attack them.

"Don't worry," Kelly assured them, seeming to read their thoughts. "They'll obey me." As an afterthought, she added, "As long as you put away your guns. Or they may feel threatened."

"Stay!" she commanded. Kenga and Rama seemed perfectly happy to continue their rest, oblivious to the moans and whimpers of Yancey and Billy Ray pleading for mercy beneath them.

The soldiers started to drop their rifles obediently. They were painstakingly careful not to make sudden moves that would frighten the tigers. Their faces drained of blood like ghosts against the dark backdrop of the forest.

"Raise your firearms! On my command, shoot to kill!" the Colonel commanded. Obediently, the men lifted their guns, looking rather displeased but taking careful aim anyway.

"Colonel," Nick yelled. "This is cold blooded murder! Those tigers aren't making a threatening move. They haven't hurt anyone."

"Speak for yourself. They're breaking our backs," Yancey grumbled, scowling at Nick.

"You want me to wait until they maul one of us before I do something about it?" the Colonel spoke disbelievingly.

"If they were going to attack, don't you think they were going to do so before now?" Kelly said, the voice of reason.

Kenga lifted her paw and licked it as if nothing unusual had happened. Her topaz eyes never left Kelly's face. Her tail lifted up and down, patting the ground as if she were swatting nonexistent flies. Rama yawned, resting his head on his paws.

Kelly kept her gaze steady on Kenga's. As long as she stayed calm, so would Kenga.

Billy Ray, beneath the heavy tiger groaned, as she shifted more weight onto him. "My leg! It's crushing my leg!"

"Shut up!" Yancey yelled.

Ferocious growls bellowed from the bushes behind the Colonel. Rama's head snapped up. His ears twitched forward. Kenga's head snapped around, her eyes pinpointed on the spot where the growls originated. Her tail froze in mid air.

"What's happening?" the Colonel asked, his attention riveted on the tigers.

An animal growled just behind the bushes. The Colonel twirled, seeking the sound.

A huge Florida panther lunged through the air, it's claws bared, it's head thrashing back and forth violently, huge fangs seeking first blood. It seemed to hang in the air above the Colonel.

The soldiers swung their rifles to shoot the creature, all gazes rapt on the scene. The Colonel froze, directly in the cat's path, his eyes wide and shocked. Nick could smell the man's fear which meant the animals could too. That was deadly.

Nick swore under his breath and his muscles coiled.

Kenga and Rama leapt into the air, their powerful haunches pushing off Yancey and Billy Ray in perfect synchronization, like a water ballet in the air. Twin growls rumbled from the depths of their bellies as they gnashed their teeth, ready to battle.

Jaws dropped. All eyes riveted to the cats poised mid-air on an irrevocable collision course. Soldiers scattered, running for the hills. Kelly jumped to her feet. "Get out of there Colonel!" she warned.

Still paralyzed with fear, the colonel remained planted to the ground.

Kelly lunged for the Colonel, knocking him out of the way a split second before the monstrous cats fell, writhing to the ground in a life and death struggle on the exact spot where the colonel had been standing.

Fur flew. Kelly couldn't discern one body from the next, the struggle was intense and fierce, yet deadly short.

Within a matter of seconds, the life and death combat ended. Kenga and Rama crawled to Kelly searching for her scent among all the strangers. Kelly knelt eye level with the cats. Rama rubbed his head against Kelly's cheek, purring like a kitten. Kenga stretched out next to Kelly, her head resting on Kelly's bent knee.

Her tortured gaze lifted to the panther, a monstrous thing, sprawled whimpering on the ground, severely injured, yet still alive. It was a pitiful sight and Kelly's heart lurched, a tear trickling down her cheek.

"Put the creature out of it's misery Colonel. Or untie me and let me do it," Nick said as Kelly opened her mouth. She shut it without a word and smiled tremulously at Nick, the sheen of unshed tears in her eyes.

Now she felt compassion for the animal that tried to kill them? Nick paused, studying her lovely face in the shadows. After deep soul searching, he realized he wouldn't have her any other way. It was her compassion, her lust for life that drew him to her. She filled that empty void that had weighed on his heart for an eternity. He was just grateful to God that she was alive and unharmed. He didn't think he could bear to lose another person he loved. Not one so young, beautiful and full of life.

The Colonel, who had crawled to the far side of the clearing during the fight rose to his feet shakily. He smoothed his hair out of his eyes with his fingers. His gaze shifted from the panther to the tigers, back to the panther a few feet from him.

"That was a mighty brave and stupid thing you did young lady. And I'm mighty grateful," the colonel said as he walked behind Nick and tugged at the ropes that bound his hands.

"Grateful enough to drop charges against us, Colonel?" Kelly asked hopefully, her heart in her eyes. She lowered her head and rubbed her cheek against Kenga's soft head, her hair red as the dusk sun against the tiger's snow white fur.

Freed, Nick rubbed his wrists where the ropes cut them. Red bruised swelled on the tender flesh. He crossed to the nearest rifle, scooped it up, aimed and put the panther out of its misery in one, swift shot.

Billy Ray and Yancey crept toward the bushes on their bellies, barely breaking a twig. She spied them from the corner of her eye.

"The poachers are getting away, Nick!" Kelly warned as he prepared himself to react.

Nick pivoted on his heel, heaving the rifle to his shoulder. He fired a warning shot a few inches to Yancey's right. "Not so fast boys. The party's not over."

"Devereaux! Gilbert!" the colonel yelled. "Take these prisoners into custody."

Soldiers tromped back to the clearing. They circled Nick and Kelly as well as Yancey and Billy Ray, their rifles raised threateningly. They looked like a Columbian death squad.

"Colonel?" Kelly implored, standing to face off against the Colonel. "Are the Lieutenant and I prisoners?" She jutted her firm jaw forward defiantly, a twinge of pride in her husky voice. Her slight breasts pushed against her green jumper and her hair swung in a silky curtain around her shoulders. Again, she struck Nick as magnificent. A rare find indeed.

The Colonel stared at the tigers contemplatively who lay passively at Kelly's side. Rama licked her hand and stared at her adoringly.

"They saved my life. I owe them."

"Does that mean you won't press charges, Sir?" Nick asked. He trudged through the clearing to where the soldiers hauled Yancey to his feet. A soldier followed Nick hitching his firearm to his shoulder. The Colonel put his hand on the barrel pushing it aside. He shook his head at the soldier. The young man stepped back, dropping his gun to his side.

"You have something of mine, Old Timer and I need it back." A ghostly smile played around the corners of Nick's lips.

Yancey stared at Nick unflinchingly. His nostrils flared.

Nick stuck his hand in Yancey's right pocket, then his left till he found the key ring that held the key to Kelly's freedom. He dangled them in front of Yancey's face. "You led me a merry chase, but the game's over."

"You didn't get us. Those cats did."

"They did, didn't they? I owe them the biggest sirloins I can find!" With that, Nick spun on his heel. He went to Kelly and unlocked the cuffs that bound her and put them back in his pocket.

Rubbing her wrists like Nick did, Kelly looked up at Nick, love brimming in her eyes. Gently, she moved Kenga's head from her knee and stretched to her full height. She bent her arms back and forth to work out the kinks in them from being forced behind her back for nearly an hour.

Nick spanned his hands around her waist and pulled her against him. "I didn't get a chance to answer your question earlier." His lips fluttered over her cheek and teased the corner of her mouth.

"What question?" she asked, gazing at Nick. Her hands crept around his neck. She let her fingers play in the soft hair at the nape of his neck. His face looked shadowy in the moonlit night, all angles and crevices. His eyes were inscrutable, his breath hot on her neck. She arched against him.

Rama got to his feet and rubbed against Nick's legs. He licked Nick's hands where they clasped Kelly.

Kelly laughed. "He likes you."

"I was so scared. I love you, Cincinnati. I thought I'd lost you."

Kelly stared at him speechlessly.

"Cat got your tongue, Cincinnati? Don't you have anything to say to me?" He trailed kisses along the hollow of her throat.

Kelly gazed at him with adoration shining from her eyes. His fingers kneaded the small of her back. "I love you too. With all my heart."

"That's what I want."

Kelly leaned into Nick, stretching up to meet his lips. His met hers halfway, capturing them, softly at first, then more demanding. They clung to each other for what seemed an eternity, until they heard someone clearing their throat nearby.

Slowly, reluctantly, Nick released Kelly's lips and lifted his head.

"We're heading out. I suggest you do the same," the colonel said in an embarrassed voice. He shuffled his feet. "We'll take the prisoners with us. Do you need a lift?"

"Our truck's just down the road. We'd appreciate an escort, Sir." Nick looked at Kelly with smoldering eyes. "Can you give us one more moment? We have unfinished business."

"At ease, lieutenant." The colonel tried to hide a grin. He turned to talk to his men who were loading the panther's body into a cage.

Nick took Kelly's hands in his and bent on one knee. "Will you marry me, Cincinnati?"

Kelly stared at Nick dumbfounded. "You hardly know me!" she gasped.

"That wasn't the answer I wanted to hear." He cracked a small smile. "I know everything I need to know. I love you." Nick kissed her hair and smoothed it away from her brow. "Do you love me?" He ripped a piece of long saw grass from its roots and tied it around her engagement ring finger.

"With all my heart."

"Well?"

"Love me, love my tigers. Can you?"

Nick glanced down at the big cats.

"No promises," he finally said.

"None?" she asked disappointed. She tried to pull away. Her hair swung in front of her face like a velvety curtain.

"Not about the tigers." He pulled her to him again and held her in an iron grip. His finger lifted her chin so that their gazes met. "When I look into your eyes, I see a paradise I never thought I'd find again. When you held me in your arms, I found my salvation." He bent his head an kissed her lips gently.

His expression was sultry when he lifted his lips. "I promise to love, honor and obey *you*. I promise I'll try to like your tigers. But tigers play too rough for me. At least most of the time." Nick reached down and scratched Kenga behind her ears to ease the harshness of his words. "Can you live with that?"

Kelly gazed deeply into his golden eyes that reminded her curiously of Kenga's when she was in a playful mood. A slow smile split her face and all the sunshine of a South Florida dawn illuminated her eyes. "It's worth a try Lieutenant. Definitely worth a try."

# Epilogue

Mattie climbed onto Kelly's legs, burrowing as close as he could get, although it looked about as impossible as cozying up to a watermelon. He knew the feeling well. A sly grin twisted his lips. He wouldn't mind trying again if they weren't celebrating Katy's birthday with her family and friends.

Oblivious to Kelly's condition, Mattie dug his elbows into Kelly's stomach for leverage, then kneed her as he strived for better position.

"Wanna see my medal again?" Mattie pulled out his blue and green striped shirt and stuck it under her nose. Proudly, he showed off his shiny medal of honor for saving his mother and sister the day of the hurricane.

"Awesome!" she enthused, peering at it closely as if she hadn't seen it at least a million times in the past year.

The boy angled on her lap for better position, not an easy task on an eight and a half month pregnant woman.

Kelly winced and her body stiffened, sending Nick's protective instincts into auto-pilot. Not that he'd ever know what it was like to be pregnant, but he knew that had to smart and it couldn't be good for the baby.

"Whoa, slugger," he said, scooping the squirrely seven-year old into his arms. "You can't pop the toaster when the doctor's out of town for the weekend."

"You're *toast*," his wife mouthed, her eyes flashing emerald fire.

Her lips twisted into a sassy grin and he bent to kiss her. "I'm not a toaster and this baby's not a pop tart."

"I'm sorry, Aunt Kelly." Mattie stared at her with big puppy dog eyes and a dimple played hide and seek in his cheek. "Did I hurt you or the baby?"

She tweaked his cheek and winked, then struggled to reposition herself in the yellow and white lawn chair as if it took major effort. "No, you didn't. Uncle Nicky's just a nervous daddy."

*Darn right.* He grew morose without warning. He wondered if he'd be a better father the second time around and knew he wasn't ready to find out, even if things were at the point of no return.

When Katy bounced into the back yard chasing a ball that Hunter tossed, his gaze followed her. Her bathing suit wedged up her baby cheeks, reminding him of the Coppertone girl. Everything else reminded him of Ashlea, especially her silky blonde tresses swinging freely across her bare back and her tinkling, carefree laughter, laughter that he thanked God for every day.

His heart lurched as it never failed to do when he watched the precious child. Although she didn't strictly resemble Ashlea, in shadow or in profile she could fool his heart into thinking she was the reincarnation. For a split second anyway. And it only took that long bring a flood of painful memories.

Kelly caught his gaze, her expression somber, thoughtful. Her slim hands spread across her bulging belly and rubbed it as she'd taken a habit to doing. Her diamond wedding ring glittered in the sunlight with each flick of her wrist. At least she wasn't chanting in meditation or listening to ocean noises.

When Sheryl Wilson slid the glass doors open, he was hit in the face with a whoosh of air-conditioning and barbecue spicy enough to make his tongue burn. Limping outside, carrying a heavy oval platter, she headed for Kelly.

Felix, one of the men who had helped rescue Katy and was now one of the group of friends, intercepted the pass and served it to Kelly. "For the little mama." The corners of his lips crooked up in amusement and sent him a conspiratorial grin. "This should be enough to start you off."

Nick suppressed a grin when he counted two ears of corn swimming in melted butter, two double-stacked hamburgers, a hot dog and assorted chips. He whistled lowly under his breath. To Sheryl he said, "You'd better bring her a bismate chaser or the baby's going to have a major case of heartburn."

Both women rounded on him and he decided he'd rather face down Kelly's tigers at dinner time.

"Bad move, teasing pregnant women," Felix said, chortling, his eyes dancing with glee.

*But it's such fun teasing the women.* He couldn't suppress the grin that sprang to his lips.

Simultaneously, the women counter-attacked. Sheryl pounced for the kill first. "Are you saying I'm a lousy cook?"

Kelly arched an exquisitely shaped brow and lunged for the jugular. "Is this another appetite crack? I *am* eating for two."

"Are you sure it's not two-hundred?" He ducked when a red and white beach ball sailed in the air straight for his face. It whizzed benignly over his head, bounced a few times then landed in the pool. The gentle evening breeze pushed it around the slowly undulating water.

"I know you thrive on danger, but antagonizing these two is suicide, guy," Hunter said then popped one chip after another into his mouth and munched happily.

Sheryl's husband, Doug, lifted the pass-through window which groaned as if it needed a dose of oil. He slid out platters filled with barbecued ribs, hamburgers and hotdogs. "Come get them while they're hot!"

No matter how long he lived, Kelly wouldn't domesticate him enough to wear a pork belly apron as Doug wore tonight. Every time he looked at poor Doug, he burst out laughing and he covered it this time by pretending to cough.

Katy appeared at his side, tugging at his arm. "Can you help me, Uncle Nick?" Her gaze slid to the hot dogs and watermelon slices.

"What are uncles for?" His good humor turned to dust when his heart lurched as it never failed to do when he glimpsed the girl from the wrong angle, caught unawares. He swallowed the basketball-sized lump in his throat, then forced a smile to his lips.

Lifting her in his arms, he held her close, feeling her heartbeat against his, and squeezed a fraction tighter than he should have until she squirmed against him. He loosened his hold. "Anything you want, birthday girl." She was the same age as Ashlea when she died. Thank Heaven she'd made it. There was a time he'd knelt at her hospital bed making deals with God that she'd live, but it had been well worth anything he'd promised.

She dove against him without warning, hugged his neck, then kissed his cheek with a big, slobbery smooch. He rocked back on his haunches, barely maintaining his balance so they didn't both topple into the pool.

"I love you, Uncle Nick and Aunt Kelly." Her voice sounded exuberant, joyous. China blue eyes glowed at him and again, he saw another set of eyes staring back.

"Much more of that and Aunt Kelly will be jealous." He tried to lighten his tone and not sound so dire. Glancing over Katy's shoulder, he met Kelly's indulgent smile. Butter dripped from her chin as she chomped happily on the last of her corn.

"She can kiss your cheek until she turns twelve, then you're off-limits. Hand-shakes only."

Groucho leapt onto the ledge on a reconnaissance mission to filch a hamburger or side of ribs. He came face to face with Nick and froze except for his the tip of his tail which swished back and forth gently.

"Scat cat!" Doug said, hissing.

The feline backed up, then jumped to the ground when Doug flicked water on him.

Despite the happy occasion, Nick didn't feel much like eating. He pushed his food around his plate and snuck piece by piece to Groucho who scrounged around his feet. He owed the big tom cat his life and Kelly's. When the food was gone, he scratched the cat behind his ears.

The impending birth had him worried. To hell with worried. Face it, he was terrified!

He'd lost Melissa in childbirth and later, he'd lost his angel. He couldn't lose Kelly, too. But she'd been adamant about having this child.

He watched his bride covertly, love welling deep inside mingled with the fear that ate at him. She'd insisted on working with her tigers until a couple of months ago and she couldn't wait to go back to work once the baby was old enough to go into daycare. Sheryl had volunteered to baby-sit.

Kelly passed her empty plate to Sheryl who heaped watermelon and ribs on it indulgently then passed it back.

Antsy, unable to wait another second, he ambled across the room, picked up a pink pearlescent package, a giant swatch of hot pink curling ribbon tumbling over the sides. He smiled when Katy's eyes grew round as saucers and stars twinkled in their depths.

Sheryl pulled a frown at him as she perched on lounge chair next to her husband. "We're not ready for presents yet. You're spoiling her."

"I owe her," he said, his voice gruff, even to his own ears. The box fairly burned his fingers and he remembered a long ago day when these people had come into his life, the day he'd fallen in love with his wife.

Katy jumped out of her chair and sprinted to him. Her cheeks glowed. Her eyes glittered. "Can I open one present now, Mommy?"

"We always wait for the cake..." Sheryl's voice drifted away hesitantly.

Katy turned her one-hundred watt smile on her father. "Please, Daddy!"

Before her father could voice a response, she tilted her urchin face to Nick. "Please, Uncle Nicky! Please, please please!"

Kelly stopped eating to watch and she nodded her assent. She reached for his hand and squeezed tightly. Her wedding ring dug into his hand, but it was exquisite torture.

He turned his over and joined his fingers with hers. His thumb rubbed concentric circles over the wedding band and surrounding flesh, feeling the sparks of electricity he felt every time he touched her.

Curious, Mattie peered over his sister's shoulder. "Hold out for toys," Mattie whispered in her ear, just loudly enough that Nick caught it. "You gotta be tough. No clothes. No jewelry. But money's okay."

The boy had a lot to learn. Someday he'd discover that jewelry meant much more than toys. Any toy.

He tousled the child's hair filled with sunlight. Handing her the gift, he whispered, "Happy birthday, Katy."

Squealing with delight and anticipation, the girl plopped to the floor with the package between her Indian crossed legs. Seconds later, ripped wrapping paper and bits of ribbon littered the patio floor as if the Cat in the Hat had spread his pink spots across the Wilson's back porch. Rover pounced on a large sheet of the discarded paper and chewed on it.

The gift beckoned him and his eyes riveted to it. When she lifted the porcelain doll out of layers of white tissue paper as carefully as if it were a real newborn infant, its china eyes fluttered open and stared at him.

The moment of truth was upon him. It wasn't the same doll his daughter had dropped in the yard the night the panther attacked her. Nor was it Katy's doll that he'd kicked that had been crushed under the weight of the Wilson's old house. But it seemed to him that china doll eyes all held the same accusations in them as if they belonged to a collective.

He expected to read that accusation in this doll's eyes. Still, he'd promised himself he'd replace the doll and it had taken him till now to make good that promise.

But the eyes were clear, actually smiling.

He sighed in relief.

Katy bulldozed into him, flinging her arms around his waist, almost knocking him backwards over a chair. "She's beautiful. I'll name her Kelly." She glanced over her shoulder at her brother. "Can I keep her? She's a toy."

"I hoped you'd get a dump truck." He kicked at the ribbon with his toe, his expression crestfallen, his hands shoved in his back pocket.

"I'll get you a dump truck for your birthday..." Nick said.

"You're spoiling the kids," Doug said, his voice booming. "Just wait till yours is born and we spoil him. Payback is sweet."

"Nicky Junior will be too busy with our tigers to be spoiled," Kelly said, smiling smugly.

"Over my dead body," Nick said. His wife merely smiled at him beguilingly.

A cellular phone shrilled, muffled by cloth. All the adults looked at each other then shifted positions to pull their phones out of their pockets.

Nick read the neon indicator panel on his but it was blank.

His wife flipped hers open. "Bradley here. What's up, Derek?" She stared into the distance, her pupil's pinpoints of light. Her lips firmed and she was in her other world. "Uh huh. When did they start?"

She patted her belly, then froze, her smile fading.

He was at her side in a flash, his insides churning like storm tossed seas, his palms clammy. "What's wrong?"

She put her hand over the receiver and whispered, "Kenga's in labor. She needs me. I have to go." She struggled to her feet.

He glowered at her in his best game commissioner's glare. "Like hell!" he hissed. "You can send flowers, or steaks, like everyone else after the blessed delivery."

"I have to go." She tried to push past him. Speaking into the phone, she said, "I'll be right there, Derek."

He plucked the phone from her hand, and held it high in the air out of reach when she tried to jump for it. Fortunately, she couldn't jump very high or with much heart in her condition.

"You'll have to handle this one yourself. We'll visit mother and baby after the birth." He severed the connection and tossed the phone to Doug.

"Who do you think you are?"

"Your husband. And you're not going into a pregnant tiger's den with my baby."

She faced off against him, her hands doubled into fists on her hips. "That pregnant tiger saved your life."

"For which I'll be forever grateful." He kissed the corner of her mouth and drew her close, taking some measure of comfort from her warmth, her exaggerated softness. "I'm scared enough as it is. Don't do this to me, too."

She pulled back and stared into his eyes, hers startled. Putting her hands on his shoulders, she tiptoed and kissed him square on his chin before she stood squarely on her flat soled water shoes again.

"I love you, Lieutenant. I'll never leave you."

"Not by choice..."

"Never by choice. I..." She paused, her lips turning downward and suddenly pinched. "I have to go." She pulled out of his embrace and wobbled towards the door.

"I thought you promised not to go?" Perplexed, he raked his hand through his hair and stared at this enigma that still constantly amazed him. He should've known better than to fall in love and then marry a redheaded woman. They were the epitome of unpredictability.

"Unless you want Nicky Junior born pool-side, we'd better go." She crooked her index finger at him.

"You're in labor?" His jaw dropped open and his feet froze. He could barely breath.

"She's not entering a dance marathon," Sheryl said wryly. She limped to Kelly's side, hugged her and kissed both cheeks. "I'm so happy for you. You'll be fine." She glanced at Nick with mock pity. "We'd better get the big He-man a wheel chair."

Kelly held out her hand to him. "I'll be with you. We'll be fine." When he still hesitated, she smiled her zoo-keeper-I-can-handle-anything-smile. "Promise."

Peering into her eyes that reflected the South Florida sun setting slowly behind him, he found calming reassurance that she and his new son would be fine. And he knew deep in his heart that the new tiger family would fare well, too. Just as their best friends, the Wilsons, had survived their near tragedies, his family would survive this.

An excerpt from

# *Next to Forever*

"What are you doing here?" she greeted him as friendly as a Rottweiler, her dark brow rising quizzically. She barred the door so he couldn't see inside. His sixth sense reeled. She was hiding something. He'd bet the school on it.

"You told me to drop by anytime. Said you have nothing to hide." He grinned wickedly. "I'm here to take you up on your offer."

"I didn't think you were serious..." If her voice turned any frostier, she'd turn him to ice. Her feet shifted and her hands clenched at her sides. A stray wisp of hair blew over her eyes and she tucked it behind her ear.

"So you are hiding something?" he challenged, trying to peer over her shoulder.

That worked like a charm. The Lawless woman moved back and beckoned him to enter, accepting his challenge, a gleam hard as diamonds flickering across her dark eyes. "My mother and grandmother have guests over today. You'll have to excuse our other company."

Kyle looked around the house unabashedly, astonished at it's understated elegance and charm. No love beads. No faded posters clinging to the walls with browning, curling cellophane tape. No loud rock and roll music—although music drifted from the back of the house. Big band music. Benny Goodman? Stained glass and Tiffany lamps lent splashes of color and elegance in unexpected corners reminding him of the prizes in Cracker Jack boxes.

And the furniture was all early American with fine upholstery. His feet sank into heavy-duty worsted pile carpeting. Fresh-baked bread and cinnamon brewing wafted around him like a warm cocoon. Lacy hand-crocheted doilies sat beneath porcelain cats.

So he'd been wrong about the house. But what about all the Pontiacs layered in bumper stickers?

"Is Josh home?" He'd work his way up to his other questions. Hopefully, his powers of observation would answer his questions. A picture was worth a thousand words.

"He's grounded to his room." She cupped her hands around her mouth and called, "Joshua, Mr. Jack —uhm sorry, what was your name?"

"Damian," he said dryly, quelling an urge to cross his arms over his chest.

"Mr. Damian's here to see you."

When no answering response came, he offered, "Why don't we go see him?"

"Want to take a peek in his room? Make sure there's no human sacrifices in the offing?" Her pouty lips twisted into a wry grimace. She lifted a finely arched eyebrow, then pivoted on her booted heel. Her long pony tail bobbed behind her beguilingly and his gaze fell fascinated on her well-proportioned back side.

Uneasiness rushed over him. This woman had an uncanny ability to read his mind. He hadn't been thinking exactly what she'd said, but she came too close for comfort. He followed her through the neat-as-a-pin house, peeking into every corner, fascinated at the stained glass. He wondered if Suki was the collector or her grandmother?

Giggling and raucous laughter drifted out from behind closed doors.

Kyle's head snapped around. "What was that?" He turned accusing eyes on Suzanne and thought he saw a flicker of guilt flit across her eyes.

"My grandmother's entertaining guests..." she said hesitantly, biting her bottom lip, looking decidedly guilty. She rapped on a closed door. "Josh? You have a visitor."

"Who is it?" Josh asked, peering out the door. His mouth dropped several notches when he spied Kyle and his eyes narrowed. "Am I under arrest?"

"Open your door, Josh. Mr. Damian wants to inspect your room. Make sure you're not sacrificing animals or growing pot..."

"You're getting really weird, Mom. Are you starting menopause?" Josh's eyebrows rose as he leaned nonchalantly against his door frame.

"Today's not the time," she warned, her voice hard as diamonds. Her eyes grew wide and she turned to Kyle.

After he let his gaze slide over Kyle insolently, Josh opened the door wide and bowed in two, waving his hand out with exaggerated mockery as if he were admitting royalty. "Enter my kingdom, but beware. My pet dragon, Beowulf, will incinerate mine enemies."

Suki slid him a reproving glance, her frown deepening. "Now who's acting strange?" she whispered, nudging her son in the ribs with her elbow.

Kyle stepped into Josh's lair and glanced around, satisfied it was an average boy's room. A computer—big surprise, he thought sarcastically. Posters of Pamela Sue, Yasmine Bleath and Kathy Ireland. A black light. A monster stereo he'd like to have in his own place. Stacks of CDs and science fiction books in semi-neat disarray. An autographed basketball on the floor in the corner. A few scattered comic books and baseball cards. Even a Bible was prominently displayed on the kid's shelves.

"Satisfied? Or are you taking me into the precinct for arrest?" She held out her hands to him as if waiting for hand-cuffs, her stance disdainful, her chin jutted high in the air. The tip of her pony tail dusted her buttocks.

"Look," Kyle said, turning to Suki. "We're getting off on the wrong foot..."

"That's not my fault..."

More laughter escaped from down the hall and he glanced at it curiously.

"Lay down and let's see what you've got," a man's voice resonated huskily, challenge lacing his tones.

Kyle frowned and he strained to hear more. Out of the corner of his eye, he noted Suki's eyes widening in alarm. Pink flush stained her high cheekbones, otherwise all color drained from her face.

"Now it's time for me to play with Wilbur and you can play with Harvey."

"It's just you and me, Baby Cakes." He swore he heard a lascivious wink in the man's teasing voice. "Let's show Maggie and Harvey how hot we are."

Just as he decided to investigate, a platinum blonde strolled into the hall. She was of indefinite age, but he judged her to be somewhere in her fifties or early sixties, a very well-kept, handsome woman with a mischievous twinkle in her china blue eyes. Her appreciative, curious gaze disconcerted him, but he stood his ground.

"Who are you?" she crooned, her smile crooked and lazy.

"This is the Jack..." Josh started to say.

Suki put her hand over Josh's mouth, pursing her lips. "Mother. This is Mr. Damian, Josh's principal..."

"Vice-principal," he corrected.

"This is my mother, Judy Woods."

"My, my, but you are a handsome buck," Judy drawled, taking his arm. She tossed her bleached blonde curls, provocatively and winked.

"Mom..." Pink stained Suki's cheeks and she looked chagrined. At least she had the good grace to look embarrassed and well she should. He wasn't exactly sure what was going on in here, but he didn't like it.

"Oh," Judy said, flirtation in her voice, "is this one yours, Suki?"